Highland Christmas

Emma Baird

BOOKS

Vinci Books

vinci-books.com

Published by Vinci Books Ltd in 2026

1

A CIP catalogue record for this book is available from the British Library.

Paperback ISBN: 9781036711221

The EU GPSR authorised representative is Logos Europe, 9 rue Nicolas Poussion, 17000 La Rochelle, France contact@logoseurope.eu

By Emma Baird

The Highland Books

Highland Fling

Highland Heart

Highland Wedding

Highland Chances

Highland Christmas

List of characters:

Gaby
A graphic designer of some talent, and a woman who staked her future on moving to a small village in Scotland.

Jack
Gaby's husband. Mean, moody, magnificent. He bears a striking resemblance to Jamie Fraser, or rather, the actor who plays him, Sam Heughan. Gaby might suggest he's the actor's much better looking younger brother.

Evie
Their one-year-old daughter and so like Jack in appearance, people often wonder aloud at her maternity.

Mildred
Their fabulous and fabulously spoiled cat.

Dr McLatchie aka Caroline aka Psychic Josie

Jack's mum, a GP who has embraced a side hustle as a psychic, one she freely admits is a complete fraud.

Ranald
Her husband. A quiet man.

Mhari
A 'friend' of Gaby's and to date the nosiest woman in the world. Complicated love life*, yet to be resolved.

Katya
Gaby's best friend. A freelance writer, Pilates aficionado and talker of much sense, bluntly, a lot of the time.

Dexter
Her boyfriend, an American too fond of hyperbole and long working hours. Katya and Dexter are new parents. Unlike as is the case with Evie, people often wonder quietly about their baby's paternity…

Xavier
A French Canadian. Definitely oui-oui. Objects to being objectified.

Jolene
A New Zealander ex-pat with a weird taste in boyfriends.

Stewart
Boyfriend of the above. Worshipper of all things porridge and newly converted to the joys of yoga.

Tamar
Their adorable child.

Lachlan*
An on-off boyfriend of Mhari. Part-owner of the Lochside
Welcome and enjoying the novelty of living life on the right
side of the law.

Mandy
Gaby's mum and someone who sees far too little of her first
granddaughter. Harbouring a secret and in need of a happy
ending.

Nanna Cooper
Gaby's grandmother. A woman with a wise saying for every
occasion.

Dylan
Gaby's brother. Also harbouring secrets and wouldn't mind
his own happy ending if they are being handed out.

Zac
Posh, blonde. Executive chef and manager of the Royal
George, Lochalshie's *other* hotel.
Falls in and out of favour with Gaby. Current status? Out.

Colm
A man keen to exchange meaningful looks with others.

Caitlin Cartier
A 'self-made' reality TV star who achieved billionaire
status at the age of 21, thanks to the beauty company she
set up. Some of you might think she is based on a real-life
person. The author refers you to the front of her book,
where she tells you everything in this book is fiction and
any resemblance to real-life characters coincidental.

Entirely. Especially any bits that might be read as libellous.

Terry
A Lochside Welcome regular. Rumour has it he's married. No-one has ever met or seen his wife.

Laney Haggerty
Just always in these books, okay?

Chapter One

THE TRUTH UNIVERSALLY KNOWN TO MOTHERS

Dear Santa, I appreciate this is a busy time of year for you, but if you could see your way to sending a few more customers to the Lochside Welcome and make this the best family Christmas we've ever had, I'd be eternally grateful...

The person meant to be making a wish as she blew out her birthday cake candles was Evie, not me. But as this was her first birthday, I thought she wouldn't mind me appropriating her request. And boy, did we need those customers... Today, however, I would not be dwelling on non-existent punters. I pursed my lips. "Blow, Evie! Like this, one, two, three!"

Ah. Too late. The village's second-youngest resident, Tamar McMillan, a year and a half older than Evie, sneaked up underneath the table, stuck his head up, blew with all his might and ducked back under again.

"Tamar!" The little scamp's mother barked at him. He ran from her, giggling. Evie wriggled in my arms, desperate to go after him. Evie loved Tamar. Her feelings weren't reciprocated. The last time Jolene and I took them swimming together, he did his best to duck her head under the water and keep it there.

"It's a phase he's going through," Jolene had said, "at least I hope so?"

I put Evie down, and she scooted off on all fours—Tamar far more enticing than the prospect of cake.

As Evie was Lochalshie's youngest resident, everyone had assumed they were invited to her birthday celebration. Our house wouldn't have handled the numbers, so we hit on holding it in the Lochside Welcome, the hotel we part-owned with six others.

Jack had strewn the bar with the pink, silver and white bunting I had designed and helium balloons. The tables had been cleared away to make enough space for party games.

Xavier, the hotel's manager and head chef, had gone to town on the food. Brought up in Canada, he was unfamiliar with traditional British party food staples. Most of it made him shudder. But he'd stumbled on an old Nancy Spain cookbook from the 1960s. "Look at zees, Gaby! You slice cucumber up very thin and put it on ze whole salmon, so people think it is scales! Shall I do zis?"

When I pointed out children weren't always the biggest fans of salmon and many people in Lochalshie promised fish "gies me the dry boak" despite fish having been a natural part of the Scots diet for centuries, he pouted. Then cheered up when he read about the hedgehog—half of a grapefruit studded with cubes of cheese and pickled onions on cocktails sticks. I'd already worked my way through far too many of them, consoling myself that the pickled onions must count as one of your five a day.

The Lochside Welcome's signature pudding was a chocolate decadence dessert. Xavier had made the dessert Evie's birthday cake, levelling up the luxury with gold leaf—

the gleam of it caught in the flickering flames of the candles.

He reappeared, knife in hand, and sliced the cake into as many pieces as there were people. Tricky given the numbers, but job done, he, Jack and I handed the plates round.

Mhari, taking a break from her semi-official role as party photographer, sat down next to me and filched my cake.

"Hey!"

"Well, my slice was titchy. Cannae expect me to survive the rest of the afternoon on just a wee bittie o' cake."

"Can I see the pictures?"

"No. I need tae touch them up. 'Specially the ones of you."

Mhari, my Lochalshie self-described best friend, was an acquired taste.

"I got a cracking shot of Jack, though. Look."

Oh, wow. That one was going on our website for sure. A tough job being the wife of a man as delectable as Jack McAllan, but someone had to do it, right? Mhari had captured him as Xavier placed the cake in front of Evie— the candle flames illuminating the planes of his face, casting exaggerated shadows that only emphasised the similarity to the ancient statues of Greek gods. She must be using an enhanced colour filter too as the red of his hair stood out in sharp relief.

"I took some o' the outside of the hotel too," she added, showing them to me. "Looks awfy Christmassy, eh?"

The lights outside the hotel were OTT, though we'd yet to get around to decorating the hotel's interior. In the garden, a reindeer pulled a sleigh at the front next to an enormous tree dotted with star lights and a gobo that projected holly leaves and berries on the white walls of the hotel. The electricity bills had soared.

"It's Christmas made camper," I'd said when we'd set them up a few days before. Jack raised an eyebrow. "Can you make Christmas camper?"

Probably not, but with any luck, the Lochside Welcome's Christmas lights would be one of those displays people drove to from miles around to see, dropping in for a drink or some food while they were in the area.

My phone buzzed as it had been doing all day—people reacting to my pictures on Instagram or phoning to wish Evie a Happy Birthday.

The screen showed my mum calling again. She'd already phoned early this morning in tears because she couldn't be here for her only grandchild's first birthday. Great Yarmouth was too far away to make visits easy, and Mum's budget too limited for her to able to afford a trip here for Evie's birthday *and* Christmas.

"Mum, hello!" I switched the phone to FaceTime mode and showed her the birthday girl now sat on the floor tearing up birthday gift wrap.

"Your brother," she replied, "wants to apologise for not having posted Evie's birthday present and card on time."

Does it count as an apology when you overhear your mum standing behind your brother, hiss-whispering that he needs to say sorry, forgetting that a mobile phone makes all background noise clear as a bell? If Dylan had remembered Evie's birthday or it crossed his mind that as her uncle, he should buy her a card and a present, I'd eat my Christmas cracker hat.

Mum came back on the line. "I'm so looking forward to Christmas! What a wonderful celebration it will be this year when we are all together."

"Me too!" We blew each other kisses and hung up. Yes, Christmas shimmered on the horizon in all its glittery glory. But that familiar prickle of worry, whenever I thought about the future started up. Money worries took the shine off somewhat.

This year's summer had been a stinker. Lochalshie's weather gods had lulled me into a false sense of security since I'd upped and moved sticks to the north of Scotland. Warm, dry-ish summers, the odd autumn storm and cold but dry winters. This year rain started mid-May, stopped for a day or two in June, and then continued into the autumn when it turned sheet-like and icy. The weather deterred everyone. We'd put up with endless cancellations and days on end when the numbers in the bar didn't surpass those working in the hotel.

Evie scuttled towards the fire, Jack swooping in to whisk her up as everyone cooed in admiration and remarked yet again on how similar they looked. It's a truth universally known to mothers... All a dad needs to do is hold his baby, jiggle her up and down a bit, and he qualifies as father of the year. Meanwhile, we women stir ourselves from sleep three hours earlier than we would like, spend our days running around after our tiny tyrants, juggling a job at the same time, and dealing with our extended family, before flopping into bed at 10pm, exhausted.

Two women sharing a bottle of wine watched him, transfixed. They nudged each other, open-mouthed. Snatches of their whispered conversation drifted over. "OMG! He can father my baby any day!" "Yeah! My ovaries have just exploded!"

Just as well I'd grown accustomed to such reactions. If Jack had been a sex god before Evie appeared on the scene, nowadays he was Zeus at the top of Olympus. Women tailed him, tongues hanging out. Even if I stood next to him, waving my left hand in the air. "Ring, fourth finger, placed on said hand by the gent you're ogling!"

"Mind and take plenty o' pics," Caroline, my mother-in-law, called out to Mhari. Jack, Evie balanced on his right hip, screwed up his face. Posing for photographs topped the list of things he hated.

Caroline joined me, waving a glass of wine at Evie, now pestering one of Laney Haggerty's ginormous Alsatians. Laney's dogs tolerated Evie to a remarkable extent, putting up with her tugging their tails and pulling their ears.

"It's good tae have a relaxed approach to parenting," Caroline said. "Evie will build up a good immune system, wi' all the exposure she has tae filthy animals. She gets that wi' Mildred too, doesn't she?"

Mildred, our ancient moggie, had yet to forgive me for Evie's usurping her rightful place as Queen of Our House.

"How are the Christmas bookings coming on?" she asked. Caroline and her husband Ranald were part of the consortium that owned the hotel.

"Three reservations for lunch," I told Caroline. "And only two of the hotel's rooms booked. Any chance you might ask the spirits to intervene and persuade people to come?"

As a sideline, my mother-in-law doubled up as a psychic. Jack and I regarded Caroline's hobby as a load of old rubbish, but any help we could get with the hotel's success, we would take. Best to cover all bases.

"I'll ask them the next time we commune," Caroline said. She'd been faking the sideline so long she'd started to believe she honestly had powers beyond the limits of rationality and logic. What harm could it do if she put forward a sincere request?

"Would you and Ranald mind having my mum and Nanna to stay on the 27th?" I asked. Our own celebrations would take place two days after Christmas once all the hotel guests had left. Last year's Christmas had been muted, thanks to Jack and I's zombie-like state as we adjusted to life as new parents. This year, I wanted the family party to be epic.

"How long for?"

The abruptness startled me. Caroline never objected to hosting my mother and Nanna. The house where Jack and I lived only had two bedrooms. Too much of a squeeze for us to fit anyone else in there.

"Um... seven days? That way they can see in the New Year with us too?"

"I'll have tae ask Ranald," she replied. "He likes his privacy, mind. I'm gonnae get a bit more food and drink."

She had a point. Much as I loved them, inflicting Mum and Nanna on anyone for seven days was a big ask. If the worst came to the worst, there was a caravan park on the other side of the loch. It closed from October to April, but the owner let out caravans to people on the proviso they kept quiet about it.

Caroline stood up and made her way toward the buffet table, its legs groaning with the effort of holding up so much food. We'd barely scratched the surface.

Evie had fallen asleep snuggled into the Alsatian's stomach, the dog curled around her. Babies were lucky that way —able, like animals, to drop off whatever noise went on around them when they were tired enough.

Mhari crept over to take her photograph. She limited her insults to me. If I died tomorrow, I knew she would leap at the chance of being Evie's guardian.

Dring! The phone again. I hit the green answer button.

"Katya! How are you? I tried to get you earlier."

My best friend's voice sounded muffled. In the background, I heard wailing—her six-month-old. "I know. I've been a bit… busy. Sorry."

"Is something wrong?" The flatness in her tone rang alarm bells in my head.

"No, no!" Fake cheery. "Is Evie there so I can say happy birthday?"

"Fast asleep, I'm afraid. But the party has been lovely. I wish you and Dexter had been here. And your little one."

"Next year, I promise. And I'll try to make it up to Lochalshie soon. Maybe for Christmas. It would be nice to escape London. The capital's hell at this time of year."

The wailing started up in earnest. Katya let out a sigh. Often, we phoned each other late at night to swap tips on childcare. More often, they ended up as mini counselling sessions, both of us reassuring each other we were not as crap at motherhood as we suspected.

"You wanted Evie, though," Katya would say. "I didn't wan—oh, it's pointless to moan. And I do love the little wretch, really."

A lot of the time she sounded as if she was trying to reassure herself, rather than me.

"I better go," she said now. "I'll be in touch soon, okay? M'wah!"

I m'wahed back and hung up, placing my phone on the table. I'll try to make it up to Lochalshie, not we'll try to make it up. "Promise you'll tell me if anything is wrong?" I fired off the message and clapped my hands.

"Anyone for musical statues?"

One hour—and a lot of cheating—later, people gathered their coats. Outside, a downpour had the rain rattling off the windows. Thickly padded coats over multiple layers, woolly hats, scarves and gloves were the only way to muddle through the winter months here. Above the smell of pizzas cooking—another Lochside Welcome speciality—I caught the distinctive aroma of damp wool.

Caroline got to her feet, her movements unsteady. A believer in strict adherence to public health guidelines on safe drinking levels, she limited herself to one glass of wine most of the time. I'd spotted her necking a second one earlier.

"I better find Ranald and head home, Gaby," she told me, indicating vaguely behind her.

The party guests streamed out, everyone calling out cheery goodbyes. The door opening and closing let in brief blasts of icy air, forcing me out of the booth where I'd taken a seat to one nearer the fire. Jack scooped up the empty plates. Evie was still slumped on Laney's dog.

"I need to wake her, up or she'll never sleep tonight," I said. Jack nodded, moving off to the kitchen, pausing next to the dog to gaze in raptures at his daughter.

Mhari, official photographer role finished for the day, took the seat opposite me.

"Something wrong wi' Katya?" she asked her attention half on me, the rest on her phone.

"Nothing at all!"

Mhari hadn't seen Katya, her erstwhile flatmate, for months. Katya made a point of never posting pictures of her child online. Mhari had cajoled, threatened and sucked up to me, desperate for me to share any photos I had. So far, I'd held out—mostly because Katya threatened to kill me if I did.

"Didnae sound like nothing to me. D'ye ken what I thought? That bairn of hers—"

The phone rang again—my mum. She must be terribly upset about missing Evie's birthday.

"Hello, you!" I said, "I was just about to send you this gorgeous pic of Evie. She's curled up asleep on—"

"Gaby, love!" my mum burst out. "Your Nanna's in hospital! You need to come down here as soon as you can!"

Chapter Two

THE HAVE A GO GRANNY

Jack materialised by my side, mouthing the words, 'What's wrong' I pointed at the phone and said 'Nanna', making my way through to the deserted conservatory, him following me.

"What happened?" I asked as Mum hiccoughed her way through an explanation, I jolted enough to worry that the all the pickled onion and chocolate cake I'd eaten might reappear.

Kathleen Millar, Nanna Cooper's oldest friend, had phoned my mum in a panic an hour earlier. She'd called around to Nanna's small, terraced house in Norwich, so the two of them could go to their weekly Tai Chi lesson and hadn't received an answer at the door. Phone calls hadn't worked either.

Kathleen knew where Nanna Cooper kept her spare key —in the plant pot at her front door. (And yes, Mum and I nagged her about the riskiness of keeping the key in the first place a potential thief would check.) On this occasion, though, the crystal-clear hiding place came in handy. Kathleen let herself in and discovered my nanna lying on the floor. She'd fallen and been unable to get up.

"She was so lucky, Gaby," Mum told me. "If Kathleen had got there any later, imagine what might have happened! Your poor gran, lying there, unable to feed herself or get to the toilet! We don't know yet if she's broken her hip. I've read the stats, Gaby! Elderly women who break their hips often end up dying after a year!"

She burst into tears, me joining in. Jack, able to hear everything, put his arm around me, dropping a kiss on the top of my head.

Elderly women. A descriptor that now applied to my nanna. The woman who'd only recently thumped a man who tried to rob her at a cashpoint, earning herself the headlines 'Have a go granny hammers hooligan' on the website of the local TV news programme.

"What have the doctors said?" I asked. Nanna was currently in Norfolk and Norwich University Hospital.

"They want to keep her in for an X-ray," my mum said, "and observation. But you should see her, Gaby! All hooked up to these machines beeping away. She's so thin too. I can't bear it."

Jack held his phone in front of me, the screen showing flight availability to Norwich. The airport wasn't a major one and flights from Edinburgh infrequent. However, there was one tomorrow at 11.15am, which would get me to Norwich an hour later.

"I'll be down as soon as I can, Mum."

And with that, I hung up and fell into Jack's arms. "Gaby, I'd come wi' you, but Monday's gonnae be full-on."

Late November wasn't a busy time in the hospitality industry. Still, we'd managed to persuade one of the local council departments to hold its annual community prize-giving event in the hotel.

Several local lollypop persons, care workers, and charity representatives were very much looking forward to the afternoon. They would eat their bodyweight in pizza and drink prodigious amounts before making their wobbly way to the front of the function room. That is where they would receive their medals and be photographed for an honorary appearance on the council's Facebook page and in the local press.

He squeezed my shoulder. "I'm sorry. I should be wi' you."

I gave him a watery smile. "Well, we knew what we were taking on when we bought a share in this place, didn't we?"

Words I said all the time to myself. Even though I'd stopped believing them a long time ago. Knew what we were doing my backside! The sheer relentlessness of hotel work threatened to grind me down all the time. And I wasn't even the person who spent the most time in here.

Nestled in the Highlands, the hotel and other local businesses relied on tourism through April to October when visitors flocked here to experience the countryside. Behind the village, the peaks of two hills, affectionately christened Maggie Broon's Boobs by the locals, offered views for miles around. The peace appealed to those who spent most of their lives crammed into the UK's overcrowded cities.

Running a small hotel in the middle of nowhere was a rollercoaster of highs and lows, where we lurched from one crisis to the next, never sure if the income from one month would keep us going another.

After a terrible summer, we needed Christmas to be mega. And to come up with a long-term plan that would keep the hotel viable in challenging times.

I blew my nose. "We better get back to the party."

Jack nodded. "Gaby, you're no' to worry about anything else except Nanna Cooper, d'ye hear me?"

Dark eyes searched mine. I nodded. "Message received and understood."

Back at the bar, everyone expressed sympathy.

"I'll babysit," Jolene volunteered. "Tamar will be so happy if Evie comes to stay with us!"

Tamar was busy plunging Evie's favourite teddy bear in and out of the giant bowl of non-alcoholic punch. What did that say for my daughter's chances of survival should she stay with them?

"Thanks, Jolene, but I'm going to bring her with me. Evie might be what Mum and Nanna Cooper need. And if I don't take her, my mum will never speak to me again."

Another unwanted thought surfaced later when Jack, Evie and I made our way home.

"If Nanna's broken her hip," I said, "she won't be able to come here for Christmas!"

"You don't know that yet," Jack pointed out.

"No, but…"

This was Evie's first Christmas. (Sort of.) I'd planned every aspect of the day. From when Evie woke up, to the nibbles we'd eat at Caroline's house where we opened the presents and the later riotous Christmas dinner eaten in the hotel with all our family and friends. The perfect Lochalshie celebration—the thought of which had cheered me up considerably in the last few weeks.

If Nanna couldn't make it, then it wasn't fair for me to expect Mum to come on her own. And if Jack, Evie and I went to Great Yarmouth instead, we'd miss celebrating with all our family and friends here, too awful a prospect to bear…

Chapter Three

INSULTING ENCOUNTERS

Eighteen hours later, I was in Edinburgh trying to stop my mind flashing up hideous images where I got to the hospital too late.

"Well, Evie. This is an adventure, isn't it?"

Solemn-eyed, my daughter took in her surroundings. Edinburgh Airport buzzed with travellers seeking a week of winter sun in the Canary Islands and suited business fliers. A family ahead of us wore sunhats, flip-flops, shorts and jaunty print T-shirts, dressed as if they were in Tenerife already. As the resident of a tiny village, Evie must find the sheer number of humans in one place unsettling.

Travel with a one-year-old brought its own challenges. What you carried on a flight. What you didn't. The pain in the butt liquid rules where anything over 100mls needed to be checked in. So far, Evie and I had made it through security. All I had to cope with now was taking her on her second flight ever and hoping her little ears could cope with the pressure in the cabinet as the plane took off and landed.

The first flight, when she was four months younger,

hadn't gone well. When we stumbled off the plane at Stansted, every other passenger hurried past, muttering about the 'worst flight ever'. Even the flight attendants' goodbyes, employees schooled in fake sincerity, rang hollow.

In the queue behind me waiting to board Flight EC9674 to Norwich, I heard muttering. "Oh God, there's a bloody baby on the flight. I'll never get tae sleep!"

About to turn around and give whoever a piece of my mind—*How dare you call my child bloody!*—I changed my mind, recalling her first flight. Until only a year ago I would have thought the same. Though I might not have said it out loud.

Evie and I made our way down the tunnel that led to the plane, her big brown eyes gazing around her in wonder. The air stewards beamed at us. "Oh my God!" one of them said, chucking Evie under the chin. "I can't believe the colour of her hair. What a lucky girl."

Seat located near the front I placed my rucksack in the overhead locker checking I had everything I needed for the flight. The Gaby flying no children version had only needed her phone, a trashy magazine and a drink. Babies required so many more 'just in case' items. Fingers crossed, toes too, that she wouldn't need her nappy changed. The prospect of doing such a thing in a tiny toilet while people queued outside appalled me.

Jack had insisted on splashing out for an upgrade for the flight, though an 'upgrade' on a bargain bucket airline meant little. All I got to do was book a specific seat and have about 10 centimetres more legroom, but I got to settle down before the rest of the passengers made their slow way onto the plane. As I fiddled with my rucksack trying to work out everything I needed to take out and what could be shoved up into the overhead lockers, I sent Jack grateful thanks.

When I finally sat down, Evie gurgling away on my lap, a man stopped in the aisle, checking his phone and the number on the row. What rotten luck. I'd ended up in the same row of seats as Mr 'I'll Never Get to Sleep on the Plane'. He looked just as dismayed, eyes lingering far too long on Evie as if he hoped glaring at her would stop her screaming her way through the entire flight.

(Mate. You've clearly never had children.)

He turned to the air steward, busy shoving handbags and carry-on suitcases in the locker. "Can I change seats?"

She took his boarding pass from him. "Sorry, Sir. You've paid for a specific seat and this is it."

He muttered a rude comment about FlyMe upgrades and how they ought to come with warnings about who you would be sitting next to.

He stretched up to put his bag in the locker, affording me a too-close glimpse of a tattoo that covered half of his torso and sat on the aisle seat. Another woman shuffled up the aisle, halting beside us. He shifted next to me.

Evie whimpered. I had one option up my sleeve for soothing her when the plane took off. But much as giving birth and motherhood had toughened me up to what embarrassed me and what didn't—tends to happen when you've had eight different people peering up your doodah— I hadn't envisaged having to sit next to a hostile man while doing it.

Great.

Evie's whimpers grew louder. The man let out an exaggerated sigh and sat down, rummaging through his bag. He took out a pair of headphones and jammed them pointedly over his ears. I recognised the brand—quality ones, but not noise-cancelling. The last time we'd flown, Evie had proved herself capable of industrial level decibel piercing.

"Look, I'm sorry, I—"

The words met empty air. The man stared fixedly at the seat in front of him. I settled for visiting all kinds of silent curses on him. May your girlfriend or boyfriend dump you. May your credit card be refused the next time you try to pay for a designer shirt (he was wearing a poplin slim fit shirt that smacked of too much money). And, my favourite one, may you step on Lego in your bare feet.

The air steward began her demo of the safety briefing. I paid attention, shivering at the bit where she instructed passengers to put on their own oxygen masks before attending to children.

"Not going to happen, Evie," I whispered to her. "I promise!"

At least her whimpering had settled down, my daughter too entranced by the slow movement of the plane along the runway as it began take-off.

The quiet didn't last. As the plane sped up, Evie opened her mouth wide and screwed her face up, shaking her little head. The screams started. Next to me, Mr Designer Shirt pulled his headphones down. Oh-oh. Emergency measures needed.

Breast-feeding, Jolene had told me beforehand, would soothe her. She should know. At nine months, young Tamar had embarked on his first flight. To visit his New Zealand maternal grandparents no less. "The sucking motion," Jolene promised me, "will ease the pressure on her ears. The flight will be a breeze!"

I was wearing a Lochside Welcome branded hoodie over a shirt. Straightforward enough to unzip, open the buttons and pop her in inconspicuously. She settled down, baby-shampoo scented soft hair brushing my skin and dark eyes meeting mine. The plane rose in the air, and she gave a little start of alarm before relaxing once more and carrying on.

I glanced sideways at my neighbour, who stared at me in horror. I glared back. What a Neanderthal creep—the type who thought women should breast-feed in the toilets. He removed his headphones. "How old is she?" his tone incredulous.

"Two," I said, betting that he had no idea what a one-year-old baby looked like. "Saves me a fortune in baby food. Not that it's any of your business. Think yourself lucky she's stopped screaming."

That said, I turned to stare out of the window, making a point of not looking at him for the rest of the flight.

Chapter Four

A PRACTISED LIAR

Miracle of miracles, my brother was waiting for me in Arrivals, waving half-heartedly as soon as he caught sight of us. Mum must have bullied him into taking me straight to the hospital.

My child-hating fellow passenger bumped into me as we exited the corridor into the arrivals hall, him too busy staring at his mobile phone. He jumped back from us as if he'd been given an electric shock. To be fair to him, Evie had thrown up just as we were coming into land, a tiny bit of milky vomit splattering onto his jeans.

I waved back at Dylan, whose eyes had darted from me to Mr Designer Shirt and back again.

"Do you know him?" I asked once I'd reached his side, the two of us watching the man as he hurried away, desperate to put distance between him and the vomit machine.

Dylan's eyes flickered once more. "No."

Did you cut all the hair off Gaby's Barbie doll, Dylan? Okay, which one of you nabbed the £20 note sitting on the coffee table?

Dylan, your teacher tells me you turned up to your English class, stoned. Is that true?

The years had given me expertise on Dylan's truth-telling. No point pushing him, however, as he'd only repeat the denial.

We hadn't seen each other since the time Dylan visited me in Lochalshie not long after Evie was born. Oh, my mistake. He didn't come to see us. My brother took after our long-absent father—tall, wiry, olive-skinned, a big believer in double denim and a non-believer in keeping in touch with your nearest and dearest. In dire need of a hair-cut, too. In my best sisterly fashion, I made the point, getting in an insult before he could.

"D'you want to give your gorgeous niece a cuddle?" I asked, and he shook his head, mouth curling up in a grimace. "Gimme your rucksack."

Safe to say, the avuncular uncle gene had body-swerved Dylan so far. Evie was strapped to my torso and fast asleep once more. I kissed the top of her head; glad she wasn't awake to discover there was a relative who didn't think she was the Bees Knees.

We headed out of the building towards the NCP carpark with its black and yellow signage, Dylan grumbling about the amount of money he'd needed to pay to leave his car for what amounted to less than 15 minutes.

"How's Nanna today?" I asked, the words sticking in my throat. Dylan had volunteered no information. A bad sign, right? "Better, according to the doctors," he said, pinging open the boot of Mum's ancient Ford Fiesta.

As luck would have it, Mr Designer Shirt I Hate Babies on Planes, also appeared. A gleaming silver Land Rover, its windows blacked out, pulled up ahead of the taxis waiting in rank. They beeped in annoyance. The man leapt in, though he managed a quick eye meet with my brother once more, Dylan's face statue still as he watched the door slam and the car roar away.

"You do know him!" I said, shutting the boot. The car had been prepped as there was a baby seat strapped on the front seat. It must have been mum as Dylan wouldn't have remembered or known. I put Evie in it, her sleeping so soundly she only grunted a little as I did so.

Dylan shook his head. "No, I don't. Anyway, get in. Visiting hours are 2-4pm, and if we don't hurry, we'll be late."

At the hospital, they ummed and ah-ed at the desk when the three of us showed up. The rule was two visitors at a time in case we all brought in germs, and my mum was already there. When I threatened a melt-down of epic proportions, the stress of the last 24 hours kicking in, the nurse at the desk relented. Permission granted for Evie and me to go in, Dylan to remain in reception.

Nanna Cooper was in a room all to herself. Was that positive or negative? I pushed open the door and braced myself.

My mum got up straight away—the bags under her eyes all too heightened and her skin the white of someone who'd spent too long indoors. She perked up when she saw Evie, holding her arms out wide. "Give granny a big cuddle!"

I handed her over. Part of me had expected Evie to yell her head off, the setting too unfamiliar. Ten out of ten to my daughter for behaving just as a granddaughter should.

Nanna, though... Attached to thrumming machines that thrummed, the veins in her hands all too prominent. Her hair had plastered itself to the pillow, yellowness streaking through the white. Her chest rose and fell in a way that made you will the machine to keep her heart going.

I puffed out air. Shut my eyes. Tried not to break down.

Nanna's hand, the one attached to the IV drip, wobbled and her eyes flashed open.

"Mum! Look!"

Mum hurried over, propping Evie up. "Your great-granddaughter has come all the way from Scotland to see you. Isn't that wonderful?"

My nanna turned her head to me. "Get me out of here, Gaby! This place is full of old people riddled with that nasty flesh-eating thing. Kathleen Millar's sister came in here six months ago and left in a coffin!"

"Mum!" My own mother shushed her. "That's not true."

"Yes, it is!" Nanna said. "You came with me to Peggy Millar's funeral, wearing that terrible dress that doesn't suit your figure and makes you look washed out."

"Better than your outfit," my mum retorted. "You went full-on Italian Mafia widow, with that ridiculous black hat, veil and evening gloves!

Peggy Millar died at home. She had a heart attack while on the toilet, remember?"

"Caused, mark my words, by the flesh-eating bug damaging the veins around her heart."

"Rubbish!"

If I remembered rightly, Peggy had been much older than my nanna's best friend—mid-90s, even. Not a bad innings, as people said...? But the pent-up stress I'd been carrying abated. If Nanna and Mum were back to insulting each other, nothing too much was wrong with Nanna.

Hooray! Epic Family Christmas in Lochalshie was still a go-go.

A nurse came in, cooing at Evie, who blew her spit bubbles back. "Do you want a cup of tea?" she asked as she took Nanna's temperature, nodding to us both when we enquired if it was okay.

"Yes, please," I said.

As soon as the nurse had left, my mum broke off her bouncing of Evie on her knee. "That was a mistake, love. The tea you get in here is the worst stuff you will ever taste."

The plastic cup the nurse handed over confirmed Mum's warning. Eau de teabag recycled far too often. I sniffed it. Chlorine?

Half an hour later—several more acrimonious exchanges having taken place, my nanna accusing my mother of keeping her in hospital deliberately out of spite —Mum and I left. We stopped outside the room to talk with the doctor, name badge 'Doctor Waveney' pinned to an unbuttoned tunic over a navy shift dress.

"Everything is going as it should," she said one eye on us, the other at the clock on the wall. No doubt she had a million more patients to deal with. "When you come back tomorrow, you'll see a vast improvement. The drip is there because she was dehydrated when she came in—probably because she'd lain in the floor for some time."

The waiting room had filled up. Dylan was flicking his way through an old copy of Woman's Own. As we made for the car park, he complained once more about the car parking charges he'd had to fork out for. My mum remained tight-lipped. They must have fallen out. Maybe he'd moaned about her not providing him with all his laundry/tidying/catering needs, seeing as she was too busy fretting about Nanna.

"Thanks for coming, love," my mum said as Dylan pulled out of the car park and onto the A47, the road back to Great Yarmouth 22 miles away. "So supportive of you!"

From the driver's seat, Dylan snorted.

"No problem," I said. It promised to be a long couple of days if I had to deal with Nanna's condition *and* Mum and Dylan sulking with each other.

By the time we arrived at Mum's house in Great Yarmouth, Dylan refusing to enter into any conversation the whole half hour journey back, I was wondering if it was too late to suggest Evie and I spend the next few days in Nanna's house instead. It was closer to the hospital for a start.

Mum lived in a semi-detached ex-council house on one of the nicer of the town's estates—her view straight onto a small play park where I planned to take Evie the following day.

Dylan dropped us off, slammed the car door as he got out and announced he was going for a walk. He strode off, hands thrust into his pockets. I unbuckled the car seat and took out Evie.

"What on earth is going on?" I asked Mum as soon as Dylan was out of hearing distance.

She buried herself in the car boot, digging out shopping bags and my stuff. "Shall we go inside first and then—"

A solitary figure pushing a buggy around the small park caught my eye—Katya, who'd said nothing about being in Great Yarmouth during our phone conversation the day before. And her expression looked far from happy. I might have been mistaken, but when Katya had clocked me, her face registered dismay for an instant before widening into what looked more like a grimace than a smile.

Dear, oh dear.

Chapter Five

A LOT OF SCREAMING AND SHOUTING

"D'you mind if I check if Katya's okay?" I asked Mum, who nodded.

"Ask her to come in. I haven't seen her little one yet."

As Katya made her way over, I stifled a sigh of envy at how stylish she appeared. Most of the time, I favoured scruffy student a-la the 90s—a look that pre-dated Evie's birth. Katya wore skin-tight jeans tucked into leopard skin ankle boots, a sweater shot through with silver threads and an almost floor-length fake fur coat.

My mum crouched down to peer at the buggy's occupant. "Blimey, love," she tipped her head up. "He's so like you!"

Katya seemed to flinch. "I suppose so. I don't see it myself."

Mum dug around in her handbag and pulled out her purse. "Here," she said, pressing two pound coins into Lucian's hand. When Evie was born, I'd made more than £100 from that old superstition. (Confession. I bought myself a new pair of winter boots…)

"Do you want to come in for a cup of tea?" I asked.

Katya shook her head. "Can we go for a wander into town? The only thing that makes Lucian sleep is endless walking."

Too used to healthy doses of fresh air throughout the day, a walk suited me also. She and I set off towards the town centre.

Late November wasn't as bitterly cold in Great Yarmouth as it was in Lochalshie, but it was dark. Our way into the town centre was lit up by the many locals who'd already put up their Christmas decorations. The shops advertised presents galore, the mannequins in New Look dressed in sequinned finery and wearing Santa hats, and a stall on the High Street was selling roasted chestnuts, the nutty smell of them drifting our way.

Great Yarmouth's heyday was the 50s before mass-market holidays abroad kicked in. By the time I grew up there, its shine had long faded away—most of the tourists older people reliving their childhoods or day-tripping families marking time until their 'real' holiday in France/Spain/Disneyland later in the year. As teenage residents too poor to afford excursions to Norwich, we hung around the pier with its ancient funfair and the roller coaster that was terrifying because of how rickety it was.

"I didn't know you were visiting your mum."

Like me, Katya had grown up in Great Yarmouth and also escaped some years ago—spending a year in Lochalshie before she and her marketing genius boyfriend returned to London.

"Ditto," she said, speeding up as Lucian whimpered. Lucian whimpered some more. From this angle, I could only see the top of his head.

Since the birth of Lucian Kubowski-Carlton six months

earlier, I'd only seen him once in the flesh and when he was only a few weeks old. Since then, he'd popped up on Face-Time, and in the pictures we shared on a WhatsApp group. But in the flesh, he was… very blonde. As is my best friend. Understandably her son favoured her looks. Blue eyes and the shape of his jaw, although baby plump now, promised similarity too. What was also apparent was how much Lucian looked nothing like his father.

Or rather, the father whose name was on his birth certificate.

If Katya noticed me shooting Lucian occasional glances, she ignored it. I filled her in on what had happened to Nanna Cooper.

"Your poor nanna," she said, blue eyes clouding over. Nanna Cooper's many words of wisdom amused Katya no end.

Update over with, I popped into the local Costas on the main street and bought us two takeaway coffees. "Here," I said, handing one over. "You get this on one condition. When I asked yesterday, you ducked the question. What is going on, and where is Dexter?"

Tumultuous was the kindest word to describe Katya and Dexter's relationship. In the time they'd been together, they'd split, what, three times? More? The original reason used to be Dexter's workaholic tendencies, but he'd stopped the 70-hour working weeks when Katya announced she was pregnant.

"Can you remember what that flat's like?" she asked me, referring to the city centre abode she and Dexter shared. "Insulated to the hilt, right? The screaming match we had last week had someone running upstairs to tell us to pipe down."

Ouch.

Katya had returned home one day to find Dexter staring moodily at their son.

"Why's Zac been in touch with you?" he asked, holding up her phone. Katya refused the thumb recognition option as she found it "too creepy", but most people's passcodes were easy to figure out. Dexter had guessed Katya's and found an unwelcome message.

"More importantly," Dexter continued, standing up, so he loomed over her. "Why have you replied to him? 'Hey, Katya—thanks for getting back to me. I can't stop thinking about you…' Then, you. 'When are you back in London? If you like, we can meet up to discuss it.' Discuss what?"

He pointed at their son. "Lucian's not mine, is he? You've been lying to me to all along. Did you sleep with Zac that time?"

"How dare you read my private messages, you rotten lousy—"

More screaming and shouting. When Katya gave in and admitted that she *had* slept with Zac that time, Dexter called her everything under the sun, slammed the front door and didn't return until two days later.

"When Dexter returned," Katya continued, "he told me to pack my bags, which was what I expected. I came here. He's phoned a few times since, but only to say 'hello' to Lucian, and when he does, he is the picture of misery."

Him and Katya both. Her cheeks slid inwards, and new lines appeared to have etched themselves around her mouth. I wondered at those phone calls. At only six months old, how much would Lucian understand or appreciate them?

Once she'd related the story, voice flat and eyes fixed at a point beyond my head, I grabbed her hand. "Katya, but I thought…"

… that deep down, Dexter knew and didn't care?

Katya's pregnancy had not been planned. She'd 'fessed up to me at the time she didn't know who the father was.

Might be Dexter, might be Zac… She'd slept with them both within days of each other. What had astonished me the more when she told me—that she was pregnant in the first place or that she'd been disorganised enough not to have used contraception on two separate occasions? The latter.

"You can't tell anyone. Promise?"

I and discretion aren't bosom buddies. Ask my family and friends. But on this occasion, I knew how important it was to stay silent.

Her eyes glistened as she shifted her attention back to me. We both glanced at Lucian, who woke up, stared at us both and burst into tears, attracting attention from shoppers drifting in and out of New Look. That set me off, letting out the pent-up stress of the past few days and fretting over Katya and Lucian, the poor, now fatherless, child.

Katya pushed the buggy back and forth once more, the motion soothing Lucian back to silence.

"Children were never my plan," she added gloomily. "And single motherhood doesn't appeal at all."

"But it's not reached that stage yet, has it?"

"I friggin' hope not!"

Dear, oh dear. In an almost lifelong friendship, my role was the cheerer-upperer. (A word? No?) "Well, if it does—a big if—think of Jack," I said, blowing my nose. "Caroline brought him up all by herself until he was eight years old and she made a brilliant job of it. And then there's Dylan and me. Our father didn't walk out until we were older, but we're still incredibly well-adjusted human beings."

Ish. Dylan wasn't an outstanding example.

Katya, too. Her mother didn't count as a single mother, as she'd had three husbands and numerous boyfriends, all of them useless on the fathering front. My little peer group appeared to be a shining (not) example of dreadful dads.

"If that's supposed to be motivational, Richardson," Katya replied. She didn't believe in women taking their husbands' names after marriage and never referred to me as McAllan. "Ten out of ten for effort, nought out of ten for effect."

"Dexter might come round," I tried, making her shake her head. Such rotten timing, too—Lucian's first Christmas. Dexter, an enthusiastic first-time father, would have spent the previous weeks planning everything he would buy for his son...

Coffees finished, we left the town centre, Lucian fast asleep in his buggy. Katya's mum lived in the opposite direction to mine. She and I hugged each other. "Phone me later, promise?" I asked.

She nodded and walked off. "Promise. Thanks for listening, Gaby. You're the best friend in the entire world."

I watched her—the way her head drooped and her feet dragging as she headed back to her mum's house. Fingers crossed none of her sisters was in residence as the four of them rubbed each other up the wrong way all the time. Her youngest sister had two kids, children so diabolical even the Super Nanny would walk away.

I must, must find some way to help.

———————————

Dylan was nowhere to be seen when I returned to Mum's house. Just as well given the atmosphere between him and my mum. I ought to ask what the latest argument was about, but Nanna's accident and Katya's revelations had exhausted my stocks of sympathy.

Upstairs, I ran Evie a bath. She splashed Mum and me with warm soapy water, laughing her head off—my mum joining in.

"Evie is exactly like you were at that age. Wait till—"

"Wait till what?" I asked, puzzled by the sudden hesitation.

"Nothing! I'll tell you later. Who's a lovely girl for your granny? Come here and give me kisses, you beautiful little angel! What shall we get you for din-dins?"

In the kitchen, dirty dishes were still piled up next to the sink—something my mum hated doing. Too busy worrying about Nanna. I pulled up my sleeves and ran the hot water, squirting in a generous amount of lemony Fairy Liquid.

Mum showed me the blender she'd splashed out on yesterday, along with a box of organic fruit and veg she'd ordered. "I can make Evie purees and things! There was a half-price sale in Jarrolds' kitchen department. The blender was half-price, and the veggie box only cost me £25."

Mum worked as a receptionist for a GP. A job not known for awarding employees with a high salary. The generosity made me guilty, realising how much she must have been looking forward to seeing Evie again.

Besides, I'd come supplied with the jars I bought. Like most new parents, I'd set out with honourable intentions. Everything my daughter eats will be 100 percent homemade and wholesome, etc. Before reality kicked in. Juggling child-care with my graphic design job for Blissful Beauty and helping at the hotel, left no time for luxuries such as cooking and pureeing veggies.

Dishes finished, Mum showed me the childcare guru's book she'd bought too. "Butternut squash puree. Says here every child in the world loves butternut squash. Do you want a shower yourself, love, while I make it? Planes always make me feel dirty."

Staying here had been the right decision, after all. I returned upstairs, checking my phone for messages from Jack. "Hope you got there safely. Will phone later xx."

By the time I'd finished, clean and fragrant once more, Dylan was letting himself in the front door, face flushed, and hair mussed up.

"Where have you been?"

"None of your business," he snapped at me. Outside the house we'd grown up in, we could be civil to each other. Once within the four walls, we regressed to our teenage selves. I stuck my tongue out. He flicked me the bird.

Mum appeared in the hallway, Evie on her hip. "You're back then. Just because it's dinner time and you expect me to put food in front of you!"

Dylan never let an atmosphere spoil his appetite, but the hostility between the two of them crackled in the air. Even Evie sensed it, her smile vanishing.

"Can someone please tell me what is going on!" I asked, swivelling around to face Mum. "Is this about Dylan still living at home despite him being the grand ol' age of 30 and someone who should have found himself some other mug, I mean a girlfriend, willing to do all the washing, cleaning and cooking, and—"

"Shut up, Gaby!" Dylan hissed. He pointed at our mum. "Ask her. Ask her what she's doing cosying up to our waste of space father. You know. The one who walked out on us years ago and hasn't bothered showing an interest ever since?"

And with that, he stormed off once more, slamming the door behind him.

Chapter Six

YOUR TYPICAL SUNDAY DAD

"What?" I spun around to face my mum, unable to believe my ears. "Are you and my dad back together?"

She ducked back into the living room, calling out, "Do you want a cup of tea? A proper one to get rid of the taste of that hospital muck?"

"No," I replied, following her into the living room. "What I want is for you to tell me if you're back with my dad and why this is the first time I've heard about it."

Evie stretched her arms out. I took her.

My mum fiddled with the rings on her right hand. "Your dad contacted me a month ago. He suggested we meet up, so I said yes, and we got together one evening in the Bricklayer's Arms. That's where we used to go all the time before we got married. Oh, that reminds me, love. The Bricklayer's Arms is doing some cracking things for Christmas. You ought to pop in and have a look. Might give you some ideas for the Lochside—"

"Mum!" I put Evie down on the floor, whisking away as many of the potential obstacles as possible. (Almost impossi-

34

ble. A one-year-old always finds something that looks innocuous and then uses it in a heart-stoppingly dangerous way.)

Mum sat down. I folded my arms. Back to thinking holing up at Nanna's house was the far better idea. Fury fizzed in my veins. How dare my disgrace of a dad turn up now and weasel his way into Mum's affections. And given the way he had treated her, why had she let him?

"Gaby, he's changed."

"A cheetah never changes his spots!" Channelling my grandmother there—a saying she used regularly.

"The word's leopard, love."

"Doesn't matter. Cheetah works just as well!"

"He has changed. And he's desperate to see you again. And be introduced to his granddaughter."

"Has Dylan met him?"

Mum hung her head. "No. He refuses."

Hence their argument. Home comforts aside, Dylan must have drawn the line at Tony's reappearance. Mum and Dad split when we were 14 and 16, blaming incompatibility which later turned out to be my mum finding Tony's many girlfriends out of step with that bit of the marriage vows that said 'forsaking all others'.

In the beginning, he made an effort to see us—a typical Sunday dad who took us to the cinema and then McDonald's. Whenever I walked past a cinema, the sickly-sweet smell of popcorn made me think of him and shudder. Occasionally, he invited Dylan and me to stay in his bachelor flat, providing we promised not to trip over any stray women hanging around there.

Then he moved abroad to run a pub in Benidorm. A few postcards later and all contact with the Father Ship ceased. No messages or phone calls when I married Jack. Ditto when Evie came along.

"Can you feed Evie for me?" I asked, grabbing my hoodie and coat. "I'm going to find Dylan."

"Oh, but love…"

But nothing. For once, I was on my brother's side.

Dylan was where I expected him. Despite the late time of year, Caesar's Fun Palace on the front was still open, its doors pushed far back to encourage punters to come in. To add a festive touch, someone had strewn the machines with gold tinsel, and an inflatable Santa wobbled back and forth on a podium at the front.

Mostly in there, were bored kids playing on the virtual racing karts or scruffy old men and women with gambling habits.

And my brother. I spotted him, up the back on the slot machines, feeding in coins and repeatedly pulling the handle down to try to score the fabled three in a row that made the machine spew out money. The overhead lighting picked out grey streaks in his hair I hadn't noticed before.

I tapped him on the shoulder. "Any luck?"

He pushed himself back and shook his head. "Nah. I take it Mum's told you."

"Yes. Honestly, what's mum thinking? Shall we stay in Nanna's house? You can use it as an opportunity to get to know your niece better."

For nostalgia's sake, I pressed some of my loose change into the machine and pulled down the handle. Three cherries. The crash rang out as coins spilled into the tray underneath, making everyone else in the arcade turn their attention to us. Two of the kids wandered over, expressions awe-struck.

'Ow much money you got, Mrs?" one asked, making me wince. A grey-haired brother and a 13-year-old addressing me as 'Mrs'. Old. Officially.

The arcade's supervisor, a battle-axe of a woman I recognised from my childhood, made her way over. We all knew they never loaded the machines in favour of punters, but the coin spill was impressive. The supervisor's eyes flashed up again, expression accusatory. "Did you kick that machine?"

"No!" The absolute cheek of her trying to accuse me of cheating. Though if she'd lobbed the accusation at Dylan, fair enough.

"Can I get it in notes, not coins?" I asked. Pound coins and small change made up the haul. If she gave me all that money, it would be far too bulky.

"No."

She unlocked the tray at the bottom and slid it out. I followed her to the booth she had at the back, watched enviously by the arcade's other customers. Coins weighed and bagged up, she handed my haul over—23 bags of small change, the total £107.31. Perhaps a career as a professional gambler beckoned. If I won this amount every time I hit the slot machines, that might help the hotel finances.

"Beginner's luck," Dylan said when I returned, handbag strap digging into my shoulder. He pointed at the coffee shop opposite the arcade. "D'you want a drink? Or a sandwich? On you, obviously."

The last thing I'd eaten had been a packet of pickled onion monster munch on the plane, earning me yet more disapproval from Mr I Hate Babies on Planes who sniffed pointedly.

"Okay then. Though I thought you might be desperate to pay for it to make up for forgetting Evie's birthday and mine and not bothering to get me a wedding present when I got married."

Far too much to hope for. As we stood at the cash desk in the coffee shop tray loaded with overpriced sandwiches, orange juice and two bits of Millionaire's shortbread, Dylan cleared his throat.

"I've lost my job."

When I'd studied him in the arcade, I noticed he looked thinner than usual and his face drawn.

"Why? You've been at The Sauce for years. I thought the company was doing well."

Dylan worked as a logistics manager for The Sauce of Life, an online alcohol retailer and distributor specialising in small vineyards and microbreweries and distilleries. Business in alcohol home deliveries had boomed in recent years. Last Christmas, Marty, the boss had given his HQ staff a four-figure bonus.

Dylan blew it on a trip to Vegas. None of it whatsoever went towards a present for his new niece.

A shifty look crossed my brother's face. "Just one of those things."

Table furthest from the door located, we sat down. Mum said she had been seeing Tony for a month, though they had spoken on the phone and emailed each other before then. All those phone calls we'd exchanged over the last few months. Not a blinkin' word said about our useless, absentee father.

"When did you hear about Tony?"

Dylan swallowed a gargantuan mouthful of ham and cheese on wholegrain. "Last week. They waltzed into the house together, not a care in the world!"

"What does he look like these days?"

"A used car salesman. Sleazy. Like an older version of your ex-boyfriend. No offence."

None taken. Ryan was a used car salesman, albeit upmarket and vintage cars. I'd walked past the showroom on my way back from the walk with Katya. I told Evie that if I hadn't inhaled helium on the night of mine and Ryan's engagement party and accidentally revealed my thoughts about marrying him, she might not have happened.

The horrors!

"I listened to his oh-so-sincere, 'Son, I know I've made such a mess of being a dad', for three minutes. Then I walked out."

I would have done the same. What was my mum thinking?

Dylan eyed my half-eaten sandwich. "Can I?"

I pushed the plate towards him. As a twenty-something, Dylan's diet had consisted of Pot Noodles until he moved back in with my mum. If he was avoiding the house, maybe he had reverted to subsisting on food with a three-year use-by date. Hence the grey look of him.

His phone rang. Dylan snatched it up before I could read the name of the caller. Whoever it was, the heaviness around his eyes and mouth lifted. He sprung out of his seat and darted outside, pacing around in animated conversation.

I snaffled the two bits of shortbread and stuffed them in my bag. Outside, Dylan said goodbye to whoever—a far cheerier man than he'd been five minutes ago.

"If you like, you can sleep in my room tonight," he said. Mum's house had one biggish bedroom, one medium-sized and the other titchy. Dylan's was the largest.

"I'm off. See you tomorrow," Dylan said, ruffling my hair, a gesture he hadn't used in years.

"But who are you—"

Pointless. When had Dylan ever shared anything about his love life? This would be one of his hundreds of booty call options. I headed back to Bath Hill Terrace once more, dreading the conversation with Mum where she tried to argue the charms of the new and improved Tony Richardson.

Sure enough, she was wringing her hands when I got back 15 minutes later. Evie waved from the mat on the floor. She'd eaten every bit of the butternut squash puree, Mum said, breaking off from angst to grandmotherly pride. Evie crawled towards me, and I swept her up.

"Gaby, I'm sorry if I sprung it on you," Mum tried, back to angst. "But if you could just meet him, you'd see for yourself how sorry your father is and how he wants to make it up to you and Dylan. I've been telling him what a wonderful place Lochalshie is and how lovely the people there are. What if he came for Chr—"

No, no, a thousand times, no.

"Mum, you are fine to do what you want"—said through gritted teeth—"but that means Dylan, and I can pick choices that contradict yours, doesn't it? He doesn't want to meet Tony again, and neither do I."

Ever, if possible. Mum bit her lip.

"What about a chat on the phone or we could Skype—"

"NO!"

Terse words exchanged, Mum asked if I wanted dinner. No thanks, I said, pleading tiredness and stomping, teenage-like, upstairs to my brother's room. It was only eight o'clock, but we'd been up since five am thanks to Lochalshie's distance from Edinburgh Airport.

Mum had put a cot in the box-sized spare room. I dragged it through into Dylan's room. The ancient wooden bars were well worn, but the mattress and blanket felt super-soft. Didn't matter, anyway. When Evie conked out on my chest after I fed her, I gave in. The two of us curled up together under Dylan's yellow and green striped Norwich City duvet, freshly laundered, thank heavens, and fell asleep.

Two hours later, the phone on top of the bedside cabinet rattled and woke me up. Jack.

Propping it up against the bedside light, I answered it in FaceTime mode. "Sorry, I'm so late calling," he said. He was in our bedroom, Mildred on his lap. (Delirious, thanks to Evie not being there.) "How's your poor nanna?"

Nanna's health explained, I filled him in on why I was hiding away in Dylan's room. Jack nodded. Last year, he'd forgiven his own father—another man who'd not lived up to the role. But it had taken a lot of time and convincing. Mine had never beaten up my mother, but his lack of interest when I married and had Evie stung too much.

She was fast asleep—her little legs and arms star-fished on the mattress and making snuffley noises. Jack blew her kisses. Evie turned him into a pile of mush—the opposite of the mean and moody Scotsman I'd assumed he was when we first met.

"Anyway, how are things with you? Are you all set for the council knees-up tomorrow night? Jolene tells me those people are rocket-like once they hit the Prosecco. Expect it to get raucous one hour in, a punch-up starts an hour after that, you threaten to call the police at 11pm, and everyone is friends again by midnight."

Jack let out a sigh. "Yes, fine, fine. But we still haven't filled the rooms or the tables for Christmas Day. And now there's a soddin' great sign outside the Royal George announcing a price cut on what they are offering on the day. A two-night gourmet experience where guests enjoy a five-course tasting menu wi' a wine flight to match, all prepared by a Michelin-starred chef."

The Royal George, the hotel at the other end of the village, described itself as a luxury, five-star Highland escape. Owned by a conglomerate, the hotel's generous advertising budget afforded widespread social media campaigns. They were likely to swoop in and nick all those who might have considered us for their festive celebrations.

Also managed by one Zac Cavanagh. Yes, that Zac. Blasted, blasted man. Causing trouble left, right and centre.

"The doctor doesn't think Nanna's broken anything," I added, crossing my fingers that were true. "So, she should be able to come for Christmas with my mu—" I stopped. Not if Mum insisted on bringing Tony with her. And I'd planned such a special celebration. God knows, we deserved it. The last time we'd had more than one day off had been back in March when Jack and I spent two nights in Edinburgh for his birthday.

"And then there's the Katya situation. She looked so miserable when I saw her earlier, I was—"

"Katya? Isn't she in London?"

"I bumped into her in Great Yarmouth. She and Dexter have had a ginormous argument."

Jack screwed his nose up. "Again?"

"Um, I think they might end up splitting permanently this time," I told Jack now, guilt making me squirm. Jack didn't know Katya's doubts about Lucian's paternity.

"Och, they'll be fine," Jack said. "He'll do the usual. Realise he misses her like a lost limb. Charter a private jet to Great Yarmouth or something." Dexter was fond of grand gestures. "They'll fall into each other's arms, swear undying love and that they'll never break up again. Until the next time."

Hmm. Not according to Katya…

"You don't think…" Jack pinched the bridge of his nose, "if Katya and Dexter split for good that he will want his share of the Lochside Welcome back, do you?"

Oh… Dexter demanding his money back was something I hadn't considered. Along with Jack and I, Lachlan, Caroline, Ranald and Jack Senior, Katya and Dexter owned a share of the Lochside Welcome. I'd always reckoned Dexter pitched in to help us because he was sentimental about the hotel—the place where he and Katya had first hooked up. But if he now considered her 'the evil witch, I hope rots in hell', what was to stop him pitching up in Lochalshie and demanding his money back?

And there was no way we could afford for anyone to pull out.

"No, no," I said, overdoing the cheeriness. "As you say, Dexter'll charter that jet or arrange for a message to be plastered on the Tower of London, 'Katya, forgive me! You're wonderful', etc., and in two months' we'll all be laughing about it."

With any luck, but the thought Jack had planted joined all the other worries whirling around my head. Nanna's health, worries that the menopause was robbing my mother of her brain cells, and fears that once again the future of the Lochside Welcome balanced on precarious foundations…

Chapter Seven

THE HANDYMAN

Evie woke me from fug-like sleep, and bad dreams at five am. The shelves in Dylan's room housed his old collection of Asterix albums, and I entertained myself with Asterix and Cleopatra—had Dylan ever moved beyond kids' cartoon books? —while I fed Evie, reading out bits of the story to her.

She fell asleep again afterwards; me brooding over Mum's revelations and trying to figure out what made her think Dylan, and I would welcome our father back with open arms.

We surfaced just after eight. "Right, Evie," I whispered as we made for the kitchen. "A bit of breakfast, some chat with your granny and let's steer the conversation well away from your nasty old grandpa!"

Mum was stirring something on the stove. "I made Evie some porridge," she said. "Thought it would remind her of home."

Fine by me. Chat about Evie's eating habits kept us clear of dangerous waters. And Nanna was, as the doctor had promised, much improved by the time the three of us turned up at the hospital. Off her drip and blinking at us, she asked if we'd bought any food with us as her breakfast had been "absolutely disgusting".

Thanks to previous NHS hospital visits, I knew most patients always begged visitors for food, darting wary glances at the nurses and dropping their voices. On our way to the hospital, I'd made Mum stop at the Marks and Spencer's Simply Food garage on the A47. She retrieved the two chicken wraps, an over-flowing bag of grapes, fresh orange juice and a packet of chocolate raisins I'd bought, from the shopping bag and put them on the table next to Nanna.

The doctor we'd spoken to yesterday came in holding a folder. Dressed in the same distinctive combo of red tights and navy shift dress, unbuttoned grubby tunic over the top, she didn't look as if she'd been home since we'd last talked, her eyes bloodshot. A nurse entered the room too, pushing a trolley loaded with equipment.

Nanna turned to him as he stopped the trolley next to her bedside and fluttered her eyelashes. "Hello, Doctor! I hope you're not looking for more blood. I've got none left."

He bit his lip, glancing over at the actual doctor, who rolled her eyes.

"Nanna, your doctor's over there." I pointed at her. Nanna glanced up before returning her attention to the nurse. "Well, I never."

My mum muttered a 'sorry' on her mother's behalf. We offered to leave, but Nanna said she didn't mind if we stayed.

The doctor cleared her throat. "Mrs Cooper, we need to do an electrocardiogram to check your heart. The process isn't painful, but we need to attach these electrodes to your chest, legs and arms. Is that okay?"

"Yes, Doctor," Nanna replied, her words directed at the nurse, "as long as you're the one who puts the patches on my chest."

Oh, for heaven's sake. The nurse took it in his stride, tearing the coverings off the patches and sticking them on. Evie gurgled. She was at that stage where she came out with a stream of sounds the whole time—goos, gaas oohs and ahs. If you listened hard enough, they made sense. Now, she was telling me she didn't think much of her current environment at all. We should leave toot sweet. She wriggled in my arms, her own stretched out towards the ground.

Test carried out—Nanna's heart function adequate, thank goodness—Doctor Waveney said she could go home in the afternoon. The X-ray had shown no broken bones. But the investigations they had carried out already, the doctor added, showed Nanna had osteoporosis. Her weakened bones had made a fall 'almost inevitable', and she had been lucky this time to avoid shattering her hips.

"But I drink milk every day!" Nanna exclaimed. "That's got calcium for your bones in it."

Doctor Waveney shook her head. "It helps, but you are quite underweight."

The Cooper genes were ones I'd always regarded as a genetic lottery win. My nanna was skinny, as was my mum and six months post-Evie's birth, I'd snapped back to my previous state. If the possibility of shattered hip bones in later life was the result, I might need to rethink the 'luck' element.

"I'll book you in for an appointment with the physiotherapist to discuss exercises you can do to strengthen your bones," the doctor said. "No jogging, though!"

Nanna shared my opinion of jogging. Painful, pointless and its proponents pitiful.

Dr Waveney spotted the food we'd brought in for Nanna. "You might want to think about upping your calorie intake. I'll ask the dietician to pop in before you leave too, to discuss what you should eat."

She looked at the chicken wrap placed on Nanna's bedside cabinet wistfully. "That will be a lot better than what you get in here."

Nanna handed her one of the chicken wraps. "Have one, Nurse. You need to keep your strength up."

"Doctor, Nanna!" I bleated, but Doctor Waveney hadn't noticed, ripping into the wrap as if terrified someone might snatch it from her. She scuttled out, the old-fashioned pager on her waistband bleeping.

I jiggled Evie up and down. The protests at being kept still intensified. No way was I letting her loose in here, with its numerous temptations to pull down on top of her.

Promising Nanna we would return that afternoon to drop her home, Mum and I left. There was no point returning to Great Yarmouth just to come back again to pick her up when she was discharged. Outside, we stopped at Mum's car, having walked back there in complete silence.

"I made some sandwiches," Mum said. "We could eat them in the car if you like...?"

"No, thank you." Too risky. I'd take a mouthful of egg mayonnaise and accidentally agree to a father-daughter reunion.

"I'm going to take Evie for a walk. See if we can find a park to play in. I'll see you back here later."

The rest of the day was little better. Nanna's exit from the hospital was not straightforward. The nurse who'd carried out the cardiogram earlier, pushed her to the car in a wheelchair, Nanna fluffing her hair out as he did so. But it took him several attempts to get her in. Then Nanna remembered she'd left her handbag beside her bed. I dashed back to the ward to locate it, only to find the hospital cleaners had already swept it up and deposited it in lost property.

Forty-five minutes later, the lost property people demanding written proof from Nanna that she authorised me to pick up her handbag, we were able to drop her off at her house. Kathleen Millar was waiting for us, her face pinched with worry. She and Nanna might pretend an age-old rivalry, but they'd been friends through marriages, children, widowhood, divorces and everything in between.

"Lillian!" she trilled, artificial cheeriness disguising anxiety, as Mum and I unpacked the foldable wheelchair the hospital had lent us. "I'm not going in that!" Nanna declared, eyeing it beadily. The wheelchair was of little use, anyway. Nanna had steps up to her front door and her house, while neat and tidy, was compact. It would be tricky to manoeuvre a wheelchair in there. Mum and I ended up standing either side of her to take her inside, while Kathleen held onto Evie, proclaiming in a loud voice about Evie's appearance.

"Goodness, she looks nothing like you, Gaby! What a little beauty!"

I gritted my teeth and thanked Kathleen for her observation. Tactlessness was meant to be a side effect of ageing.

The hospital's physiotherapist had suggested we look at adapting Nanna's old-fashioned bathroom, but the waiting list for social care services to provide the railings was months long.

"I know a man who could do it for you," my mum volunteered once we had lowered Nanna into an armchair.

Nanna and I shot her suspicious looks. "Dylan?" Nanna asked. "If you ask my grandson, Mandy, we'll be waiting longer than social services."

"No, not Dylan," my mum replied, "some-someone else."

"Who? Not Warren Marshall. I know you were friends with his sister at school, but he's the worst joiner in Norfolk," Nanna declared. "Dylan can do it."

The doorbell rang. Mum dashed past me, exchanging whispers with whoever was at the front door.

I cocked my head to one side. The whispers were inaudible, but I made out the odd sound. That once-so familiar Surrey twang, as he'd grown up in a different part of England than my mum.

I stiffened, dread curdling in my stomach.

No prizes for guessing who.

Chapter Eight

A SPOT OF UNCLE/NIECE BONDING

Nanna, whose hearing could be selective, stiffened. "That's not Tony Richardson, is it?"

Kathleen, closest to the door, stuck her head out. "Yes!"

"Is she back with him?" Nanna asked me, voice incredulous.

I nodded.

"Well, I never! That dust-bag!"

Dust-bag was Nanna's choicest insult for my absentee dad, her older person interpretation of douche bag. Also 'that niblet', which Katya and I guessed meant 'nob'.

The footsteps in the hallway got closer. Any second now and I'd be face to face with my long absentee dad. *Not* prepared.

"Mandy!" Nanna called out sharply. "If you let that man into my home, I'll disinherit you! You'll never see a penny of mine. Kathleen will get every one of the Wedg-wood ladies!"

She swept an arm behind her—the sideboard cluttered with china figurines.

Not sure how much of a threat that was, given that Kathleen looked less than thrilled. Nanna once took her figurines to the Antiques Roadshow. An expert inspected them for so long, Nanna began planning a round-the-world luxury cruise in her head, only for the expert to shake his head. "An interesting collection, but I'm afraid they are all the mass production ones, and there are signs of wear and tear. You'd be lucky to fetch a few hundred pounds for the lot."

"But Tony's volunteered to help make your house disability-friendly," Mum replied from the hallway, as more whispered exchanges took place. "I thought..."

"Thought nothing!" Nanna replied, clasping a hand to her chest. "Oooohhhh!"

"Nanna!" I darted forward and crouched down. "Are you okay?"

"My heart, my heart! The strain!"

Her spare hand gripped mine, eyes fluttering and her breath coming in gasps. I swallowed back nausea as my heart thumped too hard too. This might be the first case of grandmother and granddaughter dying of a heart attack together. Poor Evie left a motherless bairn, Jack weeping into his whisky night after night...

Kathleen, Evie still in her arms, stomped out of the room. "Mandy, get rid of that man at once! You're causing your poor mother unnecessary stress at the worst possible time."

Nanna winked at me. I stifled a grin and squeezed her hand as my heart stopped thumping in my ears.

"Nanna," I dropped my voice, "that was naughty!"

"Did the job, though, didn't it?" Nanna whispered back.

Tony dispatched, Nanna made the most of her near heart-attack status. "Mandy," she croaked when Mum let herself back in the room, expression hangdog. "Please, *never* do that again."

To me, "Gaby, is there any more of that nice Marks and Spencer's food? I might manage a little prawn sandwich. Or some cheesecake, if there is any? Keep my strength up."

Even Kathleen narrowed her eyes at that, but we escaped any further Tony talk and Mum, and I left half an hour later.

"See you soon, Nanna," I said as I kissed her goodbye, wondering if that was true.

Kathleen assured us she would stay the night with Nanna. They planned an evening catching up on all the soaps Nanna had missed while in hospital.

Mum attempted an explanation as we got into the car. "But if you would just—"

"Springing him on Nanna and me like that wasn't fair." I settled Evie in her chair. How much of today's drama had she taken in?

In the back seat, I pulled on the seatbelt. "Please can we drop the subject, Mum?"

The rest of the journey took place in silence, punctuated by heavy sighs on my mum's part. Dylan didn't bother to return to the house, phoning me later for an update on Nanna.

Aware that it was ridiculously juvenile of me to sulk in his room for yet another night, Mum and I came to a compromise that evening where Evie and I came downstairs, the three of us eating dinner together. We then watched TV while Mum played with her granddaughter.

"You don't mind what Granny Mandy does, do you my little darling?"

Evie, in the middle of a nappy change, her white skin in perfect contrast to the dark auburn locks that covered her head, gurgled something that sounded remarkably like a 'no'.

I made my best impression of a Clydesdale horse blowing out air.

In bed later, Evie asleep beside me once more, the window clattering startled me. Opening the curtains, I stared out in disbelief. Dylan.

"Are you reliving your youth?" I asked as I yanked the window up to let him in. He'd shinned up via the old elm tree next to the window, a move teenage Dylan used all the time when he sneaked out to clubs.

"The light's on in the living room," he said, collapsing onto the bed beside me. "I didn't want to risk bumping into Mum and hearing her yak on about bloody Tony. Can't believe she tried to foist him on you this afternoon."

The interruption had disturbed Evie, who woke up staring at the unfamiliar man.

"Meet your niece, Dylan. The amazing, adorable, fantastic Evie."

He turned his head to squint at Evie and me. Evie grinned at him—the move pure Jack McAllan. She reached out a hand—the gesture she used when she wanted someone else to hold her. Dylan's face battled dismay and fear.

Too bad. I picked Evie up and plopped her in his arms. "For heaven's sake. Be nice. If you ever have kids, you don't want to be anything like our father, do you?"

Tony hadn't been a hands-on dad. My mum once confessed he'd never changed a nappy when Dylan and I had been babies. Or got up at night when one of us woke up crying.

Dylan, one hand cradling her bottom and the other her

back, shook his head. "I won't be anything like Tony because I'm not going to be a dad, full stop."

My brother's 30 years on earth had so far not produced a regular girlfriend. He might deny being anything like Tony, but that lack of commitment to any woman signalled he was the same. Why have one partner when you can have many?

"You never know," I said. "Maybe the girl of your dreams is just around the corner, and in a few years', Evie will have a little cousin to play with, which would be lovely, and you would always be welcome in Lochalshie. You could pop up for family holidays, you and your partner or wife and your little one. Little twos perhaps? The experience with Evie might end up changing you so much you want to—"

"Gaby. I'm not having children. Okay?"

Wow, I'd touched a nerve there. But at least it meant that unlike Tony, he wouldn't leave abandoned children in his wake. Evie was fiddling with the rope chain around his neck, and he hoicked it out for her to grab—eyes amused. It was as if he was seeing his niece for the first time. The Evie charm trick worked its magic once more.

"D'you have anything to eat?" Dylan asked. "I'm starving."

The Millionaire's shortbread I'd snaffled from the coffee shop was still in my rucksack. There was also a small Tupperware box packed with chopped fruit. I withdrew both, removing the lid from the box and offering it to Evie.

She eyed the contents, and the slice of shortbread Dylan was unwrapping and pouted.

"Here, Evie. Delicious bananas and strawberries. Nature's yummy sweeties!"

Evie specialised in beady stares. She gave me one now,

making Dylan laugh. He broke off a bit of shortbread, gouged out a blob of caramel on his finger and held it to her mouth. Evie licked it off, her face lighting up.

The parent in me cringed. Germy fingers! A mega dose of sugar! Perhaps the sacrifice for the greater good was Dylan bonding with his niece.

Evie grabbed Dylan's hair, yanking his head towards her. "Ow!"

"I think that's her way of telling you she wants another bit of caramel," I said, the scene affecting me far more than I expected. Dylan and Evie seemed very taken with each other.

He cleared his throat. "Gaby, I've got a favour to ask. A big one."

"Not money—we've got none to spare. And I'm not phoning any of your girlfriends and pretending you've died in a tragic accident so that you don't need to tell whoever you've dumped them."

Dylan made me do that once when he was 18. The tactic might have worked if I hadn't burst into hysterical laughter after saying, 'So sorry, Lucille, but you won't be able to see my brother anymore. He farted so much last night, he gassed himself to death.'

"No, I don't want your money or help with my love life. It's, um, something else."

Talk about a build-up.

"Can I come back to Lochalshie with you for a few months?"

"Good grief! Why?"

Hard to picture Dylan in Lochalshie. Great Yarmouth was no metropolis, but I knew he hung out in Norwich a lot. How was he going to manage life in a tiny, remote village?

"I wondered…" He picked up a bit of banana and

offered it to Evie. When she spat it out, he broke her off a bit of chocolate.

"If-Jack-could-give-me-a-job."

"What as?"

"Anything. I'll work behind the bar. Or as a waiter. Whatever you need."

At this time of year? Nothing. In the last few weeks, I'd walked in on Jack a few times, his head in his hands as he studied the computer screen in front of him, trying to work out which Peter he could rob to pay Paul so that Jolene, Xavier and the two other locals who helped us out received a monthly salary. Other hotels—the Royal George, for instance—were far more ruthless, laying off staff in the quieter months and then taking them on again come the summer.

Christmas and New Year *might* up our employee needs temporarily. Unlikely, though.

"But what about all your experience? Won't employers jump at the chance of having you work for them?"

He took a deep breath. "About that…"

The rest of Dylan's sorry story emerged. He hadn't lost his job; he'd been sacked. No, Mum didn't know that bit. Hence the request for a job where people wouldn't ask for references.

"You didn't steal from the company, did you?" A joke, but if he had, I would need to reconsider. The hotel's finances couldn't handle fraud.

"No. Absolutely not! It was something else. It was— never mind. But can I?"

"C'mon, why were you sacked?"

"I'm not telling you."

His face had taken on a buttoned-up look; enough to

convince me that further questioning would get me nowhere.

"Please, Gaby. It would mean so much to me."

"Oh, all right then. The pay's rubbish and you can only stay with us for a few days. After that, you'll need to find somewhere else as we don't have room."

Dylan nodded, the lines on his forehead smoothing out. "Thanks. You're a lifesaver."

Dylan hadn't thanked me for anything in years. Decades, perhaps. Bountiful sister was a novelty position for me. He stood up, bending over to drop a kiss on Evie's head, and let himself out, saying he would sleep in the box room.

"What am I going to do about Project Amazing Christmas, Evie?" I whispered, snuggling down to lie next to her. She was at the resisting sleep stage—tiny body exhausted, developing brain terrified it would miss out on something and making her fight the urge to close her eyes.

"The time it takes to get from Norfolk to Lochalshie wouldn't help Nanna's fragile bones and weakened muscles. And then there's the sticky issue of Mum's over-eagerness to bring Tony to Lochalshie. The hotel is in trouble, my best friend's broken-hearted, and we've got ourselves a house guest."

Less than four weeks until Christmas…

Oh-oh.

Chapter Nine

WHAT A GOOD WIFE SHOULD DO

Mum's ancient Fiesta broke down on the way to the airport: Was this deliberate, I wondered, as the three of us huddled together on the hard shoulder waiting for the RAC to arrive; Mum trying to stop Dylan and I leaving before she'd forced us to sit down with our father?

The RAC van drew up. Out bounded a cheery guy dressed in a bright orange hi-vis jacket who seemed familiar. "Dylan," he nodded to my brother. "It's been ages! Have you seen Jonno and the others lately?"

Dylan shook his head. He appeared less than thrilled at the reunion, muttering that we would miss the flight. I phoned Katya. She'd decided to hide out in Lochalshie while she figured out what to do and use the peace and quiet to get on with a writing project. She was heading for the airport in an Uber. The car could swing by our way to pick us up.

My mum clasped my brother's arm. "Dylan, love. Please don't go."

You'd have thought she would leap at the chance of

offloading him. Since Dylan's return to the comforts of home at 24, my mum had moaned continually about how little he did around the house.

Dylan stared rigidly ahead. "Are you still seeing him?"

"If you mean your father, yes, I am."

She twisted to face me. "Gaby, love. He asks after you all the time."

"Sure he does," I replied, too mindful of my mum's excuses for Dylan over the years to believe her. (*Your brother sends his love. Dylan hopes you've got over the morning sickness. He had to work this weekend, so he wasn't able to come with your Nanna and me to meet his new niece.*)

Katya's Uber pulled up. I kissed my mum's cheek. "I'll call you in a few days to check on Nanna, okay? I hope it doesn't cost too much to repair the car."

And with that, we were off—Mum watching forlornly as the Uber pulled out.

As the three of us boarded the plane for Edinburgh at Norwich, I spotted Mr Designer Shirt once more. The length of his stay had coincided with mine. I nudged Dylan. "Look. There's that guy again!"

"What guy?" Dylan said, voice hyper-casual.

"Him! The one that sat next to me on the flight down and made rude comments about Evie." *Also, the one you're pretending not to know when I've already spotted the two of you meet eyes and look away*—no point pushing it. Dylan would keep pretending not to have any idea what I was talking about. I didn't see the guy get on the flight, so either he'd sneaked past us somehow, wangling a better upgrade where you got to sit at the opposite end of a plane from any children, or he wasn't returning to Edinburgh.

Either way, Evie was as good as gold—her little brow only wrinkling momentarily when the flight took off. Lucian seated with his mother at the back of the plane, however, screamed his head off, and then cried almost all the way back. By the time the plane touched down, he and his mother looked wrung out. The passengers barged past her, all of them sending Lucian dirty looks.

"Katya! Dylan too... nice to see you."

Jack, to give him credit, made it sound genuine as he greeted the party of five in the arrivals hall at Edinburgh Airport, two of them fractious. A good wife tells her husband before she springs anything on him. A dreadful wife lets her phone run out of charge, fires it up via the medium of the over-priced charging points in an airport and rattles off a text. "Jack, hi! Can't wait to get back! Got some guests with me. See you soon XXXXXXXX"

Evie stuck her arms straight out as soon as she saw him, and I handed her over. "Um, so Dylan is staying with us for a wee while, just a teeny-tiny time. We'll hardly notice him at all. He had to come back with me; otherwise, my mum will do something mad like bringing our dad home and force Dylan to listen while he harps on about how sorry he is."

As Dylan was right in front of us, Jack confined his comments on our new living arrangements to an 'Okay' and limited signalling with his eyes that this was far from ideal.

He'd driven down to Edinburgh in the Highland Tours minibus—the bright tartan logo on the side advertising sightseeing trips—so there was plenty of room for the unexpected arrivals. Being more organised than my brother, Katya had booked into the Airbnb on the High Street—its availability immediate, thanks to the time of year. Guests were much more welcome when they weren't about to take up residency in your home.

The journey back to Lochalshie in the minibus was muted—me trying to steer the conversation in a non-controversial, positive direction. The weather! Goodness me, Dylan would find it cold. I still hadn't adapted, and I'd been living in the village for three and a half years now. Christmas! Wouldn't it be wonderful now Katya and I both had children! We would spoil them something rotten. I already had my eye on this super-cute baby Santa outfit for Evie.

No reply from the back.

Sat next to Jack in the front, I noticed his jaw tighten at the mention of Christmas, now a mere 22 days away. "Are all the rooms booked out yet?" I asked, sotto voce. "And what about reservations for Christmas lunch?"

"The same. A few to fill," Jack whispered back, glancing in the mirror behind him at Katya who was staring out the window, mouth down-turned. Was he worried the information might get back to Dexter, who'd make noises about how we were running the hotel? While Katya and Dexter had little practical input into the hotel's day-to-day life, they bombarded us with promotional and marketing advice. That we, er, often ignored, too busy to face the thought of all that 24/7 social media jolliness a small business seemed to need.

"Only three of the rooms are booked up," Jack added, "and two of the six parties for Christmas Day have cancelled," Jack replied. "Hardly worth opening for."

"There's always my job," I said this so often these days it had turned into my catchphrase. I meant it as a last resort. If the hotel doesn't work out and we end up having to sell up to those evil witches who owned Hammerstone Hotels and wanted to get their greedy mitts on the land so they could knock down the hotel and build lodges on the grounds, we would at least have my job. Jack could return to Highland Tours, where he ferried people around Outlander places.

But the hotel's our dream, that persistent voice piped up, *because it's not about money and jobs, it means so much more to us…*

Jack smiled at me, the gesture not quite meeting his eyes. "I know."

The 'Welcome to Lochalshie!' sign greeted me like a long-lost friend. Katya glanced up too, pointing it out to Lucian, who snuffled in reply. We dropped her off outside the Airbnb, which was next to Jamal's General Store. The man himself appeared at that precise moment.

"Katya!" he called out. "Here are the keys to your house. I've still got stocks o' that almond milk. D'ye want some?"

Too much for Katya to hope that her sojourn in Lochalshie would pass under the radar. She took the keys and muttered that she'd pop in later.

Mhari, timing as impeccable as ever, materialised. "Hiya, Katya. Can I hae a wee peek at Lucian?"

Katya hugged Lucian tightly to her chest, so his face wasn't visible and vanished indoors, slamming the door behind her.

"Well," Mhari said, folding her arms and staring at the door. "That wasnae friendly, was it? What's she doing here?"

"Busy writing!" I announced. "Do you remember *High Heels and Pink Glitter*?"

"How could I forget? Made my life a misery for weeks reading bits o' it out loud to me and asking me what I thought."

Last year, Katya had ghost-written a book for Caitlin, a female billionaire clean romance where she had to work out how to keep the couple apart for 320 pages, after which they could kiss for the first time. ("Flamin' hardest challenge, ever!" she told me.)

The novel had proved a roaring success, sales-wise, topping the New York Times chart several weeks in a row. Caitlin's fans raved about the book on Amazon. "Best book EVAH!!!!!!! Caitlin's, like, such an awesuuuuuuuuummmm writer!"

"Katya is here writing book number two in the trilogy— *High Heels and Blue Glitter*."

"Blue?" Mhari said, brightening up. "I thought the books were no' meant tae have dirty bits in them? That's why I gave up reading the last one. But if she's gonnae write filth, I'm happy to help her out. Plenty o' experience in *that* department."

Good Lord. Did she mean what she got up to with Lachlan? All those times they used to drive out in his van together, I assumed she was helping him out with one of his criminal enterprises… maybe they were, gulp, off dogging?

Her attention landed on Dylan sat in the back of the minibus. "Dylan, aye? What brings you here?"

Dylan, thumb moving in double quick time over his phone, glanced up. "I wanted a change."

"Aye? Fae what?"

He glanced up again, taken aback. "Er… the rat race?"

Mhari nodded. "Fair dos. What are you goin' tae do about a job?"

Dylan's eyes flashed dismay, and his mouth dropped open. Mhari had a knack of sniffing out someone's weakness right from the off—Dylan's ignoble sacking, for instance.

"I'm gonna work for Jack," he said.

Next to me, Jack groaned. Terrific. We'd planned to tell

Xavier and Jolene ourselves. Stress that Dylan wasn't here to steal anyone's job at a time of year when money was tight, family member or not. No chance now. In a matter of seconds, Mhari had her phone in hand—my mistake. Now. My phone pinged. She'd just updated the Lochalshie WhatsApp group. *Gaby's brother here! The English stealing all the jobs off the locals,* which was rich given that Jolene, Xavier and I were all incomers.

"Bye, Mhari," I said, resisting the urge to poke my tongue out and flick her the vees. We drove off as she shouted something drowned out by the engine noise.

"Christ," Dylan said, "who's she? She's awful."

Plan A foiled then. Dylan would need to sleep on the sofa in the living room in our house. I had planned to offload him on Mhari asap. In my head, I even imagined them discovering they were each other's dreams come true.

Mhari, meet Dylan. As far as I'm aware, he's never been with anyone longer than a month. And he's not house-trained. Count yourself lucky if he ever lifts a finger to help you around the house. Dylan, meet Mhari. She is the nosiest woman alive and spends 90 percent of her waking hours staring at her phone. She will interrogate you to within an inch of your life, find out every one of your dirty secrets and then tell everyone about them.

Maybe not.

Mildred sat in our front window, watched the minibus balefully as we got out. I turned, Evie strapped to my chest, and she fled. The cat flap rattled open around the back. We'd be lucky to see her again before 9pm, the time she'd found out it was safe to return, as Evie was always in bed then. Whenever Evie was at her grandmother's, Mildred wandered the whole of our house, nose sniffing the air suspiciously. When she figured out her nemesis was nowhere to be seen, she took up residence on the sofa, safe for the moment from the one who enjoyed tugging her tail far too much.

In the house, I handed Evie to Jack, dumped my bags upstairs and located the sleeping bag from the cupboard under the stairs.

"Right," Jack said, watching as Dylan settled himself into an armchair muttering about how cold it was. "Gaby and I are off to the pub."

"Great!" Dylan leapt to his feet. "I don't need to get changed, do I? The Lochside Welcome's not that smart, is it?"

Jack handed Evie over and grinned at him. "Not you, mate. You're earning your keep. We're off to the pub while you babysit your niece. Cheerio!"

Chapter Ten

A RED LETTER DAY

My face fell. "Oh, but I'm—"

He whisked me out of the house before I could protest further—*But, but, but Dylan's hopeless. We'll return and find our daughter has had a terrible accident!*

Jack marched us to the Lochside Welcome in double quick time, my hand clutched in his. "What is going on with your family?" he asked as he pushed open the door. The warmth enfolded us. The log fire at the far end must have been lit a while ago, making the room hot enough for everyone to be in their shirtsleeves. Basshunter's Jingle Bell Rock belted out of the jukebox. *Let me hear you say ho, ho, ho...*

Terry and the locals, whose permanent positions in the bar never changed, day in day out, raised their pints in greeting. (We'd even painted their names on the back of the stools for them—the cushions moulded to each individual arse.) Jolene, in conversation with Laney Haggerty, broke off to ask after my nanna, and Xavier appeared from behind the kitchen door to say 'hello'.

But the total of our customers were the regulars and

four women drinking coffees. Bills of varying (horrific) amounts swam in front of my eyes. We needed the Christmas big spenders urgently.

"They appear to be falling apart," I said to Jack. First, my grandmother and her fall, then my mother and her foolish life choices. Now my brother jobless and broke.

"What are you going to do about inviting your mum and nanna for our Christmas on the 27th? You can't back out of that now."

Couldn't I? The spectre of Christmas past loomed. Dylan and I sat at the table, our mum yelling into the phone. "Where are you! The turkey's burnt, the roast potatoes have gone cold and the gravy's lumpy! Your children have brought you a nice present too!" Why should that memory hang over the day, Evie's first 'proper' Christmas that I wanted to be filled with fun, laughter and the people I loved?

"We'll see," I said. Three weeks should be enough time for Tony to give up his repentant husband/father act, Mum to see through him and my plans to be back on track.

I looked around me. "Why aren't our Christmas decorations up yet?"

Unlike the outside of the hotel, no-one had yet decked the halls with boughs and holly—no wonder we were struggling to channel Christmas.

"Ashley never put them up until ten days before," Jolene called over. I pulled up a stool at the bar and asked for a Diet Coke. "He had a thing about Christmas starting too early."

Jack climbed onto the stool next to me. "Aye. Me too: None o' this nonsense where you rev up for the festive season months in advance."

This from the man fretting about Christmas customers!

"Today is the third of December," I pointed out.

"Is it?" He looked genuinely startled.

"Doesn't the fact that it's dark outside at quarter to four give it away?" I pointed at the view behind us—the French windows that looked out at the empty beer garden and the loch beyond it, all pewter grey skies, the dark shape of the hills beyond only just visible.

"The days run away… Jolene, can I have one of those new beers? The ones from that craft brewery in Oban?"

As it was so quiet, my husband wasn't needed behind the bar. Jolene uncapped the bottle, its label bright and eye-catching, and handed it over along with a soft drink for me. I dug into my purse and gave her the money, conscious that Jack shouldn't drink our profits.

Jolene stared at the handful of coins I handed over. "What's this?"

"Slot machine win," I said. "Weighing down my bag so much I almost got charged for excess baggage flying home."

I joined Jack at the bar. "Where's the tree that goes inside the hotel?"

"No idea," he said, now on his second bottle of IPA and sheepish. His fingers crept along the bar, reaching for mine. "Do you want anything to eat? It's on the house."

Not a chance. I had all that shrapnel lying at the bottom of my bag to unload.

"Can I phone home first?" I said, holding up my phone. "Better check our daughter is still alive."

Jack snatched the phone off me. "Let me do it," he said, "I'll put the fear o' God in him."

He meant Dylan would moan. Demand to know when I was coming home. Tell me Evie was crying her little heart out. Whereas if Jack asked, he might tell the truth.

A brief exchange took place. "They won? I had an accumulator bet on that, you dancer! Aye, so Evie? Well done, she'll no' wake up now until the morning. When will we be home? Och, later. Much later. Help yersel' to anything in the fridge."

In the background, Dylan squawked a complaint and then shut up, no doubt remembering that he was meant to be sucking up to us in gratitude for free digs and a job.

Jack put the phone face down on the bar and swivelled his stool to face me, dark eyes sparkling with mischief. "Our daughter is fast asleep. Dylan managed to change her nappy and feed her. I'm up £100 in a bet. Mrs McAllan, d'ye fancy a night out?"

"All right then. It's been ages, hasn't it?"

Xavier went all out—presenting us with a 16-inch pizza lavishly covered in brie, turkey and cranberry as a nod to Christmas. I insisted on counting out the exact cost in small change, determined not to make any dents in our tiny profits.

Food finished, we parked ourselves in the prime spot—the booth nearest to the wood-burning stove pelting out heat as The Waitresses sang about sitting out Christmas this year. Jack was half-way down his fourth craft beer, the liquid disappearing at an alarming rate and the jokey, relaxed air he'd worn earlier banished.

I clasped his hand. "Are the Christmas bookings bothering you?"

He let out a sigh. "A bit. After the summer we had…"

He squeezed my fingers. "S'pose I knew what we were taking on."

True. But perhaps those previous sunny summers tricked us, persuaded Jack and me that running a small hotel in a remote area would be a challenge but doable.

"Part o' it," he added, "is provin' to my father I'm a success. God knows why."

God knows indeed. Jack's dad shared the abandon your family trait with mine. After years of alcoholism, he'd embarked on the Twelve Steps and then stepped in last year to help finance the hotel.

"Sorry, Jack." Jolene. She placed an envelope in front of him. "The postie delivered this earlier. I'd forgotten about it until now."

She scuttled off.

Jack glanced down and back up again, face serious once more. The letter bore the postmark of the Her Majesty's Revenues and Customs, colloquially known as the taxman. When sent out with the usual times of the tax year, a letter stamped HMRC was never one you welcomed. Red too.

We stared at it—perhaps in the hope that if we looked at the envelope long enough, it would disappear. Jack ripped it open and pulled out the letter, eyes scanning the contents.

He blinked. "Looks like we owe HMRC money."

"What? But how come…?"

We used an accountant in Oban, whose job it was to take care of such things. He'd submitted our annual return in October, and a letter came out soon after telling us what we owed and that had been paid up.

"HMRC has since re-investigated," Jack replied, "checking back over the last four years before we took charge. The previous owner's tax returns might have been on the creative side."

The sum the HMRC demanded now was… eye-watering.

"What are we going to do?" I asked, mind running through the options. Sell my car? The minibus? Donate my pitiful savings? Make Jack place accumulator bets every day from now on? Hunt down Ashley and make him cough up? Survive on beans on toast for the next 10 years? Pretend to Evie that birthdays and Christmases never involved presents?

"I don't know. Unless bookings miraculously shoot through the roof, I've no idea how we'll pay it…

"Oh, God, Gaby. What are we going to do?"

We both spent a wretched night tossing and turning, giving up on sleep at 3am and discussing wild plans.

"Ask Ranald," I said, knowing he would leap at the chance of helping. "Or your father." Ditto. Jack and Jack Senior's reconciliation last year meant the world to Jack's reformed alcoholic father. Thanks to a nifty investment in a salmon fish farm later sold to a successful Norwegian company, he was loaded. Ranald and Jack Senior were co-owners in the hotel anyway. If they coughed up the missing tax bill, we'd ensure they received more of the profits in the next few years.

But male pride made Jack shrink from the notion. "A man is meant to provide for his family, Gaby."

"Nonsense," I said, stroking his cheek. "This is the 21st century. If the worst comes to the worst, I can return to full-time design work and be the breadwinner. Or we can run off and join the circus as we planned when I was pregnant with Evie."

He smiled weakly. "Aye, alright. Let's hope it doesnae come to that. I haven't practised my fire swallowing skills in ages."

Everything always looks brighter in the morning. Evie

slept in too, waking up only when I let myself into her room.

"Hey, gorgeous girl! Have you got any ideas for how to make tax bills disappear?"

She goo-gooed at me, kicking her legs in the air. I picked her up. They should bottle the baby smell and hand it out to stressed executives. The day Evie lost that warm, milky aroma, I would cry. Even the wet nappy pong didn't put me off.

Downstairs, Dylan announced he was going to mooch around the village to see what passed for entertainment in this part of the world. I smiled noncommittally.

Jack, who'd been out in the garden making phone calls, let himself back in as soon as Dylan left. "I've phoned the HMRC," he told me, helping himself to coffee. "And negotiated time to pay the bill. Not nearly as much as we need, but it gives us wriggle room."

I kissed him. "Clever you."

Coffee gulped down in record time, he zipped up the Lochside Welcome dark fleece over his T-shirt. "I'll no' say anything to anyone about the tax bill just yet," he told me about to head for the hotel to cover the lunchtime shift. I nodded—no need to ruin Christmas for everyone else with worries over their livelihoods.

"Everything will be fine!" I said, dialling up the brightness as I kissed him goodbye.

"Aye, I know."

Off he went. Did his face sag the way mine did the minute he could no longer see me? Sodding Christmas. Everything had looked far more straightforward months ago when we'd launched the Lochside Welcome's brand-new festive package and envisaged a busy December catering for all those lunches and dinners, then the guests staying overnight. Waving them a fond (relieved) farewell on Boxing Day and then—boom! A traditional family Christmas where we packed the hotel with our friends and family in joyful celebration. Everyone happy and content.

We were struggling with the first goal. The second seemed impossible.

My mum—oh, I didn't want to think about that… Split from my dad? Up here with us on Christmas Day, a recovered Nanna Cooper in tow, as I'd initially imagined? Katya's situation resolved, whatever that meant. (Note to self: phone Dexter. Do my persuasive best with him. Hadn't I made the Blissful Beauty's UK launch—and bolstered his career in doing so—outstanding at the time? He owed me.)

And finally, Dylan. Who now seemed to be my responsibility. A home, a job, happiness (even if I wondered why he deserved it).

Tall orders all round.

Chapter Eleven

TINSEL, BAUBLES AND HARE-BRAINED SCHEMES

Time to super-charge the festive mood, I told myself as Evie's cries woke me the next morning. Christmas was 20 days away and still salvageable.

Besides me, Jack groaned. "Don't move. It's five o'clock in the morning. She might go back to sleep."

The whimpers intensified, followed by outright screaming.

"Gaby?" Dylan called up the stairs. "Is she meant to yell like that?"

As I let myself out of the bedroom, I met him trotting up the stairs, hair sticking on end. "God almighty," he said, "what a set of lungs she's got on her. Good job I packed those Bose headphones, eh?" He pushed past me to the bathroom.

No such luxury for Jack and me, tempting as it often was to cover our ears and wait for Evie to scream herself out. But once I'd changed the sopping nappy and settled her next to Jack, both of them facing me and snuffling in unison, I was able to squeeze in three hours of work for

Blissful Beauty, the Mac book propped up on my lap while everyone else slept. After some skilful negotiation last year, I'd persuaded my employer, Blissful Beauty, to let me job share the UK head of design post. HR wasn't keen on it, but I had friends in high places. Caitlin Cartier, who owned the company, and I had a long history together, which made my request for part-time, remote working easier to ask.

When Evie eventually woke up again protesting about her empty stomach, she and Jack were much cheerier thanks to the restorative powers of sleep.

Jack had worked ten days on the trot at the Lochside Welcome, so he was off for the day. In the kitchen, he bunged a couple of slices of leftover pizza in the microwave as Dylan stirred himself off the sofa, sniffing his air.

"Excellent breakfast choice. Can I have some?"

The microwave pinged. "Not a chance," Jack said, taking the floppy slices from the plate and cramming melty cheese into his mouth. When Dylan looked as if he might burst into tears, he sighed and handed over the second slice.

"I thought I might put up the Christmas decorations in the Lochside Welcome this morning," I announced as I warmed up a jar of baby cottage pie for Evie. "Would either of you like to help?"

Jack and Dylan, now bickering over who was going to win the English premier league at the end of the football season, paused.

"First day I've had away from that place in ages," Jack muttered, as Dylan mumbled something about interior décor not being his thing.

"Well, Evie's all yours this morning then!" I said, shoving her and the warmed-up cottage pie into Jack's arms and fleeing before he could stop me.

Bacon sizzling greeted me at the Lochside Welcome.

Xavier was on breakfast duty for the hotel's six overnight guests. He tossed me a roll straight out of the oven, the heat of it making me yelp in surprise and drop it. I snatched it off the floor. Three-second rule, right?

"Where are the Christmas decorations?" I asked through a mouthful of hot bread and jam, as Xavier watched me in fascinated disgust. A hygiene freak (useful quality in a hotel chef), he found my eating habits deplorable.

"Jolene will know," he replied as she pushed her way into the kitchen, her arms laden with dirty dishes.

Jolene dumped the plates in the dishwasher and nodded. "In the cupboard under the stairs? Shall we?"

"Don't worry about your job here," I said as I followed her into the bowels of the hotel—the storeroom at the back piled with cardboard boxes and old broken furniture, anxious that she shouldn't think Dylan was about to muscle in and steal her employment.

"Why's he moved to Lochalshie?" Jolene asked as she unearthed several plastic bags filled with the decorations. In common with other Kiwis I'd met, Jolene didn't skirt around anything.

"Did he get the sack from his last job?"

Argh. I'd planned to fudge the issue. *My brother fancied a change of scene! You don't get more of a change than moving from the south-east of England to the north-west of Scotland, right?* Trust Jolene to guess he was here because he wouldn't be able to get a job anywhere else.

"Yes," I said hurriedly, "though he won't tell me why. I checked it wasn't stealing from the company. The hotel doesn't make nearly enough money for us to afford someone skimming from it."

Jolene handed me two of the bags. "He can come and live with us if you like?"

The offer made me blink back tears. Jolene's other qualities included the ability to figure out what a person needed without asking. I don't know how I'd have coped with motherhood without her close by. Endless offers to look after Evie for me when I was flat out exhausted. Forever dropping in on the house bearing gifts. "Here. These are Tamar's old onesies. He's outgrown them? You might as well have them?"

"This isn't me being kind," Jolene threw in now as we made our way back to the public bar armed with enough tinsel and fairy lights to decorate the entire village. "We've got a spare room. Dylan can contribute to the bills and help dilute Stewart."

Stewart... Jolene's partner widely considered to be a man punching well above his weight and the second person I met when I moved to Lochalshie. Then, a prodigious drinker. Latterly, he'd given up. The man had always excelled at boring for Scotland. Recently, he'd added the Wonder of Sobriety to his repertoire. Admirable, yes, but heavy going for everyone around him.

Jolene and I spent an hour festooning the Lochside Welcome's ancient decorations all over the hotel, as Xavier, Terry and the regulars yelled useful/useless instructions from their stools.

To match the outside, I aimed for the tacky aesthetic—tasteful and Christmas aren't two words that belong together—and the riot of multi-coloured tinsel, flashing snowmen and reindeer and banners proclaiming Merry Christmas and Season's Greetings met the brief well and truly.

"Sweet as!" Jolene said as I took photos for the hotel's

Instagram account. "When people see those pictures, we'll get heaps of bookings?"

I concentrated on not letting my smile falter. Would we? And if not…

"For sure! Thanks, Jolene."

I headed back to the house. Jack met me at the door, Evie in his arms. "Sorry about this, but Lachlan's just phoned. I'm off to his for a couple of hours."

"What for?" I asked, suspicions running riot. Lachlan was only a recent convert to the side of law and order. Jack's familiarity with Lachlan's previous criminal empire was something I'd chosen never to ask questions about. There were rumours that he'd once been the sole supplier of cannabis for the entire north of Scotland.

"Male bonding," Jack said, leaping into the Highland Tours minibus. It roared off, the exhaust backfiring. Great. Another expense.

"Male bonding, Evie! What rubbish."

Dylan emerged, wrapped up so thoroughly only his face was visible.

"Where are you off to now?" I asked.

He pointed at Maggie Broon's Boobs. "Thought I might climb them," he said. "How long does it take to get to the top?"

"Three or four hours," I replied. But only if you were mega fit. In five hours, Dylan'd phone, begging me to call out Mountain Rescue, and demanding a helicopter to whisk him off those jaggy, steep peaks and drop him off back at the house.

A responsible, kind sister… Sod it, let him find out for himself.

Back inside, the bareness of our walls contrasted with what I'd just spent the morning doing in the hotel. Not very

Christmassy at all. A message on the answerphone greeted me. "Gaby, your dad and I were wondering what to get Evie for Christ—"

I deleted it. Did my parents really think they could bribe their way back into my affections that easily? It was just after 12. I could squeeze in a few hours' work, do a little light housework, find a teach your child sign language video on YouTube to help develop her communications skills… who was I kidding? When Evie started to nod off after her lunch, I lifted her out of the highchair and plodded upstairs where bed beckoned, the seductive pull of the duvet impossible to resist.

A sharp rap on the door startled Evie and me out of sleep three hours later. The curtains had been left open; dark skies outside with a tiny slither of the moon. I struggled out of bed, cursing. Evie was never going to sleep tonight. I hitched her up, and we headed downstairs.

"Let me in. I've bought you a wee pressie!" Mhari, her face poking through the branches of a Christmas tree. She and Lachlan, she said, had spent the morning fetching trees for the villagers from one of the local farmers who grew them as a sideline.

I eyed the top of it. "It's too big."

"Dinnae be silly," she said, turning the tree on its side and barging past. "I've been in this house hunners o' times. I know what size the rooms are."

Turns out she didn't. When she tried to upend the tree, it ended up on the diagonal—half a metre too tall for our ceiling. Evie watched from the floor, fascinated at the sight of two women trying to arm-wrestle an enormous tree into a limited space. Mildred hissed at it from the safety of the kitchen.

Mhari opened her rucksack. "I came prepared."

She took out a saw and proceeded the hack off the top of the tree, scattering pine needles everywhere. Evie made a beeline for them, little fingers reaching out, ready to stuff them in her mouth. I swept her up and out of the way.

"Where are your Christmas decorations for the tree then?"

Apart from tinsel, we didn't have any. Once we'd finished strewing the tree with what could only be laughingly described as decorations, it resembled the love child of Mariah Carey meets Miss Havisham and the ghost of Christmas past, while simultaneously spewing up tinsel. The angel sat at the top looked far too pleased about where that sawed-off point of the tree had ended up.

Mhari took a photo with her phone. "The Lochalshie Facebook group is havin' a wee competition—best-dressed tree in the village. I'll enter yours as a wee irony thing, eh?"

I glared at her. "Whose fault is this the rubbish tree and its décor? And look at the mess you've made!"

Mhari had spilled a lot of the earth from the bucket the tree was in to keep it alive so we could replant once Christmas was over.

"A plastic tree would have been much easier."

"Well, that's gratitude for you. We spent hours lookin' for the right trees."

"Did you?" I tipped my head to one side. "And that's all you and Lachlan did for those hours and hours and hours?"

She poked her tongue out at me. "None o' your business!"

Typical Mhari logic. She bent over and picked up some of the lumps of soil, tucking them back into the bucket. Two years ago, Lachlan had ended their on-off, mainly off, relationship when he fell in love with Nicola Milne, a woman Mhari described as a 'full-time bad hair day'. (The owner of luxuriant auburn hair that came down to her waist, Mhari could apply that comment to almost everyone.) But Mhari spent so much time in his company, they might as well have still been together.

"Oh, come on. Are you back with Lachlan? Tell me."

"Did you see that stuff about Caitlin? The Pop Sugar website says she and Donal are about tae split. Have you heard anything?"

Classic distraction technique. I fell for it, though. I was on the list of people Caitlin hit up regularly for advice on her love life, which was going through a rough patch. Like Jack and I, she had been married for two years. In celebrity terms, that equalled 20 or more normal-marriage years. Donal, a lab technician, hated the celebrity lifestyle. By my reckoning, I was due a call soon to discuss his latest meltdown, and if I thought her silly for not having insisted on a prenup as her family had advised.

"No," I said, "what does Pop Sugar have to say about it?"

"'A close friend says'—that wasnae you, was it, trying tae make a bit o' money on the side tae help fund Christmas?"

"Absolutely not!" (Though I wished I'd thought of it.)

"... 'that the couple is in crisis talks and hoping that they can make this their best Christmas ever if they stay together'. I give their marriage to the end of the year. Do you want tae put money on it? Fifty quid says they announce their separation on Christmas Day, get a quickie divorce, and she's pictured snogging some other bloke by June."

"A bet on other people's unhappiness? What a horrible idea."

She shrugged. "If you say so. Talkin' o' which. What

about a fair exchange of gossip? You must know for sure who Lucian's daddy is. That baby sure doesnae look like Dexter at a', does he?"

"That is not a fair exchange. And I don't—" I stopped. Blasted, blasted Mhari. She'd tricked me into revealing more than I should by not denying straightaway that Lucian's father was anyone other than Dexter.

She smirked. I stuck two fingers up.

There was another knock on the door. Mhari rushed off to answer it.

"Aye, so Dylan. Have you got your eye on any o' the village lassies? I can put a word in wi' them if you want?"

"You climbed Maggie Broon's Boobs in four hours!" I exclaimed, as my brother wandered in closely followed by Mhari, having ignored her question.

"Just over three, actually. After I left here, I went for a walk around the loch first."

Infuriating! I'd completed the climb twice and never managed it in under five hours. But now that he had returned and Mhari was here…

I clapped my hands. "Guys and girls! I've had this wonderful, fabulous idea!"

My audience regarded me warily—disbelief that the words 'I', 'wonderful' and 'idea' belonged together in any sentence uttered by Gaby McAllan. T'uh. I'd show *them*.

"You're soooooo similar! Mhari, you love Games of Thrones. Ditto Dylan. Dylan, you're a big fan of the Pot Noodle in all its e-number glory. Also, Mhari. Both of you are single and ready to mingle. Dylan, Mhari says she knows lots of filthy things, which would suit a man of your extensive experience. And finally, you both love slagging me off. Why don't you move in together? Perhaps true love is to be found if you're sharing the bathroom, kitchen, living room every day? We might end up as in-laws, Mhari."

Persuasion at its finest. Or maybe not, given that Dylan and Mhari both gaped at me, open-mouthed.

Mhari folded her arms. "No. I like my privacy. The only person I can live wi' is Katya."

The two of them had shared a flat for three months. I'm not sure Katya would agree to ever do it again. But Mhari had also lived with me for a while. Huh.

"And I don't need your help with my love life," Dylan added, "so no thanks either. No offence, Mhari."

"None taken. Though if we're talking about your love life, Isla Fairbairn's back in the village and years ago we used to call her the village bike, so if you're after an easy—"

Dylan thanked her for the insider info at the same time as I ticked her off. Isla Fairbairn was lovely. Everyone thought so. Even if the last time I'd seen her, she'd snuggled up to Jack, snuck her hand onto his bottoms and offered him something that should be kept between a man and the woman he was officially attached to.

"That alright, Gaby?" she asked at the time. "Might take the pressure off ye if I'm the one suck—"

Fortunately for the three of us, the jukebox exploded into an old Nirvana hit, saving us from the rest of Isla's generous bid to spare me the effort of fellating my husband.

Mission offload Dylan unsuccessful, I addressed Dylan, who looked far too ready to settle on the sofa and stay there for the rest of the day. "Can you go to Tesco's in Oban and pick up our shopping!"

To my astonishment, he didn't moan at all. Looked pleased, even, and pulled a brush through his hair. Maybe he thought Oban would prove far more exciting than Lochalshie. Fair enough, the town had far more shops, pubs and even a train station, but at this time of year, the weather made it as dank and gloomy as everywhere else in rural Scotland.

In the living room, Mhari amused Evie blowing raspberries on her bare tummy, Evie giggling her head off.

"What are you getting her for Christmas?" she asked.

"Er… haven't thought about it yet."

Evie's Christmas presents depended on what we could afford. At the moment, a tangerine.

She sat back on her haunches. "Actually, I wanted tae ask a wee favour."

"What?"

"Will-you-come-out-with-me-tonight-for-a-reccie."

Said so fast, I had to ask her to repeat it twice.

She explained what she wanted, me boggle-eyed at the request. But the way she stumbled over the words softened me up. Nosey pain in the butt as she was, she'd always made me feel welcome in the village, and I valued her friendship.

"So, I'll get you at 20 past eleven, okay?"

"But—"

Too late. The order given, Mhari was out the door before I could object. Twenty past eleven was waaaayyyy past my bedtime these days.

"Evening."

I slapped my hand to my chest. "God, where did you come from?"

Jack had sprung out of nowhere, the tips of his nose and ears red, the icy fingers he touched to my face making me jump back.

"I was hiding around the corner, waitin' for Mhari to leave."

"Thanks a lot!"

Inside, he took one look at the terrible Christmas tree

and shook his head when I explained it was an irony thing. Evie yelled when he picked her up. She wasn't fond of icy fingers either.

"Sorry, wee sweetheart! Where's Dylan?"

"I sent him to the Tesco's in Oban with a long shopping list."

"Brilliant! You, me and Evie can cuddle up on the sofa and binge-watch our way through Stranger Things 3 on Netflix.

He kissed the tip of my nose. "Do you think 'Netflix and chill' is still a thing? How about we put Evie upstairs and prove to ourselves we're still young enough not to need to do it on a bed?"

"Lovely, but I can't get too comfortable because I've promised Mhari I'll help her with something."

Jack, expression incredulous, listened while I told him what she wanted. He put Evie back down on the floor and flopped onto the sofa. "Why on earth did you agree to that?"

Because saying no was a skill I'd yet to master? And Mhari had stoked my curiosity. The woman who never asked for help or favours, seeing them as an admittance of weakness.

Evie goo-gooed at her father. He swung her up on top of his chest.

"For the love of God, Evie. I hope you havenae inherited your mother's ability to get tangled up in hare-brained schemes."

The door opened. "Gimme a hand, yeah? The car's loaded up with shopping."

Good grief. Dylan must have done the equivalent of a supermarket sweep, running up and down the aisles and shoving everything into the trolley. These days, supermarket visits took me hours, partly thanks to having to persuade Evie to put down everything she grabbed for and stopping for discussions with little old ladies commenting on her hair. Dylan's premature return put the veto on any adventurous activities on the sofa.

Jack stared at Evie once more, shaking his head. "Another thing for you not to inherit, Evie. Your mother's habit of landing things on a person without discussing them first, such as inviting her brother to move in with us."

Words ringing in my ears, I headed for the hallway to help Dylan bring everything in.

Chapter Twelve

LOW-RENT SPIES

Leaving our warm, cosy house had taken every bit of willpower I possessed. Jack, heading upstairs to bed, as I let myself out, made me promise not to be more than half an hour.

Mhari wanted to follow Lachlan when he left the hotel later that night and needed me as a back-up. If he spotted us tailing him, she planned to say we were out on a recce for scenes to include in the 'dark nights in winter' section of her photography portfolio.

"Follow him? Why?"

"To see if he's still wi' that Nicola."

On paper, Lachlan and Mhari were unsuited. Him button-lipped most of the time and her the nosiest woman in the world. When she and Lachlan split, she'd also been in a relationship with my then boss, Hyun-Ki. But she'd surprised me at the time by crying her heart out about Lachlan.

As instructed, I met Mhari outside Jamal's shop, both of us dressed head to toe in black, her in a balaclava hiding her hair. We looked like low-rent private investigators in a bargain-basement movie.

"C'mon," she said, stamping her feet. "I dinnae want to be late."

Impossible to be so, seeing as the hotel was only five minutes' walk from our house—less from Jamal's shop. We were in place bang on half-past eleven. Last orders in the pub on a Thursday night were eleven o'clock. But whoever was in charge at night needed to clean up, lock up and cash up before leaving.

Highland winter nights were hard on the body. If it wasn't howling a gale with the rain slicing through you in stair rods, the frost set in, coating the pavement in lethal slippery whiteness and every exposed bit of skin turned blue with cold. I wrapped my arms around my body and urged Lachlan to hurry up closing the hotel for the night.

We crouched behind the hedge of the house next to the Lochside Welcome, where my mother-in-law now lived. Ranald had sold his farm at the beginning of the year, and he and Caroline moved into Lochalshie's best house—the one right next to the Lochside Welcome. I'd lived in it when I first moved to Lochalshie. It was open plan downstairs with floor to ceiling windows at the front, so you had a year-round view of the loch.

If Caroline or Ranald glanced out her window now, they would see two figures. A reasonable person might draw the wrong conclusion and think we were robbers checking out either the house or the hotel and call the police. At which point, I'd deck Mhari and make a run for it.

"You owe me," I whispered to her, "loads and load and loads. Three sessions of babysitting and five compliments about what an amazing person/friend I am."

Mhari handed out compliments, on average, once a

year. Now I mulled over the last 11 months, I was yet to receive my annual word of praise.

She sniffed. "Babysitting, aye. I'm nae suckin' up to you, though. You dinnae need compliments. Anyway, shush! Lachlan's coming out. Look."

Lachlan emerged, eyes on his phone. He stopped, scanned the skies, and moved off.

"What do we do now?" I asked. Lachlan walked past his battered old Jeep parked outside the front of the hotel. Unless he was incredibly hardy and intended to walk home in freezing temperatures at this time of night, he'd need the Jeep as his house was three miles out of the village. Nicola lived in a flat tucked away in the street behind the main road through Lochalshie, Cairn Crescent.

"Follow him, obvs," Mhari let him get a head start. "C'mon. I've seen this on the telly. Ye hae to stay close to the walls and if he stops, dinnae stop. It's too obvious if you do."

Lachlan took a right turn, vanishing down the narrow alleyway on the other side of Jamal's General Store. This didn't appear promising. The alleyway led to Cairn Crescent. We let him disappear, waited a few seconds and crept down it. Mhari pointed at him. He was heading towards Nicola's flat.

"How're, Gaby, Mhari!" Laney's cheery greeting pierced the dark silence. She was out walking her dogs, one of them shoving its nose right in my crotch. Mhari swore under her breath. But Lachlan appeared to be far enough ahead not to have heard. The streetlight picked out wires hanging from his ears. He must have earphones in. Phew. Laney yanked her dogs back. The one with too much interest in my 'bits' sent me a regretful look.

Lachlan had reached Nicola's flat but didn't stop.

I snatched up Mhari's hand. "Ooh! Happy days, Mhari! He can't be with her anymore!"

She shook my hand off. "Gerroff me. Mebbe he's meeting her in the park."

Behind Cairn Crescent there was a small play park—a row of swings, a slide, a roundabout and a climbing frame. Evie loved it.

"He's meeting her in the park? It's half eleven. In the middle of winter."

"Used to meet me there. For… you know."

Play parks had nefarious uses? This I needed to discuss with my other half. Jack, should we be having marital relations in the play park late at night to pep up our love life? Given Mhari's revelations about her expertise on filthy stuff, perhaps we were missing out on hitherto unknown pleasures?

There was no sign of him in the park either. Not sure my eyes could have handled whatever he and Nicole might have been getting up to on the roundabout.

"There!" she said, pointing ahead to two figures stood where the end of the crescent met the High Street. Lachlan glanced up. Mhari and I flattened ourselves against the wall.

"Who's he talking to?" I whispered, unable to make out the other figure.

"Dunno. Havenae seen him in the village before."

We could not make out any of the conversation either, but when Lachlan held up a brown envelope, I stiffened. Money? If Lachlan was back to operating on the wrong side of the law, wouldn't that put the Lochside Welcome at risk, seeing as he was one of the owners? What if he was laundering money through the pub? Police officers might swoop. Claim it under the Proceeds of Crime Act. We'd all be out of a job and the village minus its best venue.

Lachlan moved off. The man turned.

The baby hater from the plane. What on earth was he doing here and how did he know Lachlan?

By the time I got back to the house, Dylan was glued to something on my tablet tucked up in his sleeping bag on the sofa. This week, I promised myself; he's moving out of here to stay with Jolene and Stewart whether he likes it or not.

I leant over him and plucked out one earbud. He pulled the laptop screen closer, so I couldn't see it and frowned at me.

"That guy on the plane."

"What guy?" Studied nonchalance. His eyes fixed on me, which was always, Katya told me, the sign of a liar. Truthful people didn't feel the need to impress their sincerity on you.

"The one you looked at and pretended not to know."

"Dunno what you're talking about."

"He's here—in Lochalshie. I just spotted him talking to Lachlan. All seems terrifically coincidental if you ask me."

Dylan shrugged, making a grab for his earbud. "If you say so. Do you mind? I'm in the middle of Naked Attraction, and I'm about to find out if Carson's found his soulmate."

Surprise number... what was I up to by now? 223? 372? Dylan considered a soulmate important. The non-surprise was him watching Naked Attraction, a Channel 4 game show where contestants got to date someone based purely on what they looked like naked. All that opportunity to ogle women. I left him to it.

Upstairs, Jack was fast asleep, foiling my plan to wonder

out loud and discuss in detail what the hell Lachlan was doing and who the mystery man might be.

As I hit the pillow, sleepiness zapping the strength out of me, a thought struck me.

"McAllan," I muttered to myself as his chest moved up and down, slow and steady. "If you're keeping quiet about any of Lachlan's current criminal activities or you're involved in any of them, I will kill you!"

Chapter Thirteen

UNWISE WORDS

"D'you think you could help Xavier in the kitchen today, Dylan?" Jack said as he stuck the kettle on to boil the next morning. Xavier had phoned this morning. A party of 20 had booked for lunch.

The plan had been for Dylan to start on Friday, but today's booking needed all-hands-on-deck. Xavier's news had cheered Jack up considerably, which in turn brightened me up. More parties of 20, please, and then all I needed to do was ensure peace, love and happiness for everyone...

Dylan nodded straightaway. I'd expected protests. By 'help' Jack meant 'do all the washing', but as this was now Dylan's third day in Lochalshie and it was the middle of winter, he'd run out of things to do and was getting under my feet.

I'd been working for Blissful Beauty the past few days, handing over to Trish before I started my extended holiday on Friday. Maintaining a professional reputation when your brother keeps interrupting your Zoom calls with inane questions, ("Gaby, where do you keep the coffee? I can't find it."

Or, "Is there a clothes shop in the village? I need a new pair of jeans."), was tricky.

Coffees and toast finished, I waved Jack and Dylan goodbye, my brother kitted out in the same black t-shirt and cargo pants combo that made up the official Lochside Welcome uniform.

Caroline turned up on the doorstep seconds later, dressed in her trusty Puffa jacket, her head covered by a woollen hat with a bobble on top, eyes red-rimmed and watering in the wind.

"How're Gaby?" she asked, as Evie exploded into excited gurgles. She loved Granny Caroline. I handed her over. "Not bad. Are you okay?"

"Think I've picked up a wee bittie o' a cold," she sniffed. "D'ye ken, Gaby. I sent out a' they flu reminders twice this year and still folks didnae bother. Now they're coming to me, greeting because they're loaded wi' it. Terrible."

She put her hand to her chest. "But you dinnae need to worry. Ranald and I have both had the jag this year, so we'll no' pass anything to Evie."

"Great," I said weakly, remembering me blithely taking Evie with me when we visited Nanna Cooper in hospital— and on a flight—both places germ hotbeds. Parenting, I'd worked out early on, was the non-stop realisation that you now had so many more things to fret about.

Ranald appeared too, pushing the fancy Silver Cross pushchair they splashed out on when Evie was born. Evie's gurgles increased in volume. Ranald was another of her favourites, and his face lit up when he saw her. A man of few words, I often caught Ranald chatting away to Evie about all manner of things, her listening in apparent fascination and adding the occasional "goo!", which he took as encouragement. Most of his chat centred on farming, explaining the nuts and bolts of animal husbandry to a one-year-old. If she became a farmer in later life, I would know where to lay the blame.

Caroline passed Evie to Ranald, who was also well bundled up. As a native, he dismissed thick jackets, coats and scarves, arguing it wasn't cold until the mercury plummeted to minus five.

"Aha!" I said, pointing at his coat. "Icy enough today for you to need layers, Ranald? I checked the temperature earlier. It's a balmy 5 degrees! That's not cold, according to you!"

He and Caroline flashed a look at each other. "Wind-chill," Caroline said, pulling her own scarf tightly around her neck. "Ye didnae factor that in, did ye? Makes it at least ten degrees chillier."

Ranald, his nose scarlet-tipped, nodded. Evie slotted into her chair and bundled up in blankets, they set off, Caroline calling out cheery 'hellos' to the dog walkers. Mildred joined me at the front door, caterwauling for me to let her in—the expert at figuring out the safest times to be in the house.

"Sorry, Millie-moo." I picked her up. "How about an extra breakfast this morning to prove to you I still think you're my number one?"

She yowled in response, the noise increasing once she worked out an extra breakfast meant leftover roast chicken and not cat food. The peace allowed me to make up for lost time. I fired up my iMac, wriggled my fingers and set to. Because I'd put in so much unpaid overtime in the lead up to autumn, Halloween and the festive season (all significant dates in the beauty calendar), the company owed me serious time off. And I intended to make the most of it.

Meanwhile, I had 273 emails to deal with, and a nitpicky design brief for a new subsection of the website to address. Trish, my job share partner, and I had a team of three—one of whom did as little as he could get away with. Tempting as it was to complete the Christmas campaign social media posts Marty was yet to design, I resisted. As Trish pointed out all the time, it sent out the wrong message. She was all of 23 and decades wiser than me.

The morning's work almost done, my phone, turned face down on my desk to stop it distracting me, buzzed.

Leave it. You're working…

Katya, an expert on home-working-life-hacks, counselled switching your phone off, turning it to silent, putting it on flight mode, etc., rather than relying on willpower to stop you picking it up repeatedly during the hours you were meant to be working.

Too true. I turned it over.

Mum.

Oh, dear.

The phone continued to vibrate, the motion sending it shuddering towards the iMac. I snatched it up.

"Hello…?"

"Gaby, I know it's been a long time, and I'm so sorry about that. Don't hang up but—"

Too late. I hit the red button and flung my phone onto the sofa. What a sneaky move on my mum's part. My father's various jobs over the decades had included sales in the late 1990s. She must have gambled on him talking fast enough to convince me to stay on the line and hear him out.

The phone rang again—the landline this time. I unplugged it, switched my mobile off and spent half an hour working on Marty's unfinished social media posts. When I switched the mobile back on, there was a missed call from Dexter.

Ooh! Gaby, the fixer coming up… The woman who would single-handedly persuade Dexter to see sense and bring about a reconciliation and happy Christmas for two people. When I'd visited Katya and Dexter not long after Lucian Kubowski-Carlton made his entry into the world, joy lit up Dexter's face as he held his son. "Gaby! Jack! Hey, super-amazing to see you. Come and meet Lucian—the greatest, most fantastic kid ever born!"

When she was born, Jack had been star-struck too. Not as much as Dexter. That was no reflection on Jack or Evie. Perhaps because Dexter hadn't expected him and Katya to have children, and that thunderbolt made his gratitude overwhelming—the man who'd been given the ultimate gift and then had it snatched away. The bond was there, right? All he needed was a little persuasion from me…

"Gaby."

Woo. Most of the time, Dexter spoke if he'd mainlined speed for breakfast—something I put down to his American nationality and job in marketing. Now he sounded as if he was on the long-overdue come down from it.

"Have you finished the new website pages? I want to get them signed off before I head for LA."

LA? Blissful Beauty's global HQ was in LA, as was Dexter's sister and her kids. Did this mean he was moving there sans Katya…?

"Yes, all finished and complete. But I was wondering if—"

"How's Lucian?" he asked, his voice cracking.

"Absolutely tickety-boo!" I didn't want to worry him. Though perhaps I *should*, and it would send him racing up here? "Well, not totally. Misses you horribly. I swear he said, 'Where's da-da?' the other day."

A white lie. Lucian was only six months old.

Dexter let out a sigh. "No, he didn't, Gaby."

"Well, no, but they grow so fast at this stage. You don't want to miss any of it, do you?"

Outside, Caroline and Ranald waved at me from the far end of the street. Where had the day gone?

"Do you know why we split up this time?" he asked.

Was this a trick question? If I said no, did he tell me the doubtful paternity story, and I pretended no knowledge of it? If I said yes, did I land Katya in further trouble for having confided in me and that I'd kept such a secret?

"Er... y'know Katya. Totes discreet most of the time. Tells me nothing."

The silence on the other end went on so long, I thought he had cut me off. "Dexter? Are you there? Are you okay? You're not..."

... harbouring suicidal feelings? Caroline often talked about men and mental health. "They dinnae hae our support networks, Gaby ye see. Aw those friends who ask after ye all the time."

If she meant Mhari, I wasn't sure how much of a bonus that was. Still, Dexter worked insane hours and was miles away from his own family.

"Zac's demanded a paternity test. Katya seems to think that's reasonable."

Ah. I hadn't been told that part of the argument. The curse of modernity, right? In ye olden days, you might pass off a child as belonging to the man who reckoned he was the father. Keep your gob shut for the rest of your life and no-one was any the wiser. Was it always a good thing for the truth to out?

"Dexter," I burst out, the vision of Katya's pale, tearful face swimming in front of me. "Would that be so bad? I've seen you with Lucian and from the very beginning, I said to myself—Gosh, isn't Dexter wonderful with Lucian, what does his real paternity matter, all that's important is that guy loves his little boy so much and—"

"WHAT DID YOU SAY?"

I held the phone back from my ear, startled by the outburst. What had I—oh, oh, oh dear.

There was a knock at the door, Ranald holding up Evie to wave at me through the front window.

"YOU KNEW ALL ALONG I MIGHT NOT BE LUCIAN'S FATHER AND YOU DIDN'T TELL ME!"

Caroline still in possession of a front door key, pushed open the living room door and paused, staring at the phone.

"Is that Dexter, Katya's man? He sounds awfy angry."

A few choice words at the other end of the phone confirming that my mother-in-law had a gift for stating the obvious, and he hung up.

I dropped the phone. "You could say that. Um, would you mind holding onto Evie a little longer, Caroline? I need to speak to Katya. Urgently."

———

"Katya!" I flung myself on her front door, the Airbnb property next to Jamal's shop.

Darkness had descended—a velvet blanket over the village, the moon a thin slither and stars blinking in the far distance. I'd come out without a coat, a mistake you would expect to have been hammered out of me after all this time in Lochalshie, and my teeth chattered.

Jamal wandered outside to put up a sign advertising cut-price Christmas decorations.

(Tinsel—£5.99, reduced from £6.99.)

"All right, Gaby? What's the emergency?"

"Nothing, nothing," I said, crossing my fingers I'd got there before Katya heard from Dexter. The door opened, Katya stony-faced. Too late then. Her eyes shifted, staring beyond me.

"Hi Katya, I've always wanted tae see what that house looks—"

Mhari and her magical ability to surface whenever she thought something gossip-worthy was about to happen.

Katya grabbed my arm and pulled me in, slamming the door. She stomped into the living room, me trailing behind.

The narrow Airbnb property took over two floors—two dinky bedrooms, one with an ensuite, upstairs and downstairs, an internal bathroom and a kitchen come living area. Katya's bags lay in the main room, clothing and baby stuff spilling out. She had set her Mac book up on the small dining table. Lucian was lying on a baby mat, playing with the mobile that dangled over it, his attention taken up with bashing together the toys that dangled above him.

"What did you say to Dexter?" She turned to face me.

Alarmed, I spotted what I hadn't noticed before—how much weight she'd lost. Katya and I were diametrically opposed, figure-wise—me as envious of her hourglass curves as she was of my skinniness. Now, she gave me a run for my money. Her shoulders resembled coat hangers in the loose sweater she wore, and the skin had fallen away from her cheekbones, stretched too tightly over her jawbone. Even her hair had lost its customary gloss.

"Have you been eating? Do you want me to make you something for dinner? I can pop to Jamal's shop. He keeps vegan food in stock for you—or there's always Ben and Jerry's. Not strictly plant-based, what with all that cream and eggs, but perfect in emergencies and I'll pick up some—"

Katya shook her head. "No. Just tell me what you said to Dexter? I'm just off the phone to him, and I think my eardrums might have burst."

I swallowed dread as my face flushed. "Er, I just wanted…"

Peace and love? Everyone to get their happily ever after at this time of year?

Dexter to hear my words, say, *'You're right, Gaby!' I forgive Katya everything. Tell her I'm on my way and she should remember that old army saying, Norwich!'*

(Urban legend and Nanna Cooper had it that during the Second World War, Norwich was 'code' for Knickers Off Ready for When I Come Home, a word the soldiers used when they telegrammed their wives and sweethearts ahead of their imminent return from the battlefields. Her father had used the word on her mother—she was the result.)

Gulping back shame, I repeated the conversation.

She sighed and sat down on one of the immaculate armchairs and pushed a hand through her hair. "Dexter told me how much he despises me in between wailing about how much he misses Lucian. God, I hate myself."

"Oh, I'm so sorry," I fluttered my hands. "Stupid, stupid, stupid of me to have interfered. I wish I could take it back."

Katya glanced up a watery smile in place. "No, my fault entirely. Who was it who slept with two men in the first place? And I shouldn't have told you at the time."

I dropped in front of her, putting my hands on my knees. "No, no, no, it's *my* fault. I've worked hard on trying to stop my mouth running away with me," hundreds of people might argue the opposite, "and think about what I say before I let the words out but, on this occasion—"

She put her fingers on my mouth. "Shush, Gaby! I didn't mean I was wrong to tell you because you wouldn't be able to keep the secret. I shouldn't have burdened you with it. Mine to either 'fess up or bear alone and all that."

Katya often walked a lonely path. What a rotten friend I was.

Lucian rolled onto his front. He tipped his head towards Katya. Zac looked back at me—a stripped back version of him, the eyes yet to be touched with smugness or cynicism.

"Um, d'you want me to take Lucian for the evening?" I asked. "Jack and I are happy to look after him if you want to…"

Go to the pub and drown your sorrows? Walk around the loch in the darkness? Contact Zac? Three far from ideal options.

She shook her head. "No. It's okay. I'm almost finished Caitlin's next book, and then I'm going to get an early night."

"Or what about if I stay? I'll buy the Ben and Jerry's. A tub of it each. And then we could find a horror film to watch. How about that?"

A noble sacrifice on my part: Horror films were the pits. But Katya and Mhari shared this weird predilection for horror films when they needed cheering up. They must reason that however messed up your life was, it was unlikely to be as bad as the poor soul hiding out in a deserted farmhouse, whilst an unknown, ghastly thing, prowled nearby. I would spend the entire film with my fingers plugged in my ears and a cushion on my lap to bury my face in.

Lucian pushed himself onto all fours and crawled towards Katya, startling the two of us. "He's not done that before," Katya said, holding her arms out. He crawled right into them, allowing her to scoop him up.

"That's super-advanced," I said. "Evie waited until she was ten months until she started."

She allowed her face to relax for a few seconds, cares disappearing in the wonder of what you as a woman could create and how amazing that was.

"Wait till Dex hears about... oh sod everything," she said, "Dexter loves, loved, all the stages of development Lucian goes through. He'd have been on the floor filming and sending it to all his family and friends."

I offered to stay once more. Katya shook her head. "No. I need to think."

I left, exhorting her to eat, and shut the door behind me.

"Gaby, Katya hasnae been oot the house since she arrived. Is she all right?"

Mhari. The temperature in single figures or not, the weather didn't stop her hanging about if she sniffed intrigue.

"Fine," I said. "Hectic. Writing her socks off."

I headed back to my house, Mhari clattering at my heels. I stopped. "Where are you going? Your flat's in the other direction! You're not coming back to mine. The house is overcrowded enough as it is!"

And I needed to talk to Jack. Run the day's events by him. Beg him to reassure me I wasn't the world's worst friend. Ruiner of relationships. Destroyer of people's happiness at a time of year that was meant to be jolly and jubilant.

A car sailed past us, splashing me in filthy, icy-cold water. Mhari dug an elbow in my ribs. "Did ye see who that was?"

"No."

The car had stopped in the car park outside the Royal George, right next to our house—the man's profile picked out in the streetlights as he made his way to the hotel's front door.

Zac.

"Bit o' a coincidence, eh?" Mhari said, phone out already as she typed out yet another update to the world's speediest news service. She grabbed hold of my arm. "Katya's here, and now he arrives. You'd think he'd be needed in Hammerstone Hotels' properties in London that will all be offerin' Christmas parties to boozed-up office workers. We should hang around a bit. See if he heads back along the High Street and knocks on the Airbnb's front door, eh?"

"It's far too cold!" I said, detangling her arms from mine. "Goodnight, Mhari."

And with that, I was off, thoroughly rattled.

Chapter Fourteen

ENOUGH TO PUT YOU OFF PARENTING

By the time I let myself back into the house, Caroline and Ranald had gone. Jack was lying on his front on the floor, playing with Evie. She was sat up, back against the sofa and her favourite toys scattered around her—the best one a bell on the end of a stick that she waved around, magician-style.

"Where's Dylan," I said, collapsing onto the sofa. The last few hours had been…fraught.

Jack looked up. "Still in there clearing up. He did well today."

"How did it go?" The 20 people for lunch. This morning seemed to have taken place aeons ago.

"Magnificent folk. I love every single o' them," Jack said, rolling ping pong balls along the floor to Evie. She caught one and flung it back at him. "They're still there drinking the bar dry, and they've all booked up for one-night or two-night stays next year. A weird thing though—they said they'd all—"

Evie's face reddened and screwed up. Yes, *that* expression. I struggled to my feet, but Jack managed it ahead of me, dashing up the stairs to the bathroom and reappearing with the changing mat. By the time he returned, I'd whipped off her mini jeans the stink hitting the air at once.

"Find Thomas the tank engine!" I said, doing my best to breathe through my mouth. Evie latest (and most unwelcome) phase was reaching her hands down to investigate what was in her nappy. Occasionally putting her hands to her mouth too. The first time we witnessed it, Jack and I stared at each other aghast. "Is that…?"

Cue frantic googling as we tried to work out if this was normal/harmful/merited a visit from Social Services (somehow, they were aware of us, monitoring from afar via hidden CCTV.) They hauled us in front of the Parental Court accused of serious nappy incompetence. The judge sent us down for 20 years, placed Evie with far better guardians, and ordered us never to have children again.

ScottishDaDa, an online parenting guru Jack rated (me, not so much) had posted a video on his YouTube channel discussing the very subject. Your kiddiewinkle's preoccupation with poo, as he called it. Much more common than you might think. Hence, Thomas the tank engine to keep little hands occupied.

Evie started wailing as I removed the terry-towelling nappy, regretting not for the first time my decision to go green. Nappy changes must be much simpler when all you had to do was unfasten the dirty one and fling it out with the trash.

Dylan chose that point to return, walking in, screwing his nose up in disgust and backing straight out again. "Er, I'll…"

"For goodness' sake," I shouted after him, "you changed her nappy the other night."

He came back into the room, pinching his nose between his finger and thumb. "That was a pee."

Quietened by Thomas, Evie lay still as I whipped away the filthy nappy and handed it to Jack, who gulped as he stood up, swallowing several times. How could one tiny human being produce something so enormous and foul-smelling? Evie banged Thomas to the ground, the little train tumbling over the floor as Mildred came in. She swerved to avoid it, tripping Jack up.

He fell forward, hands out wide and the nappy flying in front of him, the contents scattering into the air and hitting all of us. Dylan took the worst of the impact, his chin and coat splattered with the stuff. The subsequent wails outdid Evie.

Ever since the birth of our daughter, Jack and I had tried not to swear in front of her. We'd come up with alternative words to cover the worst excesses of Anglo-Saxon. Fudge off. Blooger it. Diggerty darn. But show me the woman, her husband and her brother who didn't yell the f-word repeatedly and altogether under such circumstances, and I'd tell you they were figments of your imagination.

No-one mentioned these bits of parenting before you set out on this path, did they?

Jack stood up slowly. "Dunno where we start, to be honest."

"No," I agreed, noting a splodge of brown on the ceiling and picking a small lump out of my hair. Evie watched all of us, wide-eyed and silent. She was the only one who'd escaped the literal shit shower. I dipped my hands in the nearby bowl of soapy water and got her into a clean nappy.

Dylan unzipped his coat. "You should have filmed that. Uploaded it onto YouTube and made it compulsory viewing for all 16-year-olds who aren't using condoms. If that's not the greatest incentive ever not to have kids, I dunno what is. I'm going for a shower."

He left before I could object.

Jack and I took almost an hour to clean the room, my husband promising me he'd research industrial firms that specialised in biohazard cleaning in the morning. Dylan returned, wet haired and fragrant, just as I set the programme on the washing machine to 90 degrees, clothes, cushion covers and everything else heaped in there.

Dylan flopped onto the sofa. He wore the air of a man about to settle in and not move for the next few hours, me or Jack expected to wait on him hand and foot the way my mum did.

"Your turn to make dinner," I announced, kicking his shins. "While I get showered and changed. Then you're free to tell me all about your first day at the Lochside Welcome."

"What, but… oh, okay. Do you mind if I fetch us something from the hotel? Xavier made vat-loads of lasagne earlier. And he knocked up a few spare chocolate decadence desserts. Though not sure if that's a good idea…"

Quite. None of us relished the thought of tucking into anything brown coloured.

"Fine," I said, "as long as you pay for it."

He set off there, grumbles kept to a minimum. I guessed he would grab a pint while he was in the pub, this time sitting at the other side of the bar. I scooped up Evie, burying my head in her tummy. She'd had her bath and was back to smelling of soothing milky warmth. "Who's Mummy's little angel? Even though you scattered us all with poop."

Our daughter must have taken one look at Jack and I (broken) and decided to suck up to us. She snuggled into me, burrowing her little head up to my chest. Upstairs, I sat on the rocking chair Ranald had made from the wood he'd foraged from his farm and fed her, typing messages to Katya on my phone and commenting on the film of Lucian she'd posted on the WhatsApp parenting group we were part of. Dexter had been one of the group's keenest posters. Not lately, though.

"Wow, he's the spitting image of Dexter, isn't he?", a blatant attempt to repair the damage I'd done earlier.

Horse. Bolted. Stable door. Shutting. Rearrange these words into a famous saying.

Jack tip-toed up the stairs. He'd stripped off his dirty clothes and wrapped himself in the floor-length blue towelling dressing gown we both used.

"Are you almost finished?" he asked.

I nodded and passed her to him. The two of them together were a sight I never tired of. The matching red hair plucked at my heartstrings every time. Evie had this way of gazing up at him—the 'I'm so thrilled you're my daddy!' expression.

He jiggled her up and down, eliciting smiles and coos. "Does Evie want to go to sleep? For hours and hours and hours? Does she think to herself, time I gave Mummy and Daddy a break? Let them sleep until, oh at least 7am tomorrow morning?"

Giggles in response. Mebbes aye, mebbes no, as people said in these parts.

He put her in the cot. She gurgled, kicked her blankets for a few seconds and then promptly dropped off.

I pushed myself out of the rocking chair. If I stayed there any longer, the motion would send me to sleep.

"I need a shower," I lifted my hands above my head and stretched out my fingers. "Please can you make sure there's a ginormous glass of wine waiting for me when I've finished?"

Jack raised an eyebrow. "On a school night? Make it a bath, and I'll join you. Tell Dylan to take his time returning."

An offer you can't refuse, right? Downstairs, I heard the clink as he set down glasses. In the bathroom, I turned the taps on and emptied in an almost entire bottle of cocoa butter scented bubble bath. The bath wasn't big enough for two of us and, like most people's, it was a bath/shower combo—practicality over romance.

I fired off a quick message to Dylan—*Stay away for an hour…* In return, he sent me the aubergine and water splash emojis. Dylan's sense of humour had never progressed beyond that of his 15-year-old self.

"Red or white?" Jack's voice drifted upwards.

"Whatever is the strongest. I've had a pig of a day."

Jack returned, a bottle of Rioja under one arm and corkscrew in hand. He poured mine to the brim, awarding himself a more modest couple of inches. One of us ought to be fit to drive should an emergency arise.

Bath at a temperature guaranteed to kill all germs and overflowing with bubbles, Jack slid in first. I stepped in front of him and lowered myself, so I could lean back against him, glass in hand. He rubbed the soapy water into the back of my neck and around my front. I closed my eyes.

"Well?" Jack asked. His hands moved, fingertips brushing my nipples. "Why was today so stressful? And you haven't drunk your wine."

I shrugged. The first sip of it had been so disgusting I gave up. Jack let me explain what had played out this afternoon with my ill-considered decision to talk to Dexter. That followed by what I'd revealed to him and then the grand finale, where I ran around to Katya's house, and she greeted me, hollow-eyed and rejecting all offers of help.

Jack's fingers stopped. "Dexter's not Lucian's father?"

Ah, whoops. The secret I'd kept from Jack too.

"Erm, no. Or maybe not. Katya doesn't know."

"She doesn't know?"

"You remember—the Highland Games, when you went to the hotel to bollock Zac for taking that wrong delivery of beer and Katya was the witness who knew for sure it was an honest mistake? She slept with him then and Dexter a few days later. Condom-free both times."

Jack cupped a hand and splashed water over my hair. My husband's many talents included a gift for hair washing, which he did now pressing down hard with his fingers as he massaged shampoo into my scalp.

"Other people's relationships…"

"Impossible to work out. Why did you keep it secret from me?"

What did that mean? Was his tone accusatory or curious? I twisted around so I could see him.

"The secret wasn't mine to tell."

Jack reached for the showerhead and turned it on to rinse my hair. The fingers returned to my nipples. His mouth landed on the back of my neck. "S'pose not. I've kept an awfy lot of secrets about Lachlan over the years."

He had? And talking of which… Lachlan and Mr Baby Hater, the other night, did Jack know something? Before I got the chance to ask, he stood up and loomed over me. Foamy water ran off him, leaving his white skin slick and gleaming, tufts of dark red body hair whorled together.

"We've got a bit of time until Dylan returns with food. Want to make Evie a wee brother or sister?"

"You're joking about a baby, aren't you?" I asked him as

he dragged me into our bedroom. The declaration alarmed and thrilled me at the same time.

"Oh aye," he said, pulling me on top of him. The heat radiating from his body was concentrated in different bits. His chest emitted it. The hands that glued themselves to my bottom were red hot. He shuffled under me. "This evening has put me off weans for life. I swear the wee minx looked up at me when I was stood there covered in shit and grinned."

Caroline warned me all the time that breastfeeding did not count as contraception. "Ye ken what men are like, Gaby," she said, me squirming in my seat. Jack was her son for heaven's sakes. "They find the woman who's just had their first child awfy difficult to resist—what wi' your breasts all swollen and your face so rounded and content. He's gonnae want to pounce aw the time!"

"Noted, Caroline," I replied, desperate to change the subject. "Everything in that department sorted, I promise."

But when I dwelt on Jack's words, had he sounded wistful? The only child hankering after a large family of his own...?

... when one of us worked part-time and the other as the manager of a hotel with an uncertain future. Evie's expenses took me back all the time. There was no way on earth we could afford another child.

Chapter Fifteen

A SALUTE TO THE SUN

The sun woke me the following morning, streaming through the window. I revelled in the novelty. It being winter, most mornings it was dark and—

Blast! I'd overslept. I leapt out of bed—no sign of Jack in it, nor Evie in her room—and clattered down the stairs.

Jack was frying bacon as Dylan entertained Evie. The trendy skeleton clock on the living room wall said nine o'clock. I hadn't got out of bed at that time in... ages. The energy top-up made me feel as if I could conquer the world. Or rather, take control of all things Christmas-related, find a way to magic up customers from thin air and convince my mum my dad was a loser to avoid at all costs...

"Morning, Sleeping Beauty!" Jack called out.

Dylan looked me up and down. I was yet to shower, hair sticking up at the front.

"Love's made you blind, mate. Beauty breaks the Trades Description Act," he told Jack, earning himself a ferocious scowl from me. And renewed determination to rid me of our house guest.

"Pack your bags," I announced, grabbing the sleeping bag off the sofa and rolling it up. "You're off to live with Jolene and Stewart. They've got more room."

Dylan's face fell. "But I don't know them."

"You've met them before."

"What about breakfast?"

"Jack can eat yours. Come on."

And with that, I pulled on my coat and boots and frog-marched him to Jolene and Stewart's house. They lived on Cairn Crescent too, reminding me I must tackle Jack about Lachlan to reassure myself he wasn't up to his old tricks and putting everyone at risk.

Stewart's outward appearance might fool most people. Shaggy haired, bearded and dressed most often in a holey T-shirt and tracksuit bottoms that should have been sent to the clothes graveyard in the sky years ago, you might mistake him for a tramp. But coding paid well. Their house was one of the bigger ones in the village. The garden at the back included extensive decking. In the summer, bushes and shrubs flowered in abundance, turning it into a wildlife haven.

Jolene swung the door open when I rang the bell. She was wrapped up in two fleeces as, like me, she found Highland winters challenging. More so, as she hailed from New Zealand. "Hey, Gaby! Dylan! Come in."

Their kitchen faced the garden. Outside, Stewart in his customary outfit (no concessions to the cold for him) stood barefoot on the decking palms together in prayer position, head tipped up towards the sun.

"What's he doing?" I asked.

Jolene flicked on the kettle switch. Tamar greeted me. He'd started talking only recently and pronounced my name as 'Gibby'. He added that question mark in there too, taking after his mother, whose Kiwi accent always made her sound as if she were asking something no matter what she said.

"Yoga. He took it up when he gave up drinking?"

She tipped her head toward Dylan. "You're welcome to join him?"

Dylan shuddered. Stewart dropped to the ground and pushed up into downward-facing dog, his tracksuit bottoms slipping down to give us the perfect view of... oh, urgh.

"Stewart!" Jolene bellowed, tapping the kitchen window. "Put your arse away!"

Her partner straightened, hoicked his tracksuit bottoms up, stretched his hands up above and gazed at the sky.

Fortified with super-strong coffee, I asked Jolene if she'd meant her promise to put Dylan up. She nodded. "No worries. He can have the spare room."

She pointed above her. "It's the one second right upstairs if you want to dump your stuff."

Dylan left us, allowing me to fill Jolene in on what I'd seen Lachlan doing the other night.

"Do you think he's up to no good?" I asked.

Jolene stirred the pot of porridge bubbling on the stove. Stewart was a porridge devotee. It did not appeal to me unless you added a vat-load of cream and sugar.

"Maybe," she said. "Lachlan's been secretive recently. Phone calls he cuts short whenever anyone gets too close, y'know?"

All too worrying. I'd need to watch Lachlan much more carefully. I also needed to make Jack promise he would tell me if he was doing anything illegal.

"So, who was that dude with him, eh?"

"See if you can make my brother confess. Dylan knows for sure but lying to his family members is his default position. If you prod him, he might reveal the guy's identity."

As we weren't siblings who hugged each other, I left without bothering to say goodbye to Dylan. Jack greeted me when I returned, pulling off my coat and desperate for a bacon sandwich. He was in his work uniform. Today's bookings included another 20-strong party who'd booked at the last minute, cheering him up immensely. "No idea where they are all coming from," he said, finishing his own sandwich in record quick time.

He waited until I'd started to eat mine until breaking the news. "Your mum called," he said. "I fired up the laptop to let her see Evie. She's awfy upset, Gaby, that you and Dylan are still no' talking to her."

I sighed. "I have spoken to Mum; the other day."

He handed me the tomato ketchup. I upended a liberal dose onto the rest of the bacon sandwich. "No, you didn't, Gaby-sketch. You said 'hello', asked after your nanna and held Evie up, so she could see her. That's not talking."

Caught! "She's still with my dad. She let him ring me yesterday from her phone to try to force me to speak to him."

All I needed to do now was stamp my foot, roll my eyes and say 'Whatevs' to complete the sulky teen impression.

"Is that so bad?"

"Yes! Tony stopped all contact with us when Dylan and I were in our early 20s. It didn't bother me that much then, but Dylan had a nasty car accident when he was 24 and ended up in the hospital for weeks. Not a card, a visit or anything! When my mum let him know I was getting married and later pregnant, nothing then either! Hurtful every time. I don't see why Tony gets to swan in now, and we forgive him, do you?"

Jack put his finger to his mouth. My voice had risen.

Evie, in the middle of sorting out her collection of trains, stared at us.

"Fair enough," he bent down and kissed my cheek, "but isn't the situation making you unhappy?"

True. Mum and I had always been close, perhaps because she had been on her own for so long.

"Okay then," I said as I walked him to the door. "I'll call Mum later today. Deal?"

"Deal," he said, setting off toward the Lochside Welcome.

Shoot. Yet again, I'd forgotten to ask Jack about Lachlan and make him swear on his daughter's life he knew nothing of any criminal enterprises that might involve Lachlan. On the other hand, Lachlan's illegally gotten gains might help pay the tax bill.

"Jack? Lachlan's not doing anything wro—"

I shut up. Caroline, booked in for babysitting to give me the chance to finish everything I needed to do for Blissful Beauty before I stopped for Christmas, opened the garden gate. Ranald would hit the roof if he thought Lachlan was up to no good. No point starting more family rows. Luckily, Caroline didn't seem to have heard me, her air distracted.

Evie packed off to her granny's, I closed the door and rattled through the work in record-quick time. Thanks to the hours of overtime I'd put in over the last few months, my Christmas holiday was due to start tomorrow. Trish called to chat through everything that needed to be done— as keen for me to go on holiday as I was so she could flex those boss muscles.

"Has Marty showed you those Instagram stories he was putting together?" I asked. Before I ticked him off, I should check with Trish in case he'd asked her for approval instead.

She shook her head.

"Heads or tails who gives him the bollocking this time?" I said, picking up the pound coin next to my keyboard.

Neither of us relished confrontation. This was the easiest way to decide who owed Marty a talking to. The coin landed tails down. Result! Trish would be the one asking Marty to follow her into the boardroom and attempting to intimidate him into obedience.

Work finished, I checked the time—ten to 12. A Katya quote borrowed from Mark Twain meant to inspire was that if your job was to eat a frog, do it in the morning. That way, the rest of the day was a breeze. Technically, it was still morning.

Next to my iMac, my phone appeared to take up all the space in the room. Phone your mother! Ask after your father! Suggest a course of HRT might make her see sense and ditch him before she gets in too deep!

I stood at the window, looking out on the loch, the rhythm of the waves and the cries of the gulls soothing me, deep breaths in and out. Promises I would listen and consider her point of view.

Mum answered at once, breathless.

"Gaby! I'm out jogging."

What? Mum believed exercise was the tool of the devil. Was she trying to improve her fitness levels to tone up for… him?

"Thanks for phoning," she added. The traffic noise in the background faded out. She must have let herself back into the house. "How's Evie?"

"Fine. Excited about Christmas."

"Is she there? Can I see her? I loved those pictures you put on Instagram."

My mum's Instagram modus operandi was to put the caps lock on so that everything she wrote came out like a yell. THAT'S MY LOVELY GRANDDAUGHTER. SHE IS THE MOST BEAUTIFUL LITTLE GIRL IN THE WORLD. LOOK AT HER AMAZING HAIR. And she needed an urgent tutorial on what the different emojis meant. Notably, when you used a combination of them in a certain way.

"No, sorry, Caroline's got her this morning."

My mum drew in a breath. If she hadn't been trying to suck up to me because it was the first time I'd phoned in a while, I know she would have thrown in a remark at that— like how spending so much time with only one grandmother was terrible for a small child. As it was, she said nothing.

"So. You and my dad."

Might as well tackle the issue head-on.

"Yes," my mum said, "we're still together but taking it slowly."

"How on earth did he convince you to take him back?" I asked. In my teenage years, Mum put up with endless absences and a lot of shouting matches late at night. Mum had been determined that when she booted him out that last time, he wasn't coming back.

"This time is different, Gaby, I swear. Your father's done a lot of growing up over the last few years."

About time, seeing as he was now closer to 60 than 50.

"And we always had the most amazing chemistry."

Eww… *really* not what you want to hear from your mum.

Mildred, by now curled up on the sofa, flicked her tail. If I'd had one, I would have done the same.

"Rebuilding your relationship will take time, I know," my mum continued, "but Tony's desperate to see you and Dylan again, and apologise. How about if we—"

The next few words were rushed out hurriedly. The gist

was—they drove up to Lochalshie asap, booked into the hotel so as not to get under our feet in the house. Then, they spent a few days with my brother and me to convince us version 2.0. Tony Richardson was a vast improvement on the last.

Mildred's tail flicked again.

Dylan had said to me that Norwich City FC would need to top the Premier League five years in a row before he spoke a word to our father ever again. An unlikely football outcome, as we both acknowledged, reluctant to show so little faith in our local football team, but their chances were... zilch.

"I don't think so," I said, "I don't understand why you're so prepared to forgive him. Aren't you frightened he'll hurt you again?"

"No, it's different this time, Gaby," Mum jumped in, "and him talking to you and your brother is one of those conversations best-done face to face."

"If we do this," I said, "and Tony walks out again in a year when he's bored with us, what then?"

"He won't!"

From the window, I spotted Caroline and Ranald. They'd stopped by the benches on the small walled-off area in front of the loch. Ranald sat down, Caroline bending her head towards him. Her face twisted to the side. I couldn't see for sure, but the look on her face alarmed me. Was something wrong with Evie?

"Mum, I need to go," I said.

"Please, Gaby—will you think about it?"

Relentless! I threw in a final killer question. "What does Nanna Cooper say? Has she come round to the idea?"

Silence. Gotcha.

"She's not best pleased."

Honest of my mum to admit. I pictured it—Nanna Cooper recovering from her fall with some light weight-lifting in the living room as the doctor has prescribed. "Mandy, I said it then, I say it now! Tony Richardson is a dust-bag through and through. Take him back. and I will never speak to you again, my girl!"

But I had more pressing concerns, such as why fear and worry etched its way across Caroline's face and what was up with Evie.

Muttering a hurried, "Okay, I'll think about it!" I rushed out to join them.

Chapter Sixteen

THE BLISS OF CHOCOLATE MILK

"Is everything alright?" I asked, the words coming in pants. I needed to begin a regular exercise programme (note to self —New Year's resolution, this time to be stuck to) if running 250 yards made me so out of breath.

Evie was tucked up in her buggy, 'speaking' to the seagulls on the shore as she liked to do. Ranald got to his feet. "She's fine, Gaby. Don't worry."

Caroline, voice bright, piped up. "He's a bit light-headed, that's all. Missed his breakfast this morning. We better get home and get some food intae him."

Jamal, in the middle of unloading stock he'd bought at the cash and carry from his van across the street from us, shouted a 'hello', reminding us he stocked a wide range of breakfast cereal choices. Caroline screwed her face up. "Aye and marked up 100 percent!" she muttered under her breath.

Ranald sat back down again, the bench creaking in protest as he thumped onto it.

"Actually, Caroline, I wouldn't mind some cocoa pops."

"Right enough," she said, darting off.

Ranald stretched his arms along the bench, eyes on the far distance. "When I was growing up, my sister and I weren't allowed to eat cocoa pops," he said, twisting his face around to smile at me. "My mother thought they were common. I discovered them as a young man in my 20s and thought I'd died and gone to heaven."

Blimey. Ranald talked in single sentences only. But he painted a compelling picture—him in his farmhouse kitchen tipping cocoa pops into one of those old crystal trifle dishes, covering them in milk fresh from his dairy, waiting for the chocolate to run into the liquid, and digging in, expression blissful.

He gestured towards Evie, still doing her best to persuade seagulls to come closer. One bold fellow edged nearer her buggy. Small children were often a safe bet for the canny gull—prone to dropping anything and everything, including food. The cheekiest of them often snatched ice-creams or sandwiches straight from their hands.

"What will we get her for Christmas?" Ranald asked. "I want to spoil her this year."

"Ranald, you spoil her enough," I said. True. The bulk of Evie's wardrobe, plenty of her toys and the trust fund maturing and multiplying (hopefully) in a bank in Oban were all down to Ranald and Caroline. I told her all the time what a lucky girl she was to have such generous grand-parents, which made me squirm now thinking of how my mum was missing out.

"Indulge me," Ranald said. "She's my first grandchild." He'd closed his eyes, but opened them once more, expression sly. "Not the last, I hope?"

I rolled my eyes. As a recently married woman, you batted off these inquiries from the villagers all the time.

Hello? Lay off asking me to confirm that Jack and I have sex. "Maybe. Though not the way we feel at present—like, permanently knackered."

And too worried about the lack of money coming in.

Caroline returned, shaking a shopping bag stuffed with three packets of cocoa pops. "Jamal had some o' that local organic milk in—the extra creamy stuff. I've stocked up on that too. Shall we head home, Ranald? I fancy a bowl o' these too."

I waved them off, oddly tearful. That story about the cocoa pops. The vision of Ranald and Caroline perched side by side on their stools in the kitchen at the free-floating table that gave you the perfect view of the loch, tucking into enormous bowls of cereal and chocolatey milk together.

I wheeled Evie home. "Let's hope Grampy Ranald eats everything up, and the light-headedness goes away, eh Evie?"

A pile of Christmas cards greeted my return to the house. The postman must have delivered them in my absence. Cards opened and displayed on the strings I put up around the living room, I updated Facebook and Instagram. "Thanks for all the lovely Christmas cards! Jack and I have donated what we would have spent on cards and postage to charity this year."

No, we hadn't, but Jack would be no more minded to write Christmas cards than I was, and this stance gave me the glow of the environmentally righteous.

"Too lazy tea write them, you mean!" commented Mhari.

My phone rang. Nanna Cooper.

"Gaby? It's your nanna."

Nanna Cooper was yet to remember mobile phones showed you the caller.

"Are you alright, Nanna? Have the bruises cleared up?"

"I'm fine," she said. "Are you free because I want to talk to you about your mum? She is making a huge mistake. I've heard a terrible thing about that dust-bag your father."

Yikes. I sat down. "What do you know, Nanna? Mum's not in danger, is she?"

Chapter Seventeen

THE RESTORATIVE POWERS OF EXERCISE

"Shall we visit Auntie Katya?" I asked Evie the following morning. "Try to repair some of the damage I caused?" Evie nodded solemnly, and we set off down the High Street.

I rang Katya's bell.

"Morning!"

Pink-cheeked and shiny-haired, she looked far better than she had two days ago.

"How is everything? Is, um, Zac here…?"

Katya screwed her face up. "No? Why would you think that?"

"You're far cheerier. And Mhari and I spotted him in the village the other night."

She rolled her eyes. "Richardson, you've been living here so long you've turned into a curtain twitcher. Any minute now you'll start saying 'you ain't from these parts, are you?' I went for a jog this morning. Put Lucian in his buggy, and we ran around the loch. Exercise is fantastic for your mental health."

It was? The restorative power of slumping in front of

the TV, with a large tub of ice-cream, was my go-to whenever I felt down.

Katya led me into the living room. I set Evie on the floor, and she made straight for Lucian, who was in his playpen.

"You look knackered," she said, handing me a cup of green tea. "Is anything wrong with you?"

Katya was far more discreet than anyone else. I told her about the unexpected tax bill and Jack's reluctance to hit up his father or stepfather for the money.

"It's all too much," I sniffed as my blasted eyes started to water once more. "I had all these brilliant plans for Christmas. The hotel would be booked solid. Then we'd have an amazing celebration with our family and friends—well, some of my family, certainly not Tony—and bring in the New Year all happy! Tell me you've spoken to Dexter, and you've kissed and made up. Give me some hope!"

Katya shrugged. "Apart from him ringing to ask about Lucian, no I haven't."

"But what…"

"We're *not* going to talk about it anymore," Katya said, eyes flashing. "And don't you dare mention anything to Caitlin the next time you speak with her because she'll only do something drastic like threaten to sack me as her ghostwriter unless Dexter and I kiss and make up."

"Oh, but what if—"

"Gaby!"

"Alright, then! Subject officially closed." I mimed zipping my mouth shut.

"The answer is to throw ourselves into work," she added. "Do you remember that life coach I did some blogs for a few years ago?"

Did I ever. Katya quoted the woman verbatim for

months afterwards. Funnily enough, the life coach via Katya had plenty to say about all the areas of life I wasn't doing well enough.

"Busyness, she says, is the cure for a broken heart. I'm taking her at her word. Do you want to see all my ideas for how we promote the Lochside Welcome for Christmas, New Year and beyond? Sounds as if we need to do this more than ever."

She had been busy. On her laptop, she pulled up a spreadsheet documenting all her ideas for publicising the hotel and a six-month content calendar for the Lochside Welcome's YouTube channel, Facebook page, Instagram and TikTok accounts. It was colour-coded, too, with the last column allocating responsibility for each task. My name popped up alarmingly often.

"Santa's grotto," she exclaimed, "combined with a Christmas fair on the 15th. What do you think?"

"That's only a week away. How on earth will we manage that?"

Evie hauled herself up, distracting me. She beamed at us both as I clapped my hands. "Oh, clever girl, Evie!"

I got down on the floor and held my arms out. "Want to walk to mummy?"

She took a few teetering steps forward, her own arms stretching towards me. Lucian had paused to watch her too. The Airbnb property had been gutted and done out a few years ago—its old-fashioned carpets ripped out. Shame: Carpets might have provided more cushioning. She thumped back down onto the floor—her face puzzled until the realisation she'd hurt herself hit her seconds later, and she started howling, setting Lucian off too.

"Sometimes," Katya said, bending over the playpen and

scooping up Lucian, "my old life flashes in front of me and I want it back so much it hurts."

I pushed Evie's little head into my chest and jiggled her up and down. "There, there, Evie! You're okay, darling. I promise."

"We'll manage a fair easily enough," Katya said as Lucian continued to yell. "Clear the dining room in the Lochside Welcome and invite local artisans to offer their stuff for sale. They'll like that idea because there will be people in the hotel drinking and there's nothing like alcohol to lower sales inhibitions, eh?"

Too right. When Jack and I celebrated his birthday sans Evie, we spent a night in Edinburgh. After a pint of lager with my lunch, we popped into Marks and Spencer's on Princes Street and spent more than £175 buying clothes for Evie.

"Charge the artisans a fee for their stalls and offer a cut-price Christmas pizza and a visit from Santa Claus. We'll attract people from miles around. I've prepared tonnes of social media posts. All I need now is some artwork from you. If you get on with it this afternoon, I can make a start."

I opened my mouth to object and shut it again. If planning an event kept Katya occupied—and even better, brought much-needed money and business into the hotel— who was I to complain?

"We better run this past Jack," I said.

"Fine. Let's do it now."

I'd forgotten how terrifying Katya was when she had a project in her sights. But the thought of a Christmas fair in a week cheered me up too. How much money might that make? Unlikely that it would equal the sum the HMRC demanded, but it would help.

Evie, recovered from her little trip, perked up once more as we headed out, Jamal calling out a cheery 'hello!' as he unpacked his van. "Got a special deal on mince pies!" he added. "They're £2.99 instead of £3.99."

"Not vegan," Katya called back, making him squint at the packet.

Dylan was behind the bar at the Lochside Welcome in earnest conversation with Terry and the other regulars when we arrived, all of them giving him tips for how to stay warm in winter.

"Start your morning wi' a brandy," Terry said, "and spend all day in the pub where someone else is paying the heating bill."

"To be fair, Terry," I said, as Katya and I dumped our stuff on the nearest table and sat down, "you do that in the summers too."

"Aye, right enough. 'Cept in the summer I sit in the beer garden."

Not true. Terry sat on the same stool all year round, too scared to risk getting off it in case someone else nabbed it, and he ended up more than a metre away from the bar.

Jack appeared, brow wrinkled in a way that made my own furl in sympathy. A Christmas fair wouldn't help that much, but it might help lift some of the weight of the world from his shoulders.

Katya whipped out the printed copy of the social media plan she'd drawn up and scribbled something on it. I cleared my throat. "Katya's had this idea. A Christmas fair and Santa's grotto. Next week. What do you think?"

Jack baulked. "Next *week*?"

"Yes," Katya said crisply. "It's perfect. You'll attract people wanting to stock up on Christmas presents and then it will be easy to persuade them to eat and drink here. I'll spread the news of it far and wide on social media."

She thrust the social media plan into Jack's hands. He peered at it, nonplussed.

Katya ran through everything she'd planned. Charge stallholders a small fee for their stalls. Turn the conservatory into a makeshift Santa's Grotto. Set up a two-tiered entry fee for those with children and those without.

"What about the presents?" Jack asked. "If you going to charge that much for Santa's Grotto, you'll need a wee bittie more than some crappy plastic toy."

"Colm might be able to help." Dylan piped up.

"Colm?" Jack and I asked, swinging around to face him. "Who's he?" I said.

My brother ducked his eyes and finished pouring Terry's pint, Guinness—its head expertly topped with white foam. "A friend of mine."

"You have a friend here?"

In the time Dylan had been in Lochalshie, he spent most of it sitting or lying on my sofa watching TV and/or scrolling through his phone. How had he managed to befriend anyone? Whoever Colm was, I thanked him. Provider of gifts for children: Supporter of community events. A veritable saint.

"He's from the brewery," Dylan added. "The one that provides the craft ale."

He held up a bottle of the beer we'd just started stocking. Xavier had met with the owner of the brewery last week. The company had offered the Lochside Welcome exclusive supply of their IPA on tap. It was also in the middle of negotiations with a supermarket and some other big company to provide beers for their subscribers. They were about to hit the big time.

"Jolene, can Stewart be Santa for the kids?"

She grinned. "Well, he's got the beard and belly for it."

True. Stewart towered over all of us, two-and-a-half metres tall and about that wide too. Dressed in the customary red and white, he'd make a convincing Santa.

"Great," I said, "so we have ourselves a date? Next Sunday? The Lochside Welcome Christmas Fair! Katya and I will start promoting it on Facebook and Instagram now."

"You don't want any photos o' me to advertise this, do you?" Jack lived in fear that photos of him would be splattered across Instagram and Facebook, given that he loathed social media, summing it up as "for big-headed eejits". Nothing I could say about its positive qualities—*keeping in touch with people far away, cat pics, spreading awareness of something*!—convinced him otherwise.

Katya hesitated. "No. Xavier can front it." She snapped her fingers. "Let's make him the Sexy Santa of Lochalshie! He's already in some of those YouTube videos, isn't he? High time we resurrected them."

Last year, Mhari had uploaded films promoting Xavier, I mean, the Lochside Welcome's charms on YouTube. Mostly, they showed the scenery and Xavier talking about life working for a small hotel in an idyllic setting and had been a great hit. They still got likes, comments and shares now but we hadn't uploaded anything for a while.

"Do you have an outfit we can dress him in?" Katya asked. A speculative look crossed her face. "Even better, what about him wearing just a Santa hat and a present held in a strategic place?"

Xavier, on his way back from delivering a pizza order, caught the tail end. Jack, huge smirk in place, explained Katya's exact suggestion to him.

"Non, non, 3,000 times non! I'm not a sex object!"

Plenty of our customers might disagree. He stormed off, the door to the kitchen slamming behind him. Jack scratched his head. "I hope he doesnae decide that's sexual harassment, Katya. We can't afford tribunal costs."

Katya cast her eye around. "What about you, Dylan? You're desperate to prove your usefulness, aren't you?"

My brother, pulling Terry yet another pint, paused. "I'm not doing a naked photoshoot."

"No need," she said.

"Do your worst," Dylan said, turning away to unload the dishwasher.

"Dylan scores a big fat zero in the sexiness stakes in my opinion," I said to Katya as we headed back out again.

"Creating the Lochside Welcome's Sexy Santa will take a bit of prep," she replied. "That's why we'll need to enlist Enisa's services. If we…"

She dropped her voice, outlining what turning Dylan from humdrum to handsome would involve.

Oh. And oh. The sister who'd put up with endless grief in her formative teenage years grinned from ear to ear.

Chapter Eighteen

TWO CONVERSATIONS

"Did you speak to your mum?" Jack asked. He'd managed to get away early, the two of us relishing the Dylan-free house. Evie, unused to seeing her father at this time, was delighted too.

Jack bounced her on his leg. Evie's favourite game was what we called the horsey ride—your leg moving progressively faster as you bounced through the way the ladies, gentlemen and farmers rode a horse.

I'd lit the fire, fake flames crackling away, and strung up the Christmas cards we'd received around the room to give our home a festive feel. The tree, shedding needles like billy-o, added to the atmosphere. The minute you opened the door, the scent of pine blasted out.

"Yes," I said, handing him a Tunnocks teacake. "But then Nanna Cooper phoned me. She reckons Tony's a gold-digger."

"… and this is the way the ladies ride, trot, trot, trot. Who telt her that?"

"Kathleen Millar. Who heard it from her daughter, who

was at school with my mum. She has a work colleague who is an old friend of my dad. Daddy dearest is skint. His old girlfriend cleared him out. Nanna says he's back in the country sucking up to my mum because he's got no money whatsoever."

Jack raised an eyebrow. "And this is the way the gentlemen ride, canter, canter, canter. Kathleen Millar's daughter's work colleague. Wow."

Was that sarcasm? So much for spousal support.

"Maybe that's why he's so keen to come up here and get his greedy grasping hands on the Lochside Welcome, hmm?"

My first thought when Nanna revealed Tony's financial credentials had been that he'd chosen the wrong woman if it was money he was after. My mum was on the minimum wage. Prodigious quantities of Prosecco and an annual week's holiday in the Canary Islands were her only extravagances.

But the Lochside Welcome... what if he got his hands on that? I'd come off the phone to Nanna more determined than ever that Tony Richardson would *not* be meeting Dylan and me anytime soon.

Jack continued bouncing Evie by now on the tenth time she'd trotted, cantered and galloped. "Mo-mo!" she bellowed.

"If you say so, Gaby."

Sarcasm for sure. I glared at Jack. He widened his eyes back, and Evie galloped on her imaginary horse once more, laughing her socks off.

"But the other thing is," I threw in before we ended up rowing, "is that Nanna can't come for Christmas!"

"Why not? Is she okay? I thought you said she'd recovered?"

"Well, she has—sort of. I invited her to visit herself. Offered to buy her a bus ticket, which won't be *too* expensive"—hopefully, I hadn't dared check—"so she doesn't have to rely on my mum to bring her. But she said sitting for that length of time wouldn't work. Her hips and knees can't take it because of the osteoporosis."

Doctor Who had been able to teleport himself for years. Why hadn't someone invented that in real life? Honestly, the science boffins in our world were such slowcoaches. If Nanna had a Tardis handy, she could be here in seconds.

"Your nanna shouldn't be travelling on her own anyway," Jack said, an edge to his voice. "If she's no' that long out of the hospital, she should have your mother with her."

"Any more Christmas bookings?" I changed tack. An argument was the last thing we needed. Though I might compose an email to Hallmark, the card company, in the morning. *Dear Whoever, why do all your cards promise Christmases filled with love, happy families, peace and contentment? So far, I have not found this to be the case and wonder if your cards spread false hope and expectations...*

He shook his head. "Nope. If I don't mention your family again, can you not talk about the hotel?"

Deal. Wouldn't stop either of us fretting though.

I spent the next day designing graphics for the Christmas Fair and posting them all over our social media accounts as per Katya's instructions, delighted to have something positive to do. When Jack let himself back in the house early evening, I was able to show him all the bookings for stalls we'd had already.

Jack ruffled my hair. "Clever you. You've got a letter. It was among the pile of Christmas cards."

The ones I'd ignored earlier, guilt-filled. But a letter. Good grief. Who got letters these days? Christmas cards aside, our mail was 90 percent junk flyers and 10 percent bills. This, though, was addressed to Dylan and me, the label handwritten. I checked the postmark. Norwich.

Oh-ho.

I put it down. "I'm not opening it."

Jack must have spotted the postmark too. "C'mon, Gaby-sketch. Reading it doesn't mean you have to *do* anything."

I blew out air, making him smile. "Oh, alright then. But not now. Dylan needs to be with me to open it, doesn't he?"

I glared at the letter. Huh, huh, huh. Dirty tricks. My mum and dad conspiring together to bulldoze Dylan and me into listening to them, seeing as we'd ignored all the phone calls, messages and emails.

Jack ruffled my hair once more and gathered up Evie for a cuddle. "How's ma wee lassie?"

"I forgot to tell you! She took her first few steps the other day!"

He grinned, the smile splitting his face in two. "Aye? Do you think she'll do it again?"

"Let's try it out."

We cleared a space, moving the coffee table out of the way and picking up the toys that littered the floor.

I put Evie on the floor in her bare feet, holding her up, so she was upright. Jack crouched down and held his arms out. "Come to your daddy, gorgeous girl!"

Our daughter beamed happily at him and jiggled up and down, bending and straightening her little legs.

"Try holding her hand," Jack suggested. "Just one. That's what ScottishDaDa recommends."

I grasped Evie's right hand. We'd worked out she was left-handed like her father. She'd want that hand free so she could use her dominant side to balance. She wavered and fell over, landing much more softly this time.

Never work with children or animals, eh?

We tried a few more times, Evie in the end, deciding she was much better off crawling as fast as her little arms and legs could carry her into her father's embrace. He swept her up, covering her in kisses.

"I promised myself this Christmas would be our best ever," I said. "The hotel busy, a riotous family and friends celebration afterwards. Not one that involved worrying about the business more than usual, my papa's far-too-late reappearance on the scene and my best friend broken-hearted."

Jack, speaking nonsense to Evie, stopped. "I did too—the amazing Christmas thing. When you've had your first child, that's what you tell yourself. She wasnae old enough last year, but this year Christmas will really mean something. Be awfy special, etc. Mebbe we've overhyped it too much. It was always going to be disappointing because we're expecting too much."

How depressing. Early on in our relationship, Jack and I worked out my role was official cheerer-upper, the one who stood on the sideline shaking the pom-poms. Jack and Gaby, rah-rah-rah. But this time, even I couldn't summon up anything. Jack's face fell: He must have been hoping for the cheerleader speech.

"What is that Colm and your brother thing about?" he changed tack, referring to the way Dylan had volunteered the mysterious Colm's services and then clammed up.

"Your guess is as good as mine. Xavier seems to have some knowledge about it. Maybe Dylan has been talking to him."

Jack's eyes scrutinised mine. "Gaby, do you think—"

His phone rang, making us both curse. Lachlan. A delivery lorry had turned up, hours later than its scheduled time thanks to the iciness of the roads. But several crates of food needed unloading into the cupboards and fridges, and Dylan was busy behind the bar and in the kitchen. Could Jack help?

"Um...?"

"Off you go," I said, taking Evie from him. "That food won't unpack itself."

Evie and I watched him from the living room window as he headed towards the hotel, his shoulders slumping the closer he got to it. "Do you know what we all need, Evie? A spot of fun and I've had an idea. A little party. What do you think?"

I picked up my phone and rang Jolene. Operation Cheer Up, coming up...

Chapter Nineteen

OPERATION CHEER UP

Operation Cheer Up got off to a shaky start when Jack point blank refused to join in. When I outlined what I had in mind, he shook his head. "No way. I disapprove. It's only fair to give him a bit o' warning."

"But it'll be hilarious!"

"Mebbe so. Anyway, if you're out for the evening, I can give Evie a bit o' quality time wi' her daddy. I'll ask Lachlan if he fancies coming round for a blether too."

The thought Lachlan might sit in our living room, pouring his heart out to Jack about... Mhari? Nicola? What he and Mhari used to get up to when they did date (dogging? Weird escapades in play parks late at night?) almost made me cancel my night out then and there.

But the greater good beckoned... the making of a poster boy for the Lochside Welcome's Christmas. Katya had already decided she was going to use the pictures and YouTube uploads well beyond the fair and to encourage interest in our hotel.

Katya and Mhari shared my enthusiasm, the former

especially when I volunteered Jack for Lucian babysitting duties seeing as he would be looking after Evie at the same time. When he overheard me making the offer on the phone, he screwed his face up, mouthing the word 'No!' repeatedly.

"That kid is a nightmare!" he muttered when I hung up.

"No, he's not! And anyway, Evie loves him, don't you, darling?"

Evie backed me up the following evening when Katya turned up at our door, giddy at the prospect of a child-free evening. My daughter held her arms out. "Ga!"

"You don't mind, do you, Jack?" she asked, as he fixed a smile in place and replied, "Not at all!"

The mood at Jolene's was festive when Katya, Mhari and I arrived. Jolene had splurged on proper decorations and had found a playlist alternating carols and songs. Their living room was three times the size of ours, dominated by a vast 75-inch TV screen. The L-shaped sofa accommodated six people, and a fair few of Jack's paintings of the local landscapes hung on the walls. Jolene's Christmas tree—the perfect size and not sawn off at the top like ours—twinkled in the corner, white lights flashing on and off.

She beckoned us in, winking when I spotted Dylan on the sofa chatting to Stewart.

"Have you plied him with Prosecco?" Katya whispered, shaking her coat off and helping herself to a large handful of crisps.

Jolene nodded. "Yeah, he's two glasses down. I reckon he's at the stage where he'd agree to anything."

Debatable… but if the worst came to the worst, Mhari, Jolene, Katya and I planned to hold him down.

There was a knock on the door ten minutes later. Enisa,

her white tunic buttoned over her hajib and loaded up with a massage table and gigantic bag of equipment, bustled in: She ran a mobile beautician business on the side and was known for one skill in particular.

"Evening all." She grinned at us as she set up the table at the back of the room. "I thought I'd start wi' your brother, Gaby?"

I nodded—maximum entertainment for everyone else.

Dylan glanced up. "Start with what?"

Mhari smiled at him. "We're havin' a wee pampering party to get ready for Christmas. And tae turn you into a Sexy Santa. We thought we'd treat you to a facial. And a chest wax."

"A chest wax?" Dylan asked, putting his Prosecco glass down. "That's not painful, is it?"

"No!" Jolene, Katya and I chorused. Like me, they must all have their fingers crossed behind their backs.

"Do you want another Prosecco, Dylan?" I asked.

"A man doesnae need alcohol," Stewart piped up. "It's a crutch that does ye nae favours."

As an ex-drinker, Stewart tended to offer such pithy observations. He didn't say 'women'. Jolene must have trained him out of that one. She poured Dylan a glass anyway, tipping the flute to an angle, so the Prosecco didn't fizz over the top. "He does when he's about to be waxed."

Dylan's eyes registered alarm. "Is this going to hurt?"

"Not at all! Katya had her full bush whipped off one time and didn't complain, did you, Katya?" I said, regretting the words as soon as I'd said them when Katya sent me dagger looks. Everyone had inadvertently glanced at her crotch the minute I said it.

She sighed. "It was fine, Dylan. And for the record, it was for a think piece I was writing for a feminist website."

She stamped on my foot. Hard. I winced but kept my mouth shut.

Enisa clapped her hand. "Right. The wax is all warmed up. Dylan, d'ye want to take your shirt off and hop up on my wee table? We'll have you done in no time."

My brother downed his Prosecco as everyone cheered (Stewart excluded) and bounded over. He stripped off his shirt and climbed onto the bed. Enisa wielded an enormous pair of scissors over him, making his face crease in alarm. "Nae need to worry," she said, opening them up and proceeding to shear her way over his chest. "I'm just cutting back a little, so we can get you smooth as a baby's bottom."

Hair cut off and gathered up, Enisa joking that he ought to sell it on eBay as somebody somewhere would be able to make a wig out of it, she stirred her pot of hot wax. "Ready?"

I'd given Dylan another Prosecco just to be on the safe side. He nodded. "Fine. Do you worst!"

Enisa pulled the roller out of the tub and applied hot wax, Dylan almost leaping off the table. "Owwwwww!"

Enisa checked the digital thermometer on her tub. "It's no' hotter than 40 degrees. It shouldnae be burning you."

"No," Dylan said, "carry on."

Bless him. He was doing the brave little soldier act I recognised from years ago. The drumming fingertips against the edge of the massage table gave it away. A man who wanted to run screaming in the opposite direction but was pinned to the table thanks to male pride.

Sympathetic sisters might say, "Dylan, don't worry! Let's forget it."

Sisters who remembered the years when brothers got their friends to ask them out and then cracked up when the said sister thought they were serious and said yes, kept her mouth zipped shut.

Enisa held up her linen strips. "Try to relax," she said. "Makes it easier."

Dylan's head swung around, eyes piercing mine in full-blown panic. Enisa used to nervy customers, slapped the strip in place, pressed down on it and ripped it off in double-quick time.

The resultant scream would haunt me till my dying day. That is when I wasn't sniggering.

Dylan bucked upright, eyes wild. "No!" he yelled, "not again! That was awful!"

The mark on his chest stuck out—a long, white rectangular space, its edges red and inflamed.

Mhari stepped forwards. She clasped Dylan's hand. "Ye hae tae. Or you'll look like an eejit the next time you strip off in front of someone."

Dylan hadn't noticed, but Mhari had filmed the whole thing on her phone. Film clips of men getting waxed were comedy gold because they almost always yelled their heads off. A terrific way to publicise the Lochside Welcome should the said film go viral…

Stewart, busy comforting Tamar who'd burst into tears when Dylan started screaming, wandered over. "I've got some codeine left over from that time I hurt ma foot. D'ye want that?"

Dylan nodded furiously. Mhari topped up his Prosecco. Tablets located and swallowed, and ten minutes passed to give them time to work, Enisa tried again. This time, the screams were more muted, Stewart taking Tamar to the other end of the house so he wouldn't be frightened.

Enisa rubbed aloe vera gel on Dylan's now bare chest. "Well done," she said, "d'ye want to book me in for six weeks to get it done again? Or what about the back, sack and crack? Jamal tells me if ye get that done, ye feel a lot more when you're having—"

Dylan leapt off the bed, grabbed his shirt, buttoned it up and put as much distance between him and Enisa as possible.

"No, no, no, no, no! Never, ever again. That must be the equivalent of childbirth for men."

Jolene, Katya and I jeered.

Enisa turned off the tub of hot wax. "Who's next? Mhari? D'ye want me to do your nails? I've got these brilliant red and green falsies wi' a wee star on them that'll look very Christmassy."

Getting a manicure didn't tear Mhari away from her phone. She held it up with her spare hand. "Ooh! You've got an admirer!"

Dylan took the phone. "You put it on YouTube?"

"Aye, 950 views already. Read that comment fae Hops236."

He squinted at the phone—thunderous expression melting away.

"What does it say?" I asked.

"Mind your own business!" Dylan snapped at me.

Mhari told us all anyway. Hops236 couldnae wait to flick her tongue over hair-free nipples and kiss her way doon—

"Stop it!" Stewart called out. "Dinnae pollute wee Tamar's ears wi' that kind o' talk."

"Who's Hops236?" I asked, yet again, being told to mind my own business. Years of experience had taught me Dylan was a quick mover when it came to the opposite sex. Now, he appeared to be moving at Red Arrows flyover speed. Blink, and you missed it.

I flicked my way through Enisa's Shellac nail varnish shades brochure, settling on a turquoise colour shot through with silver sparkles. Given everything else that was going on, at least someone was happy.

And seeing as advance ticket sales for the Christmas fair, as well as bookings for Christmas Day, were still disappointingly low, I needed to take comfort wherever possible.

———————

"Look," Mhari said, holding her phone up. The video she'd taken of Dylan screaming his head off last night had stacked up more than 3,000 views already and numerous comments, plenty of them as lewd as Hops236. And there had been a flurry of advanced ticket sales for our Christmas fair.

Result.

We were all in the Lochside Welcome's public bar for a photoshoot where Dylan would pout at the camera and (hopefully) tempt even more people to check out the hotel. He stood behind the bar, glaring at us.

"Here. Put this on." Jolene held out the Sexy Santa outfit she had sourced—loose red yoga pants, a red waistcoat trimmed with white fur and a red and white hat.

Mhari, armed with a top of the range Canon camera she'd 'borrowed' from college, fished out a dusty bottle of baby oil she'd filched from the pharmacists, and waved it in front of Dylan. "You'll need this. Want me tae rub it in for you?"

Dylan snatched the bag and bottle. "No thanks, I can do it myself."

"Has the redness died down since last night?" Jolene called as he headed for the Gents.

"Yes," Dylan shouted back, "no thanks to you, you lying bunch of bitches!"

"Language!" I put my hands over Evie's ears, but the comment set off fresh sniggers, Jolene, Mhari, Katya and I all reliving the glorious moment when Enisa whipped that first strip off.

Dylan returned a few minutes later, self-consciously clutching the sides of the waistcoat over his newly smooth chest. Mhari put her fingers in her mouth and wolf-whistled, Jolene joining in. As his sister, I wasn't about to tell him he was hot for fear of making his ego more enormous than usual. But even I had to admit he looked remarkable.

Mhari made him pull pints while she snapped away. Still sleepy-eyed thanks to too much Prosecco the night before and his hair much longer than usual, the total effect was an all-too knowing Santa leering at the camera. We gathered around the camera to study the pictures.

"Makes me want tae take a' my clothes off and fling myself at you," Mhari said to Dylan. He shook his head in faux modesty at the comment as I mimed vomiting.

But five minutes after Katya had uploaded the picture to all our social media channels, it had been liked more than 1,000 times, commented on and shared everywhere.

Dylan changed back into his regular work uniform of black T-shirt and cargo pants as Mhari joked with Xavier about missing out opportunities to share his own charms with the world, him shaking his head. "Non, non! I am 'appily loved up, as you say here. Lucas ees the only one who ogles my bare chest!"

Lochside Welcome Christmas Fair plans in hand, Katya and I took our offspring for a walk around the loch. The weather was dry but dull, a dark grey cloud looming over the hills that surrounded the loch. Rain wasn't far away.

The water was grey and choppy—two giant-sized gulls swooping in near us, hoping we might have bread with us to feed the ducks.

By the time we'd walked to the far end and back, the rain had started in earnest, turning the sky gun-metal in seconds and the spit turning to heavy drops. I popped up my umbrella—permanent umbrella carrying a behaviour hammered into me during the first six months of life in Lochalshie—and Katya pulled the clear plastic sheeting over Lucian in his buggy. Just as we re-joined the High Street, a car sailed past us—that moss green Jaguar I knew all too well. The vehicle came to an abrupt halt. The driver's door opened in almost slow motion, and a blonde head popped out. "Katya?"

"We better hurry. If we don't get indoors soon, Evie and Lucian will get soaked and maybe get colds, which would be awful," I wittered, tugging at Katya's arm. She took no notice, as the Jaguar's driver walked towards us, gaze fixed on Katya's top of the range sports buggy and the baby within it.

He crouched in front of us, eyes level with Lucian and staring at him... hungrily. "Pleased to meet you, little man," he said, holding out a finger for Lucian to grasp. Baby handshake done, he straightened up.

Zac.

"Can we talk?"

Chapter Twenty

MALE BONDING

If I'd chosen that moment to fling off all my clothes and do a little dance, I doubt Zac would have noticed. Even if I had a megaphone handy, ready to screech, "NO, NO, NO! DON'T DO THIS," neither of them would have paid any attention.

Katya agreed straightaway, ignoring my pleas we needed to go back to mine to organise all those social media posts for the Christmas Fair. She accepted Zac's offer to push the buggy for her, and they set off toward the Royal George.

When Katya moved to Lochalshie not long after I did, Zac poured an enormous amount of energy into pursuing her. When he was later exposed as a liar and a cheat, she gave up on him. But she'd always argued with me that Zac wasn't that bad...

"Well, Evie," I said. "As you know, I've always been Team Dexter, and that makes me biased, but Zac is not Katya's ideal partner at all. What do you think?"

She ignored me, too busy gazing at the lochside where Stewart paused, bending to bag dog poo.

"So, the baby daddy's come tae claim his son and heir, eh?" a voice behind me popped up.

Mhari, rumour had it, used a surveillance system on the village alerting her to incomers. The only possible explanation for her uncanny ability to surface at opportune times. Even when it was peeing down with rain as it did now.

"Don't be ridiculous," I said. "Katya and Zac are off to talk about work."

"Aye, right."

"Nae sign o' Dexter," she added, "and Katya's been here a wee while now. Have they split?"

"No. At this time of year, Dexter's super-busy persuading people to buy tonnes of make-up. And Katya is concentrating on her writing."

Mhari wrinkled her nose. I did not make a convincing liar. She headed off, promising me Zac and Katya would be an item by the end of the year.

Phone me later, promise???????? Back in the house, I typed out the message, hoping that Katya wasn't about to burn any bridges with Dexter. In the meantime, I got on with creating graphics advertising the Lochside Welcome and why it was the best place to spend Christmas. Fourteen days to go, the rooms still unfilled and Christmas Day bookings not yet at numbers high enough to stop Jack twitching every time I asked about them.

Would this be enough…?

When Jack let himself in two hours later, I handed Evie over. "She needs her nap." He took her upstairs singing Flower of Scotland to her, returning five minutes later and collapsing next to me on the sofa.

"Isn't it great to have the house to ourselves again?" I

spread my arms out. Hours stretched in front of us, the possibilities endless…

(Who was I kidding? The possibilities, me and him finding something on Netflix and falling asleep half-way through.)

Jack hugged me. I found myself enveloped in black cotton, the smell of pinecones and warmth. "The greatest."

His phone trilled, both of us cursing. If whoever had woken up Evie, we would kill them, single-handedly. Also, points deducted from Jack. Rookie mistake. Always turn your phone to silent when you put your small child to sleep.

He hoicked it out of his pocket, face screwing up in puzzlement as he studied the screen. "It's Dexter."

I drew back. Maybe Dexter wanted a one-to-one male conversation. A discussion about what you did when you didn't know if your baby momma *was* your baby momma.

Jack moved into the kitchen. I heard the back door open. Ayes, no's and 'I completely understand, mate' drifted through. I lay on the sofa and pointed the remote control at the TV to avoid overhearing half a conversation and jumping to conclusions.

Bonus! I found an episode of *Don't Tell the Bride* on More 4 themed around Christmas. As someone who'd married in December, I loved Christmas weddings. This one featured elves, a menu leaning heavily on turkey, pigs in blankets and Yule Logs, and a Santa. I welled up as the bride put her hands to her face when she saw it and bursting into tears. She even liked the dress the groom had picked for her.

The kitchen door opened. Jack, grim-faced, stepped through.

"Oh!" I sat up. "Was Dexter distraught? Did you tell him Katya is amazing, wonderful, kind and generous, and she just made one idiotic mistake?"

He shook his head. "He's split with Katya for good."

Curse him to hell and back—what a time of year to drop that bombshell on a person. I took back every pleasant thing I'd ever said about him. May he rot in hell.

Jack sat down, head bent forwards. He tipped his face up, expression bleak.

"Worse, Gaby. He wants out of the hotel partnership. And is demanding his money now."

Chapter Twenty-One

TOO MUCH GIN; NOT ENOUGH CRISPS

"He's a broken man, Gaby," Jack told me after I'd called Dexter every name under the sun. He sat down on the sofa, wrapping an arm around me. "I've never heard him sound so down."

Maybe so, but all my sympathies lay with my best friend. A knock on the door startled us both—the 'yoo-hoo!' shouted out, all too familiar.

As I stood up, Jack caught hold of my hand. "There's nothing you can do, Gaby."

"I know, but—"

He shook his head—a warning. Katya was at the door, eyes shiny and cheeks too red. Had the dreaded Zac put the sparkle in her eyes? She hugged herself. "Can I come in? What about if we get Mhari to take photos of all the children with Santa at the Christmas Fair and then charge them £20 for the prints?"

Oh-oh… spoken like the person who didn't know what her boyfriend (now ex) was planning. How rotten of him not to tell her before he broke the news to us. She pushed the buggy into the hallway and lifted Lucian out.

"Do you want a glass of wine?" I asked, following her into our living room. Jack caught my eye—dismay, embarrassment, horror at the prospect of having to break the news to Katya vis-a-vis her boyfriend. He stood up hastily— a man planning a rapid exit.

"Delicious, yummy red wine?" I continued, gesturing towards the kitchen. "Or a G&T? The gin's made by this small distillery nearby and——"

Lucian deposited on the floor, she straightened up. "No, thanks. Are you bracing yourself to tell me something, Gaby?"

That's the trouble with best friends, especially someone you've known for the best part of 20 years. She was too aware of how my mouth ran away with me when in a tricky position. "Possibly. Sure about that G&T?"

Mildred wandered into the living room, took one look at the baby and bolted into the kitchen and up on top of the fridge, Lucian turning his face to his mother, dismayed. A furry, cuddly thing he couldn't touch. As Lucian screwed up his face in preparation to scream his head off (and wake Evie), Jack grabbed him. He swung Lucian up in the air, holding him above his head and blowing raspberries at him. Lucian giggled.

Katya watched him playing with Lucian, a wistful expression on her face. She might have turned down the G&T, but no reason for me to do so. I gulped back a large mouthful in the kitchen and took a deep breath.

"Has your phone been off?"

She fished the phone out of her handbag. "Yes. Oh. Dexter's been trying to get hold of me."

Her expression brightened.

I looked away. "Um, well. Better phone Dexter back then."

Conversation number two held in our back garden. Jack and I grimaced at each other, me silently begging Dexter to change his mind, mainly for Katya's sake but also for the Lochside Welcome's future.

"Please can I have that gin and tonic after all?" Katya asked as she returned to the living room, voice small.

"Of course!" Jack leapt up.

"He's spoken to you about his share in the hotel?"

"Yes." Jack handed over the G&T.

"How much is Dexter's share? It's so long ago, I've forgotten what we put in."

Figuring out what percentage of the profits we'd since made and then working out how much we owed Dexter would be tricky. And the share might end up a substantial sum, at a time of year when money wasn't flooding into the coffers, and we had a ginormous tax bill to deal with.

"What if I—"

"No," Jack and I said together, anticipating the offer to buy him out herself. "No-one is asking you to do that."

Doubtful Katya would be able to afford his share anyway, and if she were about to become a single parent, she'd need to keep a tighter grip on her finances.

Jack still bouncing Lucian up and down offered to take him upstairs, so that Katya and I could talk. As soon as I said 'yes', he shot up the stairs, obviously terrified that Katya might force him to give a male perspective on what Dexter might think/feel. ('I'm Scottish, Gaby! We dinnae do feelings!')

"Have you eaten today? Did Zac give you anything?" I asked Katya, whose face appeared even more pinched than when I'd seen it earlier. The G&T was finished already. On an empty stomach, that stuff was lethal.

"No, I'm not hungry," she replied, topping up her glass from the bottle on the coffee table.

I dug out tortilla chips and hummus from the fridge, placing the food in front of her.

"I don't understand," I burst out. "Dexter loves Lucian. You don't abandon a baby you've spent six months loving, do you?"

Katya shrugged. "I didn't think so either."

"Would it help if Lucian had a DNA test?"

Katya took another far too large gulp of G&T. I'd abandoned my glass after the second mouthful made me want to heave. "What if he is Zac's? Dexter will never change his mind. And…"

She started to cry—something I had never witnessed. Ridiculous, given the length of our friendship and how often Katya had provided me with tissues and sympathy, but it was the truth. I hugged her as she turned my shoulder soggy, wishing there was something I could do.

Crying fit over, she asked me for another gin.

"Only if you eat those tortilla chips!"

The warning fell on deaf ears. When Jack crept downstairs an hour and a half later, he found her fast asleep on the sofa, and me on the hunt for blankets to heap around her and a bucket to put by her head in case she needed it through the night.

"Lucian's fast asleep," Jack said. "I changed his nappy and stuck him in wi' Evie."

He picked up the bottle of gin and squinted at it. "How much did Katya have to drink?"

"Not a vast amount," I said, placing a glass of water next to her, "but she's not been eating much. She banged on and on about how monogamy is a patriarchal construct designed to oppress women and then added that if Dexter ever dates anyone else, she'll kill him. With her bare hands."

On the floor next to her, Katya's phone vibrated. She didn't stir. I picked it up, hoping it might be Dexter—a good sign, right?—and dropped it. Zac. *Thanks for seeing me. So amazing to finally meet Lucian and I'm over the moon you…* was all I could read without unlocking it.

Jack shook his head. Tucking the blankets around Katya, I kissed my fingertips and pressed them to her hollowed-out cheek.

Chapter Twenty-Two

THE BLUSHING BEAUTY

We were all up early the next morning—courtesy of Lucian waking up at 6am and showing no inclination to go back to sleep. Jack and I resorted to taking him into bed with us, which necessitated bringing in Evie too, who was wide awake and wondrous at this addition to her bed. "You little tart," I told her, "you needn't think your daddy, and I condone sleeping with boys!"

As they both sat between Jack and I having a 'who could yell the loudest' competition, there was a knock on the door. Jack yanked the purple and silver duvet up over his chest, making me smile. "What are you? A Victorian maiden?"

A mussy-haired, green-tinged face poked around the door. The gin fumes hit me from where Katya stood.

"God," she said, "I'm so, so sorry! Motherhood's meant to make you a grown-up, isn't it, and here I am drinking too much on an empty stomach and passing out. How is Lucian?"

Lucian was gazing at her, a puzzled look on his face. Not used to his mother being so dishevelled, perhaps.

"All the happier for having slept with our daughter," I said, patting the bed. "Sit down, and I'll heat his bottle if you like?"

She nodded, then grimaced. "Oh dear, I'm sorry but—

And with that, she fled—the sound of retching coming from the bathroom. Jack pulled the sheet over his head. "You're clearing that up if she's made a mess."

The remark prompted a retaliation from me—the state of Stewart in his drinking days and what I'd put up with. Katya returned, white now instead of green.

"Again," she said, "a thousand apologies."

She teetered, stumbling forward, her hands grabbing at the air. I leapt out of bed, pulling back the duvet with me and treating everyone to the sight of... a rampant lion who then had to seize the bed linen back, all the time watched by two wide-eyed infants. Lucian might even have reached for it.

Katya, on her hands and knees and me beside her, put a hand over her eyes. "I didn't see anything! Anything!"

(The lady doth protest too much me thinks)

I'd never seen Jack McAllan flush so spectacularly, the redness flooding his cheeks, throat and chest.

"Are you okay?" The question could apply to both. My husband had disappeared, the sheets pulled over his face.

Katya stood up. "A bit faint. Can I make myself something to eat?"

"Sure. Then you better go back to bed."

Evie left with her now normal-coloured papa, I took Lucian with us downstairs and piled toast under the grill. The slices slathered in butter and honey, Katya managed two of them before dashing up the stairs for the bathroom once more. About to phone my mother-in-law—it wasn't normal to be this sick, surely?—she promised she didn't need a doctor, but would it be okay if I looked after Lucian for the morning and she slept it off?

A challenge. But Jack had managed to care for both Evie and Lucian the other night, and if I phoned Jolene, she might help. I nodded. As Jack had got up, we put her in our bed, and she fell asleep straight away.

I crept out of the room and downstairs.

"Will you be okay?" Jack asked, nodding towards Evie and Lucian who were squabbling over the toys on the floor. "I need to go to the cash and carry. I cannae get out of it. Then I'll have to see the accountant in Oban to find out what we owe Dexter and how we can pay him."

Lucian snatched a teddy bear from Evie, who screeched in response. "Fine. I'll enlist Jolene as soon as the hour reaches a civilised time."

Off Jack went. I swear to God there was a bounce in his step as he left the house, jubilant, no doubt, to be escaping a morning of screaming weans.

When Katya surfaced at midday, apologetic once more, Evie and Lucian were showing their best impressions of impeccable behaviour. Fed washed and changed thanks to Jolene's help, Lucian was fast asleep on the sofa: Evie was rearranging her teddies. Katya had slept through hours of screaming, and my head was fit to explode.

"Can you eat something now?" I asked, and she nodded gratefully. Toast round two successfully kept down, she told me she planned to return to London as soon as possible.

"Are you going to try to see Dexter?"

… on the off chance that he might find you and Lucian too much to resist?

"I don't know. Everything points to Dexter not wanting anything more to do with us. We've split before, but this seems permanent."

I grabbed hold of her arm while we stood at the front door. At least the rain held off, weak sunlight brightening the choppy waves on the loch. "Promise me you'll try to talk to Dexter? No matter how much he refuses to listen?"

Misplaced pride, I reckoned, was stopping Katya from making an impassioned plea for him to return. Silly to let that stand in the way. As someone who made a Grade A twit of herself far too often, I knew what I was talking about. When you let your guard drop, fantastic things could happen.

Katya wriggled free. She found a packet of tissues in her handbag and blew her nose hard. "Why? Just for some ridiculous notion of not being alone at Christmas?"

My plans for happy endings of any kind rumbled, then. But Katya's unhappiness when everyone was supposed to be celebrating cut me up. There's a saying that you're only as happy as your unhappiest child. Here, it was my unhappiest friend.

"It won't do any good. I've given up, Gaby. I made a mistake, a terrible one I know, but I've apologised until I'm blue in the face. There's nothing more I can do to make him change his mind, is there? If he wants to throw away what he once told me had been the best, most amazing and super fantastic few months of his life ever"—Dexter was prone to hyperbole—"who am I to stop him?"

"Please. Promise me. Cross your heart and hope to die. Swear on your mum and all your sisters' lives to do it!"

Katya smiled. As teenagers, we made those dramatic overstatements all the time—no harm in reminding her.

"I know you and Dexter were meant to be going to your mum's for Christmas this year, but you'll come here no matter what won't you? No offence to your mum, but I think you'll have a better time with us."

Guaranteed. The Kubowski Christmases were like those of the Cartiers. Fights and dramas from the outset. Epic arguments about who got to eat the toffee sticks from the tin of Quality Street. Liable to end in tears. Talking of the Cartiers...

An idea struck me. Ninety-five percent of me shook my head in horror. *"Do not do that! Stupid!"* The remaining 5 percent said, *"I'm desperate, I have to."*

Katya gave me a wobbly smile. "Okay. I'll phone you later."

I nodded. I hugged my friend goodbye and hurried inside, determined to talk to Caitlin and get her on board.

"I've fallen out with my mom," Caitlin replied when I asked how she was. Miraculously, I'd got hold of Caitlin the first time I Skyped her. And Jack was still out, which was as well. He wouldn't approve of this in a million billion years.

"You and me both," I told Caitlin. "What was your argument about?"

Caitlin was at the hairdressers—or, instead, this being Caitlin, the hairdresser had packed his industrial drier, toolbox and bag of tricks and decamped to hers. Stylist to the Stars Jerry attended to her locks once a week. Made sure the extensions stayed in place and her roots never emerged more than a millimetre. Katya and I once tried working out how much time it took to be Caitlin if you counted up all the hours spent on hairdressing, facials, personal training. Then add the weird therapies designed to banish any fat cell that dared stake a claim on the wrong bit of her body. And, of course, manicures and pedicures.

"A lot," was our not very scientific answer, but it

explained why Zoom chats so often took place to the back-drop of yoga lessons, hairdressing and beauty treatments. She'd once called Katya during a Brazilian wax while on all fours. ("Didn't even blink when the therapist ripped the strip off her bum hole!" Katya said, awe-struck.)

My surroundings were, as usual, far less salubrious. The living room where my iMac lived, its cables kept well out of the way of crawling babies though it had become increasingly difficult to stop her making straight for it, small hands on a mission to yank out plugs and worse.

Video calls meant you only had to tidy a small part of your house—the bit visible in the webcam—and only bothering to smarten your appearance from the waist up. I wore a jumper on top of my pyjamas.

Jerry lifted Caitlin's hair up at the back, making her wince. Her extensions were attached through a tight skull cap, the individual locks woven through the holes in the mesh. It looked excruciating.

I held up Evie, so Caitlin could blow her kisses. "Too, too cute! I've got her some super-amazing presents for Christmas. She'll be so excited when she opens them!"

Excellent. Jack and I wouldn't be able to afford anything once we'd paid off the tax bill and Dexter.

"My mom's demanding Donal, and I attend the Cartier family Christmas gathering. And that we say on the show that we're trying for a baby," she added, screwing her face up. This was a familiar argument. While Caitlin's spin-off show was the more popular of the Cartiers' reality TV franchise these days, she still made regular guest appearances on the programme that had made her famous.

Adrienne had been urging her daughter to give her a grandchild for years now. Not because she longed for another baby in the family, but because she knew it would push the ratings up. Millions more would tune in to watch Caitlin's stomach swell week by week. If she had a baby shower, it would bring in even more viewers—ordinary people happy to watch as hundreds of celebrities swanned up the drive bearing ridiculously overpriced gifts.

"And er… are you trying?"

"No. I'm crazy busy right now. As I keep telling Mom. Apart from that, Donal and I aren't talking to each other, much less sleeping with each other. I didn't finish high school, but I'm 100 percent sure baby-making needs the mom and dad to be in the same room instead of opposite ends of the house."

She pouted. "And Donal says if he has to do another Christmas with the Cartiers, he'll leave me."

Ah. The article in Pop Sugar Mhari had shown me where 'a close friend' claimed Caitlin and Donal were at 'breaking point'.

"What was your argument about?" Caitlin asked.

The gist of it explained—I didn't want to take up too much time talking about my family when I had urgent news to pass on—I moved onto the real reason I'd called. Katya had ordered me not to speak with our shared celebrity friend about her and Dexter just in case Caitlin threatened to sack Katya as her ghostwriter unless she kissed and made up with Dexter.

She hadn't, however, said anything about me ringing Caitlin and suggesting she threaten to unemploy Dexter instead…

News of Katya's predicament cheered Caitlin up. Not because she was a nasty person, but when you have troubles of your own, hearing about someone else's serves as a distraction.

"But that's so awful!!!!" she exclaimed. "Poor little

Lucian abandoned like that. My heart breaks for him!!!!!! He such a super-cute baby too, like the best!!!!!"

I stifled an objection there. Caitlin only called mine 'cute'.

"Terrible. Dexter's so unhappy. He loves Lucian so much."

Caitlin nodded. "I always think of Johnno as my real dad."

The Cartiers thrived on drama. It was why they were reality TV stars. Contentment and couples getting along well together did not make for exciting viewing. Caitlin was used to stories about infidelity. One sister's ex-partner had slept with four of her so-called friends while with her. Adrienne was on her fourth (or was it fifth?) husband, but husband number three—the one after Caitlin's actual father —was the one she'd stayed married to the longest, a whole seven years. Jonno had been around for all of Caitlin's childhood. He had also attempted to see her after he and Adrienne split. More than could be said for her actual dad.

Hence, my attempts to get her onboard with persuading Dexter splitting up with Katya would be the biggest mistake he ever made.

"Exactly. No stronger bond than with the one who brings you up, right? Not the dude who provides the sperm. Would you talk to him—stress how important that is?"

"Hey, of course. Why don't I tell Dexter he's fired if he doesn't phone Katya and beg her to take him back? That might work, right?"

Sound reasons to get back together with your girlfriend: You will lose your job if you don't. No relationship expert ever put that at the top of their list of the criteria for lasting love, did they? But didn't I owe it to my best friend to try?

"Well, maybe use that as a last resort. But if you speak

to Dexter, could you mention how much you adore Jonno and that he's not your real dad, but it doesn't matter a jot? Or could Jonno have a heart to heart with him?"

"Sure, honey! I'm in London in a coupla days' time. I'll tell Dexter he is super-crazy if he chucks everything away. And then order him to speak to Jonno. And if he's still determined to throw everything away, I'll threaten to fire him. How about that?"

"Thank you."

We blew kisses at each other and hit the 'leave meeting' button.

Fingers crossed that Dexter listened.

Chapter Twenty-Three

NEWS DELIVERED BY THE SOBER SUITED

"What did the accountant say?" I asked as I nailed up a Santa's Grotto wooden sign on the door of the conservatory in the Lochside Welcome. We'd heaped dark blankets around the place to make it look cave-like and strung fairy lights all around the walls.

I was helping put the finishing touches to the hotel ahead of the Christmas Fair in two days' time. In the background, Andy Williams sang about the most wonderful time of the year, making me grit my teeth. Not here, mate, I told him. We're all as miserable as sin. Christmas can stuff itself where the sun doesn't shine.

There had been no call from Dexter to say he had changed his mind. Either Caitlin hadn't talked to him, or the threat hadn't worked—the latter more likely.

Jack leant against the door, tipping his head back against it and staring at the ceiling. Gareth Murdoch in Oban embraced every accountant cliché out there—sober-suited, glasses and 100 percent serious all the time. Sitting in front of him was like being summoned by the headmaster and ordered to explain yourself. He'd shuffled papers in front of Jack and peered at him over the top of his glasses.

"I've been studying your accounts and your net profits," he'd told him. "Not good news, I'm afraid."

Tourism is a frail business in Scotland, overdependent on something we had no control over—the weather. The wet summer had discouraged day-trippers and last-minute bookings. Those in our partnership understood the Lochside Welcome was a long-term investment unlikely to profit by much in the first few years, and none of us was in it to make substantial amounts of money. But there was only so much of a hit we could take.

"That tax bill will swallow up all your profits. If your American friend pulls out," Gareth had added, pushing one of the papers towards Jack. "This is how much you'll need to pay him back."

Jack's face said it all now. There were far too many noughts in the sum.

Dear, oh dear…

"He said we should have drawn up a penalty clause should any investors wish to leave early," Jack said. "It's standard in financial schemes. We were foolishly optimistic, according to him, and we should have envisaged this situation right from the start. Or used a better lawyer. If we could persuade Dexter to hold off until the end of the financial year in April, we might be in a better position to pay him back."

"Can we?"

"No. Dexter's adamant he wants his money asap. Flower, his oldest niece, is university age and he wants to cover her tuition fees. Otherwise, she won't be able to go. She needs that money in place before she applies."

I stopped what I was doing and took his hands. "We'll be fine."

What rubbish. Jack glanced up, dark eyes searching mine. Most of me wanted to say, "Let Ranald do it. He and Caroline have plenty of money."

Dylan, Evie in his arms, joined us. "She needs changing," he told me, relieving himself of my daughter who stank to high heaven. I reached for my bag and pulled out the changing mat, Jack crouching down to help me.

"Is my job at risk?" Dylan's question sounded regretful —as if he loved working and living here. To everyone's surprise, not least his, he'd taken to his new job like a duck to water. Because the business was so small, no-one had just one position in the Lochside Welcome. Dylan doubled up as a barman, waiter, cleaner, occasional sous-chef and handyman.

Jack and I stared at him. We'd kept the Dexter conversation quiet, only sharing the news with the co-owners, but any information didn't stay secret for long in Lochalshie.

"Hopefully not," Jack said. We'd need to talk to Xavier, Jolene, Tina and Russell too, warn them they might need to think about looking for other jobs if they wanted greater security.

Dylan screwed up his nose. "God, what *are* you feeding her? I've got a bit of money."

He had? But now I thought about it, that made sense. This was the man who'd lived with his mother for the last six years paying a peppercorn rent (the word was too generous; it had been miniscule). The logistics job had paid well.

"Thanks, mate," Jack said, bagging the dirty nappy. "With any luck, it won't come to that."

"Well," Dylan shrugged. "It's there if you want it. I can take on Dexter's share. But I'd like more responsibility if I did. Got a few ideas about how you can cut costs to improve efficiency and utilise some of the underused spaces in here."

And with that, he walked off, leaving me and Jack agape. "Blimey," I said, "he's fallen hook, line and sinker for this place, hasn't he?"

Jack nodded. "Wonder what those ideas are. Dunno if I'm cut out for hotel management. Someone else might be able to do it much better than I can. Sometimes I wish I was back doing the Highland Tours. They were much easier."

When I'd first met him, Jack had run Highland Tours where he took visitors to north-west Scotland's most picturesque lochs, castles and viewpoints. Lucan, Xavier's boyfriend, now ran the tours, though he'd never bought the business off Jack.

"That's not true!"

Jack kissed my cheek. "Bless you, Gaby. I'm needed behind the bar. See you later."

And with that, he was off. Despondency radiated off him. I hugged Evie tightly.

"The fair will be an enormous success!" I whispered to her, "and loads of people will book in for Christmas and January and February and March and April and May..."

You could act in front of a loved one. When your audience was a one-year-old and yourself, not that easy. Even Evie didn't look convinced.

Chapter Twenty-Four

TEAM LOCHSIDE WELCOME FOR THE WIN

The day of the fair dawned—bright and sunny, which would help with visitor numbers. In winter, when the skies were grey, and the rain stair-rod-like, the overwhelming temptation was to lock the front door and stay inside.

I threw back the covers. Downstairs, Evie was in her highchair go-gooing at her father.

"Today," I told Evie as I accepted a cup of tea from Jack, "is going to be amazing, awesome and wonderful. And we'll make so much money from the fair, we'll be able to pay off all our debts."

The advance ticket sales had proved disappointing. Thanks to the photos and videos of Dylan simmering at the camera, the hotel's social media accounts had all gained thousands more followers.

"Come and meet the Lochside Welcome's Sexy Santa! He wants to know if you've been naughty or nice…"

The comments below the pictures ranged from "Ooh, I've been very naughty! Will Santa punish me?" to suggestions I had to delete as soon as they appeared. But they didn't seem to be following through on the sales.

"See you there in half an hour?" Jack asked, and I nodded, calling out that I hoped we were about to be run off our feet. He smiled. "Aye. Here's hoping."

My phone pinged.

Your dad and I were wondering if we could come up to Lochalshie next week to see you and Dylan....?

Gold-digging Tony and Menopausal Madness Mandy? Absolutely not.

Did you get your dad's letter?

Shoot! I'd stuck it in the magazine rack and forgotten about it. Today I'd take it with me, and Dylan and I could open it together once the fair was over.

Perhaps after the New Year? I typed back, ignoring the letter question. After New Year would give Tony enough time to realise Mum was as skint as he was and ditch her.

Thank you, love. That means a lot to us.

Grr. Now I'd be guilt-tripping all day.

Another ping. Katya had taken a picture of the hotel, the sign outside advertising The Best Christmas Fair in the Highlands.

"It's on! Team Lochside Welcome for the win!"

"Right, my gorgeous girl," I swirled Evie in the air. "Today's a big day. A Christmas Fair and Santa too. How amazing."

She gurgled. I couldn't wait to see how she reacted to Santa. The non-sexy version in the form of Stewart. The other Santa had been strong-armed into donning that waistcoat and loose pants once more to stand behind the bar and attract customers. Hops236 still pined after him. *You can slide into my Christmas stocking any day...*

"Do you know this woman?" I'd asked him, and he'd

given me an all-too knowing smile. "No. Seems dead keen, though, eh?"

At the Lochside Welcome, someone had set the jukebox to *Now That's What I Call Christmas Music*, Slade playing on a loop. People bustled all around us. Dylan and Xavier had cleared the dining/function room to allow local artisans to set their stalls up. Different smells competed for domination —Laney Haggerty's side-line of home-made soaps clashed with scented candles, pizza, pine needles, and the cinnamon and cloves of mulled wine.

My mother-in-law wandered over, reaching out her arms for Evie. Dressed in her Psychic Josie 'uniform'—a long, layered skirt with tiny mirrors attached, a printed blouse with billowing sleeves and a veiled scarf that hid her hair—strangers would take her for the real thing.

"Are you expecting lots of customers today?" I asked. To avoid disappointment, Psychic Josie's clientele needed to book in advance, which gave her enough time to look people up on social media. Then, she could say something profound, which left them open-mouthed at her perception skills, everyone forgetting that everyone already knew about their relationship splits/dead grannies via Facebook and Instagram.

"Aye, a fair few. All the lovelorn wanting to know if they'll be able tae get a partner in time for Christmas."

"Christmas is less than two weeks away," I said. Katya, helping Mhari's mother drape her hand-knitted scarves all over one stall, waved at me. Maybe Caroline might direct a few of the lovelorn Katya's way, seeing as my chat with Caitlin had yet to produce any results.

"What time's Santa due?" I asked Jolene, who was replacing the optics at the bar. We'd created a special Christmas cocktail—clementine martinis served in old-fashioned champagne saucers and topped with a little sugared peel.

"Eleven o'clock," she said, decanting one into a saucer and handing it to Terry at the bar for taste testing. "I've got a job for you."

"Me? But aren't I supposed to be—"

She ignored me. I followed her through the back to the small conservatory that faced onto the beer garden on the shores of the loch., hoping that whatever she wanted me to do involved no serving people food and drink. A job allocation that would end in tears for all of us.

Jolene unfolded a small portable table and set it at the front. She thrust a plastic bag at me.

"What's this?" I asked, realisation and dismay dawning as I took in green and red fabric.

"An elf's outfit. Santa's gonna need a helper. There's no-one else to do it—I'll be too busy serving customers. Ranald can babysit Evie."

"But…"

She was right. Someone had to organise the queue, so overexcited small children didn't stampede the conservatory as soon as Santa arrived. "I'd better get changed."

The outfit—green and red striped tights, a green velvet dress trimmed with red fur, a cowl hood and black high-heeled boots—looked ridiculous on. The dress was far too short, and the bodice strained across my chest.

"I can't wear this!" The mirrors in the women's toilets didn't allow me to see my full-length appearance, but I'd a nasty suspicion my bottom would be on display if I bent over. "What kind of elf outfit is it?"

Jolene looked sheepish. "The only elf's outfit I could get at short notice—the female sexy one. I've got some blusher here so we can give you red cheeks to make you look the part. Anyway, I need to get back behind the bar. Have fun!"

Mhari came in with her phone in hand. She peeked up. "Dinnae get that outfit dirty, will ye, Gaby? I had a lot of fun wi' it. I want it back clean, all in one piece and nae dodgy stains on it."

The day stretched ahead—me having to bat off endless rude comments and worrying about everyone being able to see my knickers.

Mhari glanced around her. "There are loads o' cars in the car park and along the main street. You're gonnae get plenty of people in. Want me to take photos for Instagram? Especially ones o' your brother, Gaby. He looks amazing."

Too much to ask that she might add, "And you look alright yourself."

The day had stayed dry. A crowd gathered outside to wait as Xavier and Jack wove around them, offering the hot chocolates and sausage rolls included in the entry fee. Which reminded me. Dylan had volunteered Colm for the presents. I hadn't organised that part of the day (and would not have ended up in this ridiculous elf outfit if that had been the case) so I wasn't sure if our benefactor had delivered.

Dylan was at the bar. It wouldn't open until 11 o'clock, but he and Jolene were busy stocking the fridges with bottled beer, cans and soft drinks. He straightened up.

"Wow—is that the uniform of choice for prostitutes in Lapland?"

"You can talk 'Mr I'm Covered in Baby Oil'. Did your Colm come up with presents for all the kids?"

"He's not my Colm!"

Touchy. Jolene nodded. "Yeah. We got a huge sack of stuff. Decent of him. It's loaded in the sleigh for Stewart to throw over his shoulder when he comes in, which will be," she glanced upwards at the clock above the bar, "in five minutes". I'm taking Tamar out to see Santa arrive. Want to come?"

Too right. Katya also joined us, Lucian strapped to her chest. Outside, the crowd had swelled. Jack, hot chocolate and sausage rolls dispersed wandered over. I handed Evie to him. "What are you wearing?"

I'd put a coat on, but the boots and the tights were visible.

"I'm one of Santa's elves."

Jack's eyes dropped to the thigh-high stiletto-heeled boots. "Not one Will Ferrell would recognise."

"Can you hear him?" one father asked his overexcited little boy. Their heads whipped to the sound of sleighbells to the right.

"Ho, ho, ho!!"

The 'sleigh' was a two-seater-four-wheel carriage, its sides deep red paintwork and gold piping. Laney Haggerty sat at the front of the carriage, bundled up in furs and a blanket, Russian style. Fake reindeer horns had been stuck on her two ponies. Behind her, Stewart-Santa, his beard whitened, waved at the crowd as he bellowed out more ho, ho, hos. The man behind me lifted his son onto his shoulders. The little boy clapping his hands, enchanted.

The sleigh came to a halt. Stewart stood up, the move unsettling the carriage, which hadn't been built with men of Stewart's size and girth in mind. It wobbled alarmingly, Laney sliding along the bench she sat on and Stewart swaying from side to side.

He righted himself—all those years of drunkenness must have given him superior balancing skills—and hauled up the bulging sack by his side, swinging it up and over his shoulder.

"So, have ye aw' been naughty or nice this year?"

"Nice!" the children chorused.

Jack, Evie wearing a bemused expression in his arms, smiled. "You, my little love, have been exceptionally nice. And you're going to get tonnes of presents."

Not from us. We hadn't bought Evie anything yet, too overwhelmed by horrible bills.

Tamar, in his mum's arms, pointed straight at Stewart. "My daddy!" he announced gleefully. "That's my daddy!"

"No, Tamar," Jolene threw in hurriedly as every child in the crowd turned to him, their little mouths hanging open. "That's not your daddy! That's Santa Claus."

"No. My daddy. My daddy, Stewart. He's my da—"

Jolene vanished, bundling Tamar out of the crowd before he could destroy the magic of Christmas for all the other children. "That's Santa, alright!" I exclaimed. "I'm his elf, so I should know!"

The man who'd put his son on his shoulders, turned to stare, eyes scanning up and down, landing on my thighs. "Bet you know lots of tricks, sweetheart, eh?"

Jack sent him 'back off' vibes the man ignored as he and his son headed back into the hotel.

The crowd built up behind Stewart at he entered the Lochside Welcome. We slipped around the side to the doors at the back. The mass had flooded into the reception area, the hall and the corridors, children demanding they see Santa at once.

"I'll offload Evie on Ranald," Jack said, disappearing among the throng. I pushed my way through to the conservatory. Stewart had taken a seat in there, the sack dumped beside him. Three children and their parents burst in.

"I'm first!"

"No, I am!"

"Me, me, me!!!"

"That's my dad—"

Jolene pelted in and grabbed up Tamar. "Sorry. I'm gonna dump him with his gran. Can you manage them?"

Wrestling my coat off, I acknowledged that I could, heart sinking. Angus appeared, perking me up. Farmer, rugby player and part-time bouncer for the Lochside Welcome, he was the best option for crowd control. He squatted to his haunches and eyeballed the children. "Ye've gottae wait in line for Santa. That's the rule. Understand?"

The children nodded, accepting his orders when he numbered them one, two, three. The mother of tiny tot three leant in. "Please come around to my house at bedtime every night and put my son to bed, I'm begging you!"

She put her hand on his arm. "You could always stay for a beer afterwards...?"

With order established the next two hours flew by. Stewart asked each child if they'd been naughty or nice—kid said nice, parents said the opposite—what they wanted for Christmas and told them to eat up all their porridge. Not your usual Santa script, granted, but porridge made with milk or water and no added sugar was a parentally approved breakfast option. The sack of Colm-supplied presents—a never-ending supply of Lego, toy cars and cuddly bears—lasted too.

Two hours later, Stewart declared himself exhausted and announced he was off to find Tamar and head home for a snooze. No offer to help me tidy up or with the rest of the fair. I stuck my head around the door to the hall. Most of the stalls were empty—their holders having sold all their stock. Splendid for them. Not so good for me and my Christmas present buying plans.

In the public bar, Xavier, Jack and Jolene were doing a roaring trade. Beers, mulled wine and glasses of Prosecco were everywhere, and the Christmas special pizza (turkey, cranberry sauce and Stilton) was in high demand.

Dylan wove in and out of tables, picking up glasses and wiping up. I'd underestimated my brother, thinking he would turn his nose up at such menial work. However, he wore an air of general contentment exchanging jokey comments with both the regulars and the out-of-towners.

Ranald, Evie in his arms, wandered over. "Shall we hide out in the conservatory?"

The words smacked of desperation. Ranald hated crowds.

We left everyone to it and parked ourselves on two of the substantial wicker armchairs in the conservatory: a low winter sun trying to break through the clouds. Ranald handed Evie over. He was back to looking knackered, wearing that same grey-skinned, yellow-eyed look I remembered from when Ashley had been ill a few years ago. Odd, considering that Ranald had retired from farming more than a year ago.

I kicked the door shut. No-one would miss us if we dozed off for a while.

"HOW DARE YOU, YOU MAN-STEALING BITCH!"

I snapped awake, Ranald's eyes meeting mine. A second later, the door to the conservatory burst open, as Mhari rugby-tackled Nicola Milne to the floor. The two of them landed with a thump in front of Ranald, Mhari's hair flying up halo-like around her head.

Ranald drew his feet out of the way. "Ladies, what are—"

"HE WAS MINE, AW' MINE BUT YOU HAD TAE INTERFERE POURING POISON INTO HIS EARS ABOUT ME!"

Mhari scrambled on top of Nicola, her hands pushing her shoulders to the floor, Nicola wriggled around underneath her. In the struggle, Nicola's false eyelashes came off, laying spider-like on her cheeks. Mhari yanked at her hair, making her scream. She fired a clumsy punch at Mhari, knocking her jaw and eliciting name-calling, not at all suitable for a family hotel.

Evie stared at me. "Ooo!"

I stood up. "Mhari, Nicola! Stop this!"

A small crowd had gathered outside. "Fifty to one," I heard someone say, "on Mhari Colquhoun to win."

"What's all this about?" I asked.

Mhari whipped her head around, her face curled up in a snarl. "This stupid bint telt Lachlan I daubed him in, to the cops for dealin' cannabis! I've just found out. And she said I'd told everyone he only lasted two minutes tops whenever we—"

"Okay! I get the picture! But I'm not sure this—"

"… when everyone knows Lachlan's the best sha—"

"Mhari, shut up!" Lachlan had pushed his way into the room, cheeks dotted with two bright red spots that matched the ones Jolene had painted my cheeks earlier. I swallowed hard. The crowd sniggered. "Speedy Gonzales, eh?" someone murmured. "Easy come, easy go…"

"Is that why you broke up with me?" Mhari screeched at him. "Because you listened to her lies!"

Nicola took advantage of Mhari's distraction to knock her to one side. She struggled to her feet and aimed a kick at Mhari's backside, sending her toppling flat onto her front. Mhari stood up, hands in front of her, false nails pointing forwards. Those mini weapons literally could scratch a person's eyes out.

"Stop it, the pair of you!" Lachlan hissed, planting himself between them. Jack slid in behind me, muttering, "He's a brave man!" in my ear. Then, "That elf outfit... don't hand it back until tomorrow, okay?"

"He dumped you, you slag," Nicola cried, "because you can't keep your legs closed! You were having it off wi' that Hyun-Ki yin at the same time!"

Mhari launched herself forward, knocking Lachlan off to the side. Nicola sidestepped her, picked up an armchair and thrust it at her, Mhari ducking down to avoid it.

"Oh, heck," I muttered in alarm, patting Ranald's arm. He'd tried to get out of his seat but collapsed back, the effort too much for him. Debatable what emergency service I called first—the police or an ambulance.

Jack took Evie from me and handed her to Jolene, so she'd be out of the way. He grabbed Nicola's arms as she made to thrust the chair again, yanking her back. The chair flew out of her hands and straight through the conservatory window, the smash of glass silencing everyone and flooding the room with cold air.

"Whoops," she said, as it landed upside down in the children's sandpit.

Whoops indeed.

Chapter Twenty-Five

AN OVERACTIVE IMAGINATION

"When did you find out about what Nicola had said to Lachlan?" I whispered as Mhari, and I swept up the broken glass. Ranald was still in his armchair nursing a hot chocolate and a plate of sausage rolls, batting away my offer to fetch Caroline.

The damage done, Nicola Milne, eyelashes still stuck to her cheeks, had fled the scene seconds afterwards. Jack and Lachlan placed temporary boarding over the broken window to keep out the worst of the weather. They'd enticed the crowd back to the public bar with the offer of free mince pies. Perhaps the afternoon's unscheduled drama as a plus would encourage our visitors to stay in the bar discussing the fight's finer details over food and drink.

Mhari sniffed. "None o' your business."

I sat back on my heels, shivering. Sexy elf costumes were not draught-proof at all. "Are you kidding? You shoot your mouth off, get into a fight that ends up costing us money—"

"That was Nicola, no' me!"

"Same difference! And then you refuse to talk about it. Ranald can't hear you if that's what you're worried about."

I tipped my head towards him. Sure enough, he'd fallen asleep, his head lolled forward onto his chest.

"When I was taking photos of Dylan, I overheard her talking tae someone," she said, sniffing. "Eh... sorry about everything."

Not much of an apology, but that was the best I would get.

I held out the box for her to dispose of the glass.

"Is it awfy expensive to get the window fixed?" she asked, and I sighed. The insurance might cover the repairs. Hotels, usually those popular with hen or stag night bookings, often took out policies for guest damage. We hadn't. Oh well. Perhaps some of today's profits might cover it.

I stood up as that all too familiar dampness made its presence known. Great. To add to the sexy elf effect, I now had two wet circles on the front where my boobs had leaked. "Give me that scarf."

Mhari treasured her scarf collection. Today's offering was a cashmere mauve and silver one. She unwound it. Any other day, the request would have met a flat refusal: A person suffering qualms of conscience. I tied it around my neck, adjusting the ends to hide the wet patches.

"D'ye think Lachlan will ever speak to me again? Or will he think I'm a bunny boiler?"

No, and yes? I struggled to think up something positive to say.

Katya materialised at the door, Lucian in his buggy. "I missed all the excitement by the sounds of it. Mhari, do you want to come back to mine? We could watch Scream if you like?"

Mhari's face brightened. "Aye, alright."

They headed off, Katya waggling her eyebrows at me over her shoulder. The ideal solution—she kept Mhari out of harm's way, and they cheered themselves up with a horror fest. Mhari might even confide in Katya. Ask for tips on how to win Lachlan back, or maybe she and Katya would settle for consoling each other with discussions about the awfulness of men.

My handbag had tipped on its side—the contents spilling onto the floor. That blasted letter sat on top of everything and hollered at me to open it. I set off to find Dylan. Might as well get it over with.

Evie retrieved from Jolene, I headed for the public bar, which was pleasingly full.

"We have taken tonnes of money," Xavier told me, as he uncapped a round of craft lagers pushing them towards the two women waiting at the bar who fluttered their eyelashes at him.

Jack dumped a crate of lager on the bar, bottles rattling, and lowered his voice. "Tonnes of money minus window repairs, repayment of that tax bill and Dexter's share."

"I'm sure we've made much more today than you think!" I said, the over-brightness giving me away. He pecked me on the mouth, ruffling Evie's hair at the same time.

One of the women at the bar did a double-take. "Are you Sam Heughan? Because we're, like, Outlander's biggest fans! Can we get a selfie with you?"

As was always the case with the Sam Heughan fans, they never noticed me or the wedding ring Jack wore, sidling up to him, hands sneaking everywhere. I shuffled out of the way.

"Where's Dylan?" I asked Xavier.

A shifty look passed across his face. "In the kitchen. Do you want me to get heem for you?"

That smacked of someone covering up for another person. What was Dylan up to? Siphoning off all the food to sell it on to another place?

"No thanks, Xavier. I can find him myself" I walked past him as he umm-ed and ah-ed, heading for the kitchen.

Dylan had his back to me, talking in a low voice to someone. They stopped as soon as I came in, turning to face me—one face registering dismay, the other surprise and then recognition.

"You!" I said. 'Mr Designer Shirt I Hate Babies on Planes, and I Meet up with Men Late at Night who Hand me Envelopes'. Here, talking to my brother who had stated vehemently he did not know him when asked even though I could tell he was lying…

Did this have something to do with Dylan's sacking? Perhaps mystery man was a criminal, and he and Dylan had hatched some mad plan in Norwich that they were now masterminding from Lochalshie? As if my day hadn't been dramatic enough.

"I won't," I said, hugging Evie to me, "sanction any criminal wrongdoings, Dylan Richardson! If you, Lachlan and this man are planning to turn the hotel into a drugs den by growing weed in the attic because it gets super-hot in there, I refuse to be a party to it. Even if you're growing it to benefit cancer patients because the effects are proven to help with pain relief, and perhaps the Government's criminalisation of cannabis is misguided and doesn't—"

"Gaby!" Dylan glared at me. His friend's brow wrinkled, nonplussed.

"For God's sake, shut up! I'd forgotten how weird your

thought processes are. This is Colm. Y'know. The guy who donated tonnes of presents for Santa's grotto."

Oops.

"Sorry about that" I held my hand out. Colm regarded it warily. "There is no baby sick on there, promise."

When I'd seen him at the airport, he had been wearing designer gear. Today he was far scruffier—an ancient polo top under a hoodie and ripped jeans. I guessed him to be Dylan's age perhaps; small lines at the corners of his eyes fanning out.

"The last time we met," he said, "I was a bit rude."

A bit?

"Blame it on the stress o' flying." Colm had the west coast Scottish accent. Soft and lilting, the words almost sing-song. I hadn't noticed it when we were on the flight together seeing as he had been so disparaging about Evie.

"Twice as stressful when you're travelling with a baby."

He had the grace to look shamefaced. "Aye. Sorry."

"How do you two know each other?" I asked. There were far too many coincidences for any of them to be one. He and my brother exchanged some silent communication impossible to work out.

"Colm manages the microbrewery in Oban—the one that's just started supplying the Lochside Welcome," Dylan said. "It's also a distillery. He and I met when he came down to Norwich to discuss supplying Marty's business with lagers and gin."

Marty had been Dylan's boss until he sacked him for whatever mysterious reasons Dylan wasn't prepared to go into.

Colm checked his watch. "Dylan, I need tae go. Will ye tell Jack I'll be in touch about setting up regular deliveries?

Nice to meet you again, Gaby. And eh… your wee daughter is gorgeous."

I smiled, much mollified. Evie gurgled in response, proof as if I needed it, of my child's brilliance. She understood every word.

Dylan followed Colm as he left. A man desperate to escape further questioning, such as, *Why didn't you tell me that from the start?*

"Dylan! Tony's sent us a letter. I've got it with me."

He stopped, hand on the door handle. "I'm not interested."

"Me neither, but it only seems fair to read it. As Jack said to me, we don't need to do anything."

He sighed. "Okay."

As I took the letter from my bag, Evie snatched it from me, flinging it in the tub of tomato sauce base for pizza set on the kitchen counter.

Dylan slow hand-clapped her. "Well done, Evie. That's the right place for it. Well, there or as emergency bog roll supply if you run out of things to wipe your arse with."

Evie clapped back. I handed her to her uncle. "You two share a common maturity, though I might argue Evie is more advanced."

The letter floated on top of the sauce. Xavier's recipe for pizza base was decadent on tomatoes, red wine and olive oil which made for lethal staining. I fished it out as the smell of garlic wafted around me. The handwritten address on the front had already started to run.

I opened the envelope. *Dear Dylan and Gaby, I know that I have not…* The rest of it was unreadable thanks to virulent orange staining. There were three pages, too, all as unclear.

Dylan jigged Evie up and down, smiling with her as she giggled away. He'd lost that haunted, hollowed-out air he'd had when he first arrived in the village. Lochalshie magic working once more and turning stressed-out city types into relaxed dudes? Jolene told me he made a cheerful enough housemate—helpful, even. When my mother came to her senses and ditched my father, I would pass the news to pass on. *Mum, surprise, surprise! Dylan only acts like a lazy slob with you and me. He's a model citizen around anyone else.*

Jack, arms loaded with trays of dirty plates, came in. He spotted the letter. "What happened there?"

"Evie took matters into her own hands," I said; Dylan adding, "and now we can't read Daddy dearest's grovelling apology for the last ten years. Pity."

Jack shot me one of those 'Gaby, you're kidding yourself' looks. "Dylan, you're needed behind the bar."

Dylan nodded and made his way back into the fray.

"What can I do?" I asked. The punters were still packed out in the bar and dining room.

"Would you mind checking up on my mum?" he said. "She seems awfy keen on those clementine martinis, and I'm no' sure her system's up for them."

Oh dear. Visions of Psychic Josie advising all and sundry on how they should sort out their lives while half-cut swam in front of me. Best I sort that out before her clients cottoned onto her not being that psychic after all.

———

"Aye so, the stars hae it clear what ye need to do. And that is, leave him at once!" The words accompanied by table-thumping. "He's a bad yin who deserves to be strung up fae the nearest lamppost and left there as a warnin' tae men who are tempted tae stray…"

Oh dear. Psychic Josie's 'stall' was a booth in the public

bar she'd draped with swathes of star-studded dark velvet material to provide privacy. Those clementine martinis had altered Caroline's volume control. Her voice boomed out. There were enough people and chatter to hide the worst of it, but anyone at the adjacent tables could pick up every word.

The woman she'd been advising emerged, dazed expression in place. Her friend darted forward. "What did Psychic Josie say?"

"Ordered me to leave him," the woman replied, "even though Chris only said to me there was a rumour that Kay at his work is dynamite in the sack."

Her friend took her hand. "But Psychic Josie must know something! She advises that Caitlin Cartier, doesn't she? Chris is either cheating, or he's gonnae do it. Best to cut your losses and run."

Crossing my fingers that Chris *was* a lousy yin and that my mother-in-law hadn't just ruined two people's prospects at everlasting love, I pushed my way in through the drapes and drew them shut hiding us from sight. Caroline glanced up, the veil not disguising the beam of joy she directed towards her granddaughter.

"Gaby! D'ye want me to read Evie's horoscope? The stars are all aligned, and the moon in Mercury means amazin' things for a'body born in November!"

How much had she had to drink? The words were slurred, and there were two empty clementine saucers in front of her. She breathed out pure Cointreau fumes. The offer to read Evie's horoscope was one oft repeated. I always said no because a) astrology was a crock, and b) while Jack and I would do our best to give Evie a solid start in life, she'd be making her own luck.

"No, no," I said, sitting down, Evie on my knee. She

made a grab for the nearest saucer. Caroline tried to swipe the glass out of reach, knocking it over and smashing it. Sugared peel soaked in vodka and Cointreau spun across the table, landing in front of Evie who picked it up and stuck it in her mouth before I could stop her. My life often felt like a never-ending plea to people not to judge me for rubbish parenting abilities.

"Oops," Caroline said, "bit silly o' me. Mind, Gaby. In the old days, folks used to gie their kids a wee bittie o' whisky to ease their gums when they were teething."

Nevertheless, she leant over, took hold of the strip of peel and pulled it out of Evie's mouth. My daughter wailed. I shoogled her up and down, scant consolation for the sweet, sugary and alcoholic treat her granny had whipped away from her.

"Caroline," I asked, "are you okay? Jack said he was worried about you. When you're on Psychic Josie duty, you don't usually drink."

Or at all. Come to think about it, hadn't I noticed Caroline knocking back the wine the day of Evie's birthday party? And when we'd visited her and Ranald for dinner the other week, I'd caught her topping her glass up in the kitchen when I walked in looking for a cloth to wipe up baby vomit.

"Any chance o' another of they clementine martinis?" Caroline asked, turning her head to glance over her shoulder even though the velvet drapes made us invisible to the bar staff.

Evie's whimpers died down. She plucked at my top—the gesture all too recognisable. Sexy elf suits might look the part, but this one lacked the all-essential discreet front access. I would need to unbutton the bodice and peel it open.

"I'll order you one in a minute," I told Caroline as I wriggled out of the top, pulling the sleeve off my left shoulder. Evie latched on, her mouth puckering up rosebud style and her eyes closing. "But I wonder if it's wise to—"

Caroline burst into noisy tears, eyes spilling and her hiccoughing so much that what she said was indecipherable. I caught the odd word—Ranald, awfy young, couldnae bear to…

The noise around us had died down. Four o'clock—the lull between people having overstayed the lunchtime slot to those about to descend on the pub for a night spent eating pizza and boozing.

"What's that about Ranald?" I asked, wondering if I should mention how tired he'd been earlier. Caroline glanced up, mascara streaks making their way down her cheeks to the veil that covered her nose and mouth. She pushed the heel of her hand into one eye, a lock of dark, greying hair escaping from the scarf around her head.

"Jack's gonnae be devastated," she said, tipping her head to the side. "Terrible time tae put him under any more pressure or stress. At this time o' year too."

Evie had fallen asleep, a somnambulant, milky Cointreau scented bundle in my arms. Everyone told me all the time how much she resembled Jack. I thought she was the spitting image of the woman in front of me. The shape of her head and the colour of her eyes. The way she fixed her eyes on everything around her, trying to take it all in.

"What is wrong with Ranald, Caroline?"

"He's got cancer!" Caroline burst out.

Jolene, holding a tray bearing two clementine martinis, whipped back the drapes covering the front of the booth.

"Oh!" her hand flew to her mouth. "Sorry, I hadn't realised…"

Behind the drapes would be my mother-in-law and me in the middle of a private conversation about her husband? Or that there would be a half-naked woman, thanks to me having stripped off most of the stupid sexy elf top, Evie now asleep and me with my right breast and nipple on show?

The drapes, too feebly constructed to withstand such treatment, fell over. They landed on Caroline, leaving the topless bit of me still exposed to the outside world and subjecting Terry, the regulars, Xavier and Dylan and three people queueing at the bar to the view.

Evie, miraculously, remained asleep. Heat flooded my face, turning my cheeks scarlet.

Jolene dumped the tray, bent over and pulled the material over me. "God, I'm so sorry."

But the words came from far off—Caroline's bombshell all too prominent. Ranald had been a comforting backdrop in my life ever since Jack and I had got together. I'd come to adore him latterly. The help he provided with Evie and the way the two of them interacted would melt the stoniest heart. My own grandfathers hadn't been around—one died before I was born, the other a distant figure we had seen little of and even less when my dad abandoned Dylan and me. Evie needed the solidity of Ranald's presence for years to come.

Jolene picked up the tray and touched my shoulder gently before walking off. Caroline had pushed back the drapes, her head spinning wildly around her.

She leant in. "Gaby, d'ye think anyone heard?"

I squeezed Caroline's hand in mine. "I don't think so, Caroline. But you must tell Jack. He'll want to know. Do you want me to do it? And, um, what should I say to Ranald?"

Weeks earlier, I'd been out of my mind worried about Nanna Cooper and her fall, the overwhelming relief that set in when I realised her condition wasn't serious.

There would be no such easy escape here. I had no precedent for someone close to me being this ill. How did you talk to them about it? A tricky prospect when that person was non-conversational at the best of times. My tendency to verbal diarrhoea made this delicate too. What if my mouth ran away with me as I tried to discuss Ranald's prognosis with him?

Caroline got to her feet, collapsing on the first attempt, her bottom landing with a thump on the chair. Second time around, she managed to scrape the chair back from the table and stand up.

"We better find ma son," she said, "I'll tell him, but I'll need you wi' me, Gaby. Come on."

Heart in my far too uncomfortable boots, I struggled back into the stupid bodice top and followed her out of the bar and into the storeroom stroke office out the back.

Chapter Twenty-Six

PROJECT OVER-OPTIMISM

Jack met us in the corridor, sardonic grin in place. "Gaby! Sources tell me you've just treated our customers to a view o' a wee bit more of you than I'm comfortable with. Xavier says Terry's had to go home, he's that traumatised."

He raised an eyebrow. "Traumatised, eh? I hope that's the right word for it. If he has disappeared for any other reason, I'll never let him back in the bar again."

"Can we talk to you?" I said, tipping my head towards the back office. "Your mum's got something she needs to tell you."

The smirk fell away at once, Jack's gaze flickering to his mother, who was red-eyed and reeking of Cointreau. On the way here, she'd snaffled the two saucers of clementine martinis Jolene had brought to our table when she inadvertently turned me into a flasher.

Caroline drained one glass—the other tilting towards the carpet. Thanks to its sugary stickiness that stuff was murder to clean up.

Jack took the glass from her hand, darting a sideways

glance at me. The 'office' required expert navigational skills to weave your way around old chairs and tables, empty boxes, crates and the files and ledgers that should have been on shelves. The room smelt of stale beer, damp cardboard and pizza. An ancient computer was parked on a desk at the front, the screen flickering artificial light in the gloom. Yet again, the decrepit overhead light had blown three of its bulbs.

Jack turned. "Should we sit down?"

I nodded. Caroline fell back into one of the plastic chairs. I took the one on the other side, and Jack leant against the desk, arms folded.

"Son, it's Ranald," Caroline began.

"He's ill, isn't he?" Jack asked, startling me. He ran his fingers through his hair—a stress gesture I knew all too well. "He's no' looked right for some time, but I thought if I ignored…"

Me too. My subconscious had been absorbing Ranald's appearance for weeks now. The greyness of his skin and the yellow tinge to his eyes. The tiredness and the weight-loss. That time he'd collapsed onto the bench when he and Caroline were returning with Evie. And today when he'd struggled to get to his feet during the Mhari/Nicola fight.

Project Gaby Optimism I convinced myself; *He's fine, fine! He's married to a doctor. Nothing can happen.* As if such things conferred immortality on a person.

"Stage 4 bowel cancer," Caroline said. "Ranald bein' Ranald didnae want to worry me, so he kept quiet about his symptoms."

Jack screwed his face up. "But what about the screening programme? Don't they start testing you every two years once you're over 50?"

Caroline nodded glumly. "Aye, they do. Ranald must

hae been awfy unlucky. He was last screened 20 months ago, but he started feelin' ill nine months ago. Said nothing to me about blood in his poo, having a bloated tummy and him losin' weight despite no' changing his diet."

"What do the doctors say?" Jack asked. "Chemo? Radiotherapy? I'm happy to run him to the hospital in Oban whenever you cannae manage it, Mum."

The cracks in his voice cut through me.

"Nae point in it," Caroline said, tears starting up again. I got up and located one of the packets of spare toilet roll we stored in here for the hotel toilets, passing her a handful of tissues. She blew her nose noisily.

"The tumour's too big. And it's spread to Ranald's liver."

She broke off, the sobs starting in earnest. Jack crouched down, throwing his arms around her, his head on her shoulder. Evie stirred, kicking one little leg out and twisting to snuggle into me further. Almost as if she knew I needed comfort.

Crying fit finished, Caroline sat back, and Jack unfolded himself, glassy-eyed.

"What… what does that mean?" I asked, pretty sure of the answer. Biology wasn't something I knew much about, but I understood the importance of the liver in human function.

"It's terminal," Caroline said, clasping Jack's forearm once more. "The oncologist says he's got six months left, tops."

"Xavier, we need to head home," I said. "Will you manage?"

Xavier looked as if he wanted to object. The bar had busied once more. We'd asked Caroline if we should drop by the conservatory to say something (what?) to Ranald, but she'd shaken her head. Tomorrow would do.

"Mais oui," Xavier replied. The sight of us in the corridor must have stopped him—me tearful, Jack splotchy-faced and eyes unfocused. "Off you go!"

At home, I set Evie on the floor and put the kettle on to boil.

"Tea?"

Jack nodded, but when I handed it over, complete with the prescribed three spoonfuls of sugar supposed to help with shock, he didn't touch it.

"He's only 60!" The words bleated; a man demanding the universe answer to unfairness. "I thought…"

He would live forever? Or at least die years and years and years into the future when such things were easier to face? (Were they?) I sat down, a loud rip as the bodice of the sexy elf's outfit parted company with the skirt. So much for my promise to Mhari to return it intact.

"Did I ever tell you about the first time Ranald taught me how to make shortbread?"

"No." I'd known that's where Jack's talents as a baker came from—a bonding exercise the younger Ranald carried out years ago with his new stepson, but I'd never heard the exact circumstances of the first time.

"Mum was studying to be a GP, and she was away for the afternoon. I told Ranald I was bored. Mum and I had lived in the village until then, and Ranald's farmhouse was out in the middle of nowhere. Nae friends nearby. I'd been playin' up all week.

"He said to me, 'how about I teach you to make the best biscuits in the world?', so I agreed, expecting us to make chocolate covered cookies with loads of fancy decoration. 'No, no, Jack', he said, 'the best things in life are simple. But they must be made with love. Who do you love most in the world?'"

"I said 'my mum', and he smiled at that. 'Well, when you cream the butter and sugar, tell yourself you're mixing it for your mum and imagine what her face will look like when she eats them.'"

The rest of the story…a farmhouse kitchen heated by an Aga cooker: A man and a young boy waiting for the shortbread to emerge, lightly browned, the air rich with vanilla and butter.

"That was the first time I called him Dad."

At that, he pitched forward, burying his head in my lap —the sobs making his body shudder. Evie, busy crawling after Mildred who leapt out of her way, paused, grabbed hold of my leg, and hauled herself up.

She patted Jack's head, which set me off—tears dripping off the end of my nose. Jack shifted his head, so he faced her, the two of them mirroring sombre expressions. Ranald wasn't biologically related to Jack, but for a few seconds, I saw it—generations of stoic Scottishness passing from parent to child, Ranald's shiny-cheeked face imprinting on Jack's and then Evie's.

In the years to come, Evie wouldn't remember him, but I hoped some trace of that extensive time she had spent him with as a baby would remain—an indelible touch that lasted a lifetime.

I threaded my fingers through Jack's hair. "We'll talk to her all the time about him."

He nodded the corners of his mouth lifting. Evie flopped back onto her bottom and crawled back to her play-mat. Mildred waited until Evie was safely distracted by her

Barney the Dinosaur toy and jumped on top of Jack's chest, settling her head to the side of his neck. It looked as if we wouldn't be moving anytime soon. Just as well the living room was warm, the fake flames flickering from the electric heater soothing to watch.

"When Evie's old enough," I said, Jack's eyes meeting mine in understanding. We finished the sentence together. "... you'll teach her how to make the best shortbread in Scotland."

Chapter Twenty-Seven

AN UNEXPECTED OFFER

When she heard about Ranald, Katya cancelled her return to London. I told her she didn't need to stay, but I found her presence comforting.

On Wednesday, the two of us took Evie and Lucian for a long walk around the loch, Katya asking gentle questions and then distracting me with embarrassing stories from our Great Yarmouth teenage years. (The person who'd made a twit of herself most of the time had been me.)

"What are you going to do for Christmas?" she asked as we paused at the far side of the loch. From here, the village almost looked toy-like, bookended by the lights of the Lochside Welcome and the Royal George glittering in the distance.

"No idea," I said. Despite the Christmas Fair and Katya's push of the hotel on social media,

no-one else had booked rooms for the two-night festival package and Christmas day lunch reservations remained low. However, bookings for the new year looked healthier. The tax bill repayments would eat up all those profits, though. Jolene, Tina and Russell's Christmas gifts might end up being their P45s.

"Jack, Xavier, Dylan and Lachlan are supposed to be working Christmas and Boxing Day, with Jolene, Tina and Russell waiting on and me lending a hand if required."

Jack and I had discussed it the night before. "How am I gonnae manage the jolly mine host act when all I'm thinking about is Ranald and my mum and you and Evie?" he'd asked me. "I'll be a spectre at the feast."

"I s'pose we can do what we'd originally planned," I told Katya. "The family celebration in the hotel on the 27th. By then, I might feel Christmassy."

Doubtful. In my pocket, my phone vibrated. My mum had been trying to get hold of me for the last few days. She would want to discuss my half-assed agreement she and Tony come to Lochalshie. I ignored it.

"Dexter rang Jack. Was that your doing?" I asked Katya, who nodded. Her ex had told Jack he was fine to wait for his share of the hotel money. Katya must have called him.

"Did he...?"

Katya shook her head. Oh well. Daft of me to have hoped the news would shock him into a 'life's too short' realisation that sent him back into Katya's arms. Or that my silly chat with Caitlin would have any effect.

We let our offspring out of their buggies, Evie and Lucian bundled up in thick padded all-in-one waterproofs making them resemble a pair of mini Michelin men. Evie toddled on the sand. Since taking her first steps earlier in the month, she'd advanced quickly, and the sand on the shore made for a soft landing should she get too enthusiastic.

Lucian, only at the crawling stage, set off after her.

A figure jogged towards us.

"Katya, tell me that's not who I think it is."

"Hear him out, Gaby. Please?"

I sighed as Zac came to a halt, panting. As another non-Scot, he had yet to adjust to the Highland winters and was as thickly bundled up as Evie and Lucian.

"Sorry about Ranald, Gaby," he said, teeth chattering, and I nodded. Zac excelled at fake sincerity. Today's efforts merited a nine out of ten. No mistaking the genuine emotion, though, that crossed his face when he exchanged some unspoken communication with Katya, and she nodded.

He scooped up Lucian, face the picture of sheer wonder. "Hello, little man. Aren't you a bit cold?"

"I've got something to confess, Gaby," he said, swirling around. Lucian's resemblance to him was all the starker when they were together—same hair and eyes, and even the way Lucian's mouth dropped open.

"What?" I snapped.

"Mena. Your first cat."

Good grief. This was old news. Mena had died in a hit and run two years ago. On Christmas Day, I'd found out Zac had been the driver of the car that ran her down (and didn't stop) when Jamal spotted it on his CCTV footage.

"I'm not sure how much better this makes the story, but I wasn't the one driving the car," he continued. "That was Lois."

One half of the Hammerstone Hotels partnership: "Who wasn't insured at the time. But I covered up for her. That was wrong. I'm sorry—I know Mena meant a lot to you."

"And I knew," Katya piped up, astonishing me. She

shrugged. "It was one of those things I kept meaning to tell you. Proof that Zac's not that bad after all."

Blimey. If I'd been standing between Zac and Katya, Zac's eyes would have lasered straight through me. Hard to guess what entranced him the most—Lucian or Katya, that faint bit of praise enough to make him think he stood a chance with her once more.

"Fair enough," I said, not that convinced. Zac had still covered for someone committing a crime. "Thanks for telling me. How are your Christmas plans coming on? Is the George fully booked?"

Only courteous that I showed an interest in our rivals, even if it came out through gritted teeth. Night after night, cars and minibuses crammed the car park in front of the George.

He cleared his throat once more. "Just about, but I've got a proposal for you. If you like, you can all have Christmas dinner at the Royal George once Jack's finished his shift. Save you having to make anything. We've got a private room that's used by corporates when they have their away days. It seats ten people."

Gosh. Generous, or generous-ish. I doubt Zac had come up with the idea all by himself.

He jiggled Lucian on his hip, a smirk crossing his face once more. "You and Jack might learn something, Gaby. Find out how a professionally run hotel works."

"Don't spoil it!" Katya said, but the words made me snort.

"Will you serve us that poncy tasting menu?" I asked. "All teeny-tiny portions and stupid foams and swirls served on slate plates?"

"Absolutely not. I don't waste food like that on peasants," he grinned back at me. "You'd be on the coach party menu."

Decades ago, coaches took pensioners on tours of the Highlands. They dropped them off for hour-long stops at hotels where they were served 'soup of the day' (almost always tomato), followed by wafer-thin slices of meat drowned in gravy with lumpy mash and frozen peas, and finished with tinned peaches and ice-cream.

He handed Lucian back, doing his best to hide the tiny kiss he dropped on the baby's head.

"I'll speak to Jack," I said, guessing what the response would be but no need to mention that now, "and ask him what he thinks. Thanks, though."

"Well," I said, as Katya and I watched him go. Lucian and Evie popped back in their buggies, we set off back towards the village too. "That was unexpected."

She let out a sigh. "Underneath all that over-entitled rich white boy privilege, a decent guy lurks. Not much of the time, but when it counts."

"One who'd be the happiest man in the world if you agreed to be his girlfriend."

Which would be a happy ending of sorts, seeing as they seemed to be in short supply.

"I know. But I don't think…" She let the wind swallow the rest of whatever she'd been about to say. I could guess.

… *he's who I want.*

"He is Lucian's dad in case you were wondering."

"Wait, what? Did you agree to a DNA test?"

"No need. Zac showed me pictures of himself at the same age. Lucian's Zac's absolute double. And I think I've always known."

I nodded. Katya wouldn't want me to make too much

of her news. "There's a saying," I said, "about how it takes a village to raise a child…"

Dexter might have abandoned her, and Zac might not be the one she wanted. But if Katya moved back to Lochalshie permanently—and her ghost-writing career made that possible because she could work anywhere—everyone would pitch in to help.

"Perhaps," she shrugged.

On the High Street, Lochalshie's pharmacy advertised a half-price Christmas sale on perfumes. Most of them dated back to the 1980s and had probably been in the shop since then—super-potent scents you recognised at once and guaranteed to kill off the smell of anything else for at least five hours.

"Do you fancy some Christmas perfume?" Katya asked, the smile putting a dimple in her cheeks.

"Only if that means we get to torture Mhari."

"Deal! If I buy you a bottle of Poison, you can get me the Obsession."

Bickering about who would be getting the Poison, the bell above the door clanged as we walked into the shop. Mhari, eyes glued to her phone, as usual, glanced up, a sly grin spreading from ear to ear.

Katya grinned back. "Mhari, hi! I hear the WWE's been in touch, asking if you want to audition for their next SmackDown women's championship. Mind you, hair pulling is forbidden. That might hamper your chances."

"Katya, hi!" Mhari replied, smile not faltering in the least. "Is that so? A wee birdie tells me you and Zac have just had a wee cosy-up on the beach. Is Lucian gonnae be a chef like his daddy when he grows up?"

Sometimes, you have to say to yourself, *if you can't beat 'em, join 'em.*

Katya picked up a dusty packet of condoms and lube and placed them on the counter.

"Who knows! Anyway, you're the first to hear the news. Dexter, Zac and I are all going to live together. D'you know of any houses for rent we can live in? One bedroom will be plenty…"

Chapter Twenty-Eight

MEMORY SLIPS

Jack spent the following day with Ranald. "How is he?" I asked when he returned early that evening, bearing a still warm tray of the shortbread he and Ranald had baked. I bit into a piece, spilling crumbs down my front.

"Aye, okay," Jack said. "Lachlan dropped by too. He's gutted."

As Ranald's nephew, Lachlan was close to his uncle—more so than he was to his father, a once upon a time head-teacher who disapproved of all Lachlan's lifestyle choices. "He's trying tae convince Ranald to have chemo," Jack added. Not the only one. Caroline had tried, as had Jack. Me too, all of us meeting a brick wall. Ranald wasn't deliberately obtuse, but he'd had a long conversation with the oncologist. Chemo would give him only a few more months and would be unpleasant and inconvenient.

"Who wants to spend the rest of their life," Ranald told Caroline, "going to and from the hospital and feeling sick?"

He was adamant too that he would die at home. No hospitals, no hospices.

"The Macmillan nurse came to the house today while I was there," Jack added. "Lisa. Awfy cheery lady—made Ranald laugh quite a few times. Turns out she once dated Mhari's cousin's husband."

Everyone in this area had some connection to Mhari's family.

"What will she do?" Back in September, we'd held a fundraising pub quiz in the bar for Macmillan nurses, but I was unclear about their exact role.

"Support Ranald through his cancer experience," Jack put the words in air quotes, "which is one way o' saying, helping him prepare to die."

What a job.

"She does the practical stuff with my mum and the psychological and pain management support wi' Ranald."

He got down on the floor, flattening himself, so he was level with Evie, lying on her front and playing with Thomas and his friends. "Um… I asked her if she wouldnae mind givin' me a bit o' help too. Y'know, help me wi' knowing what to do and say."

I scooted across the floor to join him. I leaned against his side, reaching over to brush my hand against his. "Maybe we could ask Lisa here to have a session with us, as I need that too."

He nodded, teary eyes fixing on Evie. "Best fucking grandfather Evie's got. Sorry about the f-word."

I ruffled his hair. "Understandable in the circumstances. Katya and I ran into Zac this afternoon, who offered me one of the private dining rooms in the George on Christmas Day for the whole family. Save us having to do anything. What do you think?"

Jack screwed his face up. "Generous o' him, I suppose."

Perhaps. Zac hadn't said anything about it being free,

and the sign advertising the George's Christmas lunches said they were £125 per person.

"But it wouldn't feel right, would it?"

"No. I'll send him a 'thanks ever so much but no thanks' message, okay?"

The doorbell rang, and we looked at each other and grimaced. Jack rolled onto his back and put his hands over his face. "Don't answer it."

I jumped up. "Whoever it is will know we're in." That was the advantage and drawback of living in a village filled with neighbours as community-spirited (nosey) as Lochalshie's residents. "I'll say we're about to have our dinner."

Dylan was at the door, hopping from foot to foot, the scarf around his throat at chokehold to keep out the wind. "Hey, let me in! It's Baltic out here."

"Must you?" I asked. "We're about to eat."

"Excellent," Dylan said, pushing past me and heading for the living room. "What are you having?" he threw over his shoulder, pausing at the door.

"Nothing you like," I said, "because you're not getting any of it. Cheerio, Dylan."

Jack swung open the door to the living room, the veins at his temples pulsating.

"Dylan," voice deceptively quiet, "we're no' in the mood."

"That's what your mum said you'd say," Dylan replied as he unwrapped his scarf and hung it on the hooks on the hallway wall, "when she asked me to babysit for the two of you. She thought you might like a night out, seeing as you won't get that much time together alone over the next week. And it's your wedding anniversary."

I clapped my hand to my mouth. How could I have forgotten? We only married two years ago! When Jack blinked and mouthed the word 'sorry' I realised he hadn't remembered either.

Dylan peeled off his coat, wrapping his arms around his body. "Is that fire going? Otherwise, I'm going to freeze to death."

Jack's eyes met mine, both of us shaking our heads. A night out? Was she mad? Where would we go? In winter-time, night-time attractions in rural areas were few and far between.

Dylan slipped past Jack and settled himself on the sofa, stretched out full-length. Evie chirped at him, her little face widening into a smile when he whisked her up beside him.

"She also said you wouldn't be able to think of what do to do with yourselves. That's what happens when two people have been together forever. There's no excitement anymore."

"Thanks, Dylan." I folded my arms.

"Better hurry. Your taxi's outside."

I peered through the curtains. Sure enough, Lachlan's Jeep was parked on the roadside. He gave me a cheery wave, as I did my best not to think 'Hello, Two-minute Thomas!'. (Not right, remember! False rumour started by Nicola Milne to discredit Mhari in Lachlan's eyes.)

Dylan aimed the remote at the TV, clicking on the Netflix app and scrolling through the options. "Nothing too violent in front of Evie, please!" I bleated as he paused on Sons of Anarchy, Charlie Hunnam's brooding face domi-nating the screen.

Jack slung an arm around my shoulders. "Do you want a night out?"

Oh, why not? We were two people craving distraction. I nodded, and he took my hand, pulling me towards the stairs. "Come on. Let's get changed. All the better to paint the village red and prove to my mum and your brother we're not boring after all."

Jack persuaded me to wear my 'wedding' dress. My actual wedding outfit ended up being a sweatshirt and jeans, the flowery headdress my only concession to finery. But when Jack and I attended Caitlin's wedding the next day, I wore a turquoise silk, empire-line dress that had seen few outings ever since. It almost did a dance of joy when I took it out of the wardrobe.

He was in his kilt, the plaid matched with a plain black shirt, and those muscular, fabulous knees on show. This was the most glamorous we'd been in... forever. I climbed into the back of Lachlan's Jeep gingerly. He had two very smelly dogs that often sat behind him, covering the seat in mud and hairs.

Jack snuggled up to me, recoiling immediately. "Jesus. What is that perfume?"

"Poison. Everyone wore it in the olden days."

"What—as a midge repellent?"

I play thumped him. "Where are we going?"

Lachlan caught my eye in the mirror. "It's a surprise."

Not much of one. When Lachlan stopped outside the Lochside Welcome three minutes later, I let out a groan.

"No, you've got to be kidding! This is a busman's holiday for us, isn't it?"

He jumped out of the Jeep and opened the door for me. "Everyone put their heads together and have come up with a wee treat for you both. Be open-minded. And at least you won't have far to stumble home."

Jack shrugged. "S'pose it's fine seeing as we both forgot our anniversary."

Jolene met us inside, holding out her arms for our coats. "Congratulations, you two! I've dug out the champagne?" She paused. "What's that perfume, Gaby? It's disgusting."

Terry and the regulars were the only other people in as it was a Thursday night and so close to Christmas. A small table covered in a white linen tablecloth stood in the middle of the room. The song on the jukebox was Billy Idol's White Wedding. Lachlan must have dreamt that one up. On the day of our wedding, he drove us to the registry office in Oban and put the song on. I'd argued in favour of something more suitable (Bruno Mars' *Marry You*, say), Jack and Lachlan both claiming that song made them want to vomit. Jack's lips twitched as Billy sang about nice days to start again.

He pulled out the seat for me, his attention caught by something behind me.

"Look!"

I turned. All around the walls were blown-up pictures of Jack and me. Our wedding—the two of us in the registry office. Another one was taken in here. Then Jack, Evie and I walking along the loch shores and one from her birthday. Some sneaky ones where I hadn't realised a camera was nearby and that I might not have sanctioned had I known. That one where I was eight months pregnant, double-chinned and sporting my best hot and bothered face, for instance.

"Where did you get the pictures from?" I asked as Jolene returned with the champagne in an ice bucket and two flutes. "Mhari. She's much better now than when she started out, right?"

She nodded towards the photo taken in the registry office. It was a little blurry, but there was no mistaking the expression on our faces—utter bliss.

My eyes watered, remembering how blessed I'd felt

surrounded by family and friends, and grateful that our wedding had ended up as small and intimate as it did.

"Gosh, I'm so lucky!" The words seemed to come out of nowhere. Mum and I standing in the registry office, her about to walk me 'up the aisle'. *"To have been blessed with the best, most wonderful, most beautiful daughter in the world."*

She nudged Ranald, who'd just picked her, Dylan and Nanna Cooper up from the airport. *"Don't you think?"*

Ranald smiled. *"Absolutely, Mrs Richardson."*

"It's Mandy, you silly-billy! We're about to be in-laws. We can't be Mr McLatchie and Mrs Richardson, can we?"

Ranald shook his head, amusement making his eyes gleam.

A moment in time. One I'd never see again—a stupidly obvious thing to say, but Ranald's death kept looming over me, tinting everything in a sepia-like fog, where people froze in the moment, and I viewed them from the outside.

Tears trickled down my cheeks. That Blissful Beauty waterproof mascara better live up to its extravagant claims.

"You're not meant to be crying, Gaby-sketch," Jack said, reaching across the table to crush my fingers in a tight grip.

"I know!" I sniffed. At the moment, if he cried, I did and vice versa. But as we were in the hotel and Jack still subscribed to old-fashioned notions of masculinity where men didn't cry in public, he blinked several times and held it back.

There was soft pfft as Jolene uncorked the champagne, pouring Jack a full glass hesitating before she poured mine. Just as well.

"Half a glass for me," I said, "or I'll end up a blubbering wreck, and I need to get up early tomorrow. Loads to do."

Xavier appeared, dressed in immaculate chef's whites

and a skull cap. Most of the time, he only bothered with an apron. He gave us a mock bow.

"Madam. Sir. For tonight, I 'ave prepared you a special deesh to celebrate the occasion of your wedding anniversary."

"Is it a wedding pizza?" I asked, heart sinking. Not that Xavier's pizzas weren't the most delicious food you could eat in Lochalshie, but out of necessity, I ate a lot of them.

He shook his head. "Non, non! Sometheeng much better. Are you ready?"

The dish shouldn't have come as a surprise. Xavier re-emerged minutes later bearing two plates piled high with fish and chips—the exact meal we'd eaten with family and friends post our wedding. Xavier had always turned his nose up at fish and chips, telling us it was an overrated dish popular in the UK because British people all had such low standards for food. (This from the man who'd given the Lochside Welcome the Canadian classic, Poutine—cheese, chips and gravy.)

He'd outdone himself. The batter was crisp, the fish flaky and the chips triple cooked. The smell of vinegar did its best to compete with Poison and lost.

Food swiftly polished off, I reached for Jack's chips. He smacked my hand away lightly before giving in. Behind us, the door opened, and Mhari walked over.

"You ate aw' that?" she asked, her face wrinkling in disbelief. "That portion was so big I'd a bet wi' Xavier you'd no' manage it all. Now I owe him a tenner."

"Thanks for the lovely pictures. They're amazing. Can we keep that one of the three of us with Evie?" I pointed to the most prominent picture on the far wall. It wasn't a studio shot but had been taken a few months after she was born. Jack was holding her; he and his daughter's eyes locked together. I was turned to my side watching them, my mouth wide open saying something.

"Aye. No bother. Is £250 okay?"

"*How* much?"

"I'm settin' myself up as a professional, aren't I? Think yourself lucky. That's mates' rates."

Jack shook his head. He kicked me under the table. I doubt he wanted that picture, disliking the idea of people walking into our living room to the sight of it. Jack lived in fear of being judged big-headed—the worst crime a man in Scotland could commit.

"Got another wee thing you can keep for free though," Mhari said, as Jolene flipped up the bar hatch and pulled down the large screen in front of the bar we used whenever there was a premier football match on.

Mhari pulled over a table and set up a laptop. The screen flickered to life—the Lochside Welcome photographed in the height of summer, its planters and baskets a riot of pinks, oranges, reds and purples and the blue of the loch's waters in the background. Cut-outs of our faces floated either side of a text box, Jack and Gaby, two years on.

The first film started up. Suspicions confirmed. The YouTube video Mhari had taken when I rescued Scottie from the loch, the cold water making my nipples stand to attention and all too obvious. The film had earned me the nickname Nora Nipples.

I put my hand over my face. "Oh God." Terry and the regulars cheered.

The rest, though, was far more comfortable to watch—particularly the one of Jack and Xavier when they waded into the loch themselves to save the drunken women who'd underestimated the strength of the current in there. Jack hated that video almost as much as I hated the nipples one of me. Another clip was of Evie's recent birthday.

The film finished, and Mhari took out a memory stick and handed it over. "There ye go. Are you greetin' again?"

"No." Yes. Jack handed me tissues, and I wiped my eyes. But the films had made me laugh too, everyone else joining in at the clip where I was filmed at a ceilidh falling flat on my face after being whirled around far too fast during an eightsome reel.

Jolene returned with two large helpings of chocolate cake. "I couldn't possibly…"

But when she put the plate in front of me and topped it with a generous scoosh of squirty cream, I gave in, wondering if Jack would need to roll me down the street back to our house afterwards.

"The Argyll Room's free upstairs," Jolene said as she cleared the table, "if you can't be bothered staggering home."

Oh…Jack's fingertips crept towards mine. "What do you reckon?"

"Can I ring Dylan?" I asked, "and check on Evie just in case."

"Go for it," Jack handed over my phone.

"Gaby, she's fine," Dylan told me as soon as he answered. "Look."

He jogged up the stairs to Evie's room. There she was, still fast asleep.

"Put the phone right next to her so I can hear her breathing," I insisted. Better safe than sorry. The small sighs and snuffles convinced me.

"I'll see you tomorrow morning," he added, remarkably cheerful. Of all the surprises Dylan had presented me with so far, discovering he rated in the higher bit of one to ten on the babysitting abilities had to be the biggest.

The whole night smacked of a set-up—from the babysitting to the taxi, the photos, the food and the room's availability, everyone seemed to have been in on it. Village life often took…

"Please don't cry again," Jack begged as he stood up, my hand in his. "C'mon. We ought to make the most of this. I can't remember the last time we had a dirty stop-out, can you?"

Chapter Twenty-Nine

SACRIFICES TO THE WEATHER GODS

We left to a chorus of ribald remarks, Terry calling out after us that he gave it five minutes until they were all subjected to the sounds of a bed squeaking overhead. Which would last thirty seconds tops, max? Jack flipped up his middle finger, re-joining that he doubted Mrs Terry had seen any action this century.

The night's unanticipated excitement was a welcome relief. "The bed doesn't squeak, does it?" I asked as we headed upstairs. Jolene and I had threaded the dark wooden stair rails with tinsel when we'd decorated the hotel weeks ago. Jack dragged me to the honeymoon suite at the far end, and pulled me in for a kiss, lips pressing against mine. Underneath the lemony aftershave, he wore lay the heady combination of pizza dough and beer.

"Nope," he drew back, unlocking the door. "But even if it did, this room is above the storeroom and the manager's office. You can yell your head off, Gaby-sketch," he smirked at me, "and no-one will be any the wiser."

I raised my eyebrows. "That better be a promise you live up to, McAllan!"

The Argyll Room, so-called because of the clan tartan of the curtains that matched the cushions strewn over the bed, enticed a person in. A sign on the wall said, Bide awhile and rest, weary traveller. The room looked out over the loch. We left the curtains open. In any other place but Lochalshie, such a tactic would be risky. What if, say, you made your husband do a striptease for your own amusement?

(Oooohhh—the slow unbuttoning of a shirt still had the power to set my pulse racing even after all this time.)

But here, unless someone in the houses in the small hamlet at the far side of the loch owned an industrial tele-scope, the bit where Jack then stepped out of his boxers had been for my eyes only. He dived onto the bed beside me. I snuggled closer to him, soothing myself by listening to the slow and steady beat of his heart. He settled his hand on my hair, smoothing it back off my face.

I shuffled back under Jack's arm as we lay back and gazed at the ceiling. Once upon a time, those swirls of plaster had been fashionable. Then they'd been naff, and now they qualified as vintage shabby chic.

"Have you made your mind up about what we do on Christmas Day?"

"Och, let's go wi' the original plan," he said now. The one where he would manage the hotel on Christmas Day, then the three of us would take leftover food to Caroline and Ranald's house, and we'd hold the party 'proper' in the Lochside Welcome on the 27th.

Jack turned on his side, propping himself up on his elbow as his fingers sketched their way down my throat and onto my chest. "Awfy nice that we can take advantage of the hotel's empty rooms, but I'd rather they were filled wi' other people. I keep coming round to the idea hotel ownership's no' for me."

He heaved another sigh. "I think we give it some serious thought in January. Keeping it or not. Find out if that Hammerstone Hotels' offer is still on the table."

Oh. The Lochside Welcome had been our dream. Jack might give it up and heave a sigh of relief, but no-one would buy the business as is, and certainly not Hammerstone Hotels. The venue where we'd shared so much history, as did most of the villagers, would disappear forever.

"Hotel ownership is about living from day to day," I said, back to my role as chief cheerer upper. "And trying to do what we can. The weather might be much, much better in January! And February, and March, and April, and bring in tonnes and tonnes of visitors all eager to spend their dosh."

"The weather's a bittie beyond our control, Gaby-sketch."

"Believe me, if there was a way to improve the weather in Lochalshie, I'd sacrifice anything."

The fingers now drawing gentle circles on my abdomen paused. "Aye? Like what?"

"No more coffee."

A big ask. Love of espressos was obligatory for graphic designers. They fuelled those all-nighters when deadlines loomed.

"Anything else?"

The fingers edged lower down.

"Chips. Not a single, solitary slice of crispy, deep-fried potato doused in vinegar and salt would cross my lips ever again."

Jack squinted at me.

"Well, limit them to once a month. Self-denial at its finest."

"Mmm. If you say so. But if you want sunshine and a lot less shivering, shouldn't a sacrifice be more worthwhile?"

I grabbed his hand once more. "You're right. Martial relations on high days and holidays only, which means your wild oats are now off-limits until Christmas Day."

As expected, I found myself half-smothered by a body that landed on top of me—every part of Jack signalling precisely what he thought of that pronouncement.

"The weather gods will need to settle for some other sacrifice." Warm words tickled my ear. "If that's okay by you…?"

"I'll think of something," I whispered back, "and in the meantime, if you wouldn't mind getting on with it, let's find out just how sound-proof this room really is."

Force of habit woke me early the next morning. Jack was already up.

Tempting as it was to make the most of a power shower uninterrupted by baby yells, I stuck to three minutes and made it downstairs in time to find Jack and Xavier in the kitchen unloading a food delivery from numerous crates and boxes. Food stacked in the cupboards and fridges, Xavier shifted from foot to foot.

"Ah, I have sometheeng to tell you. Two theengs."

The first was that Lucas had proposed. Would it be okay for the Lochside Welcome to host its first gay wedding next year?

"That would be a great honour!" I said, Jack nodding agreement. Perhaps we could use that as a marketing angle:

The Lochside Welcome—Scotland's best gay wedding venue.

"And also, we got a booking late last night for two rooms, which means ze hotel is four-sevenths booked for Christmas!"

Jack high-fived him. Four rooms were much better than two, but the money would barely cover the staffing, heating and food costs.

"Next year, my friend," Xavier clapped Jack on the back, "will be much better. I can feel eet in my bones! Guests will…"

He trailed off, dismay replacing cheeriness as he remembered Jack's stepfather's situation. "I'm sorry. I did not mean… Do you want breakfast?"

The heavenly smell of sausages and bacon pervaded the hotel. Xavier might turn his nose up at most British food, but he embraced the fried breakfast in all its greasy glory.

"Better not," I said, "our daughter awaits."

Jack grabbed his coat too. We made our way home, the skies still dark. A minibus passed us, engine purring, and drove into the George's carpark. Great. Bound to be yet more people desperate to spend their Christmas, not at our hotel.

"You still stink of that perfume," Jack said. A man trying to avoid dwelling on our lack of customers too.

"Tell me about it. I want to throw up, it's so horrible. Lucky for me, though, that it only doubles up as a midge repellent, and not a man one, hmm?"

"Lucky, aye."

To prove it, he pulled me in for a snog. Those full-on snogs had fallen by the wayside of late. Time I reacquainted myself with the heady feeling of losing yourself in a kiss— all the sweeter when done outside in the depths of winter,

Jack's body sheltering me from the worst of the wind. A fantastic kiss has the power to make you believe most things are possible. A Happy Christmas, for one thing...

Laney Haggerty, out for an early morning walk with her dogs, navigated around us. "For goodness' sake, do that in the privacy o' your own hame!"

Laughing, despite everything, we spilled into the house and into the living room. "Off you go Dylan and thanks ever so—oh!"

"You're early! I thought you wouldn't be back until seven o'clock at least!"

Two half-naked men doing their best to pull on their T-shirts and jumpers greeted us, my brother's expression a mix of dismay and resignation.

Chapter Thirty

ENOUGH INFO, THANKS

Man number two was Colm who, I told myself later, should not have come as that much of a surprise given the way Dylan had behaved around him right from the start. Pretending he didn't know him. Bumping into him up here. Hiding away in kitchens having private conversations.

Really, Gaby, I told myself; *you are sooooooo slow on the uptake. Not a sodding clue when it comes to other people's love lives.*

Respectable once more—though Dylan had put his sweater on inside out—Dylan promised Evie was still fast asleep upstairs and had witnessed no shenanigans.

"But that doesn't matter!" I trilled, anxious Dylan and his 'friend' didn't think me a homophobe. "Jack and I plan to bring up Evie to be kind, tolerant and understanding, don't we, Jack?"

Jack nodded, pointing out that even if she had witnessed anything, it was unlikely she would have understood what was going on, given that she was only a year old.

The shock was more to do with what I'd assumed about Dylan over the years. A commitment-phobe. Secretive about his love life. Mum had only ever met two of his girlfriends years ago when he was in his teens/early 20s. The jokes I'd made about the hundreds of booty call options he had any evening he didn't fancy a night in with Mum, where I'd pictured lots of identikit false-eye lashed, fake-tanned women opening the door and beckoning him in.

"Does Mum know?" I asked, taking the armchair as Jack made us coffees. Given that he'd chosen to invite Colm here and 'entertain' him, an interrogation was my due.

Dylan shook his head.

"And is Colm," I nodded in his direction, him tipping his head back at me, "your, um, first?"

"No," Dylan said. "I've been on Grindr," the dating app for gay men, "for years, but Colm's the first guy I've been serious about."

He blushed. Dylan. The man I'd always assumed incapable of embarrassment and now pink-cheeked and biting his bottom lip. Colm slid closer to him on the sofa.

"And you met at work?" I asked. Jack brought a tray of coffees in and handed them out. He perched next to me on the armchair.

"Aye," Colm took up the story. "I'd been down to Norwich a few times to talk to The Sauce about ma business. The Grindr app…"

Ah. The app told you who was in the vicinity and up for a… fun time. "So, Dylan and I met up and, er, Marty caught us and sacked Dylan."

He took hold of Dylan's hand. "So, it was all my fault he got fired."

"No, it wasn't!" Dylan said. "Marty's gay himself. He's had the hots for me for years, but I always knocked him back. He fired me out of spite."

"Is that legal?" I piped up. Colm and Dylan exchanged guarded looks.

"Um, when he interrupted us, Colm was going do—"

"Okay! Enough info, thanks." Family members were, without question, people you *never* wanted to picture having sex.

Next to me, Jack shook. Someone trying to suppress laughter. My lips twitched, me desperate to burst into hysteria too, imagining Marty's outrage.

Colm addressed me, expression earnest. "But I felt bad about Dylan getting sacked. When he said Jack had given him a job, and me having a wee connection through the brewery, I tried to help. If the hotel does well, Dylan can work there and stay in the area, can't he?"

He'd held my gaze throughout that brief speech, but the words done, his eyes returned to Dylan. The image of a man who'd won a fantastic prize. As Dylan's sister, I'd question Colm's judgement—*mate, I've known him for 28 years, and I'd award him a measly 2 out of 10 in the best people to love stakes*—but the sincerity touched me. Might even have made my eyes prickle.

"Sorry I was so rude about your daughter," he repeated. "Dylan talks about her a lot and what a wee sweetheart she is."

He does? My mouth dropped open.

"Help with the hotel?" Jack asked, returning to something else Colm had said. "How?"

Colm grinned. This must be the first time I'd been able to study him properly. He was ruddy-faced, strawberry blonde and green-eyed, compact and muscular, the perfect contrast to my brother's dark-haired, olive-skinned swarthiness on a long, lean body.

"A mate of mine owns a digital marketing business," he

said, "so I persuaded her to run a few campaigns on behalf of the Lochside Welcome. When people Google places to visit/stay in December, the hotel appears near the top of the list."

Those mysterious parties of 20 that kept turning up in the depths of winter.

"But," Colm continued, "I needed a wee bit o' money for it because those pay per click AdWords are expensive. Lachlan slipped me some. He had some spare cash going."

"We saw you!" I burst out, "when Mhari and I followed Lachlan one night because she wanted to check if he was still dating Nicole. We thought the two of you must be up to no good."

Dylan stared at me. "That's what you were doing that night? Is this what happens when you move to a tiny village? You spend your time stalking people?"

"No!" (Yes.)

Colm cleared his throat. "I've a wee proposition for you, Jack," he said, swivelling to look at me too. "You as well, Gaby. D'ye want to invest in the brewery? We've just landed a contract with Wetherspoons."

Jack gaped at him. Wetherspoons were all over the UK, dominating the UK pub scene. In Lochalshie, we were too small a place to attract their attention (thank goodness). But a contract with the mighty 'Spoons was an excellent way to secure a small brewery/distillery's future.

"Gies you another income stream," Colm added, "as it's always wise no' to put all your eggs in one basket, eh?"

True. If we scraped together enough money to invest, that might buffer us against future bad summers.

He got to his feet. "Have a think about it. I'd better head home."

Dylan saw him to the door, Jack and I exchanging shakes of the head.

"Colm's asked me to move in with him," Dylan said as he walked back into the living room. "In Oban."

Good grief. If anyone had told me a month ago that a) my brother was about to find love, b) would embrace his niece wholeheartedly, and c) end up moving to Scotland permanently, I would have assumed it was an elaborate joke.

"Fabulous!" I said. "Whenever Jack and I fancy a night away somewhere, you can have Evie to stay!"

To be fair to Dylan, enthusiasm replaced alarm in record quick time.

Jack stood too. "What are you two going to do about your Mum?"

Oh. That I hadn't been expecting. Dylan met my eyes. I sighed. "She's still seeing my dad! And Nanna warned me he's after her money, remember?"

Dylan's puzzled expression reminded me I hadn't told him about that conversation I'd had with Nanna. I related it now.

"Kathleen Millar's daughter's friend's work colleague," Jack said, the edge to his voice making me jump. "Wouldn't it be better to listen to what your mum has to say? She was supposed to be coming here for Christmas. Bringing your Nanna, too. It's no' fair of you to keep punishing her this way."

Harsh. Dylan's expression reflected mine—dismay at the unexpected ticking off.

I folded my arms. "Why now? Tony Richardson doesn't get to waltz back into our lives when it suits him. What interest has he shown in us over the years? Nothing. Mum will see sense soon enough, and he'll disappear again."

"But he might not," Jack's voice had taken on a deceptive softness—a tone I ought to know by now and might have reacted to sooner if I hadn't been part astonishing revelations befuddled.

"He will!" I countered. "There's no point to this discussion."

"And it's none of your business, mate," Dylan threw in.

Jack's eyes flashed. "Jesus! The two of you. Here I am bargaining wi' the universe it grants my stepdad more than the six months the oncologist's predicted, and you're too proud even to talk to the man or meet up wi' him again."

His voice had risen—the noise setting off cries in the bedroom above.

"Now look what you've done!" I shouted back at him.

He pushed past Dylan and I and stomped up the stairs. "I'll sort her."

Dylan met my eyes. "Do you think Jack's right?"

"No! I know the Ranald situation is awful for Jack, for me too, but it's not the same."

Dylan shrugged. He'd filled out again, and the extra kilos suited him. That and the glow of contentment he radiated. An air that nothing could touch him—not an argument with his brother-in-law, nor estrangement with his mother and father.

He yawned, stretching his arms to the ceiling. "I better head off. I'm due at the hotel in an hour."

At the door, he paused once more. "Thanks, Gaby."

Upstairs, Evie was still crying, Jack shoogling her on his hip. "She's wet," he said, handing her over. I was prepared to be conciliatory, but the comment riled me.

"What? And it's my job to change her? Mum once told me Tony never changed a single nappy when me and Dylan were babies."

His eyes flashed. "Xavier's just texted me. Tina's phoned in sick. He needs my help."

"Parenting is meant to be a two-person job, remember?" I said, rolling out the changing mat and dumping Evie on it. Her eyes darted between the two of us. "And you promised me you were off today! The man who spends so much time working, his daughter is looked after by me the bulk of the time! So much for you being a fantastic 21st-century dad! I'm like every other woman on the planet, doing the bulk of the childcare while you get the oohs and the ahs just for giving her a cuddle in public from time to time!"

In life, there are times you say words you wish you could claw back the minute they leave your mouth. They fly towards their target—tiny devastating missiles you are powerless to stop.

Jack's face crumbled. His hands flew over his eyes, nose, mouth, and he turned away.

"I didn't…"

My apology fizzled out. Many a true word said in anger? Another one of Nanna Cooper's pearls of wisdom.

He let himself out, hurrying downstairs. The door opened and closed softly.

Great. What a start to the day.

Chapter Thirty-One

THE TRUTH SERUM OVERDOSE

"I wanted your first, well second, Christmas to be so special!"

I'd spent the last ten minutes sniffling while Evie watched, bemused. From the safety of the top of the sofa, Mildred's tail swished.

"The best Christmas ever!"

Evie returned her attention to Thomas the tank engine, smashing him into the fireplace. Oh heck. Jack and I hadn't even bought her anything yet—the money worries and then the Ranald situation all-consuming. Much as I suspected Evie wouldn't care about presents given her age, when I pictured her opening nothing on Christmas morning, my insides curdled in shame.

The Parental Court was coming for us for sure, the jury flashing us accusatory glares when the judge read from a scroll in front of him—*Gabrielle Amelia McAllan and Jack Alexander McAllan, you stand before us accused of buying your daughter sod all for Christmas, and screaming and shouting in front of her. How do you plead?*

"Shall we visit Grampy?" I asked Evie, who clapped her hands. And then I'd swing by the Lochside Welcome, find Jack and talk. The accusation I'd let rip had been exaggerated, but there was a kernel of truth in there and the hotel taking up so much of his time was something we needed to discuss.

The last two days had been Arctic cold—a warning that snow was due, the elements preparing the ground to make it icy enough for the snow to settle. Evie in her buggy, I picked my way along the High Street trying to avoid any black ice. Thursday was Mhari's day off, making the pharmacy a safe place for me to pop in without alerting her to what I was up to.

Alison, the pharmacist, greeted me cheerily. "Hiya, Gaby? D'ye want some Calpol for the wee yin?"

I shook my head, reaching for what I wanted. Items purchased, we headed for Caroline and Ranald's. Caroline, eyes red-rimmed, let me in. I followed her through to the kitchen where a heap of sodden tissues lay on the central unit. The 'are you okay' dim-witted question died on my lips.

"Where's Ranald?"

"Upstairs. If you wait here, I'll fetch him doon. It'll fair cheer him up tae see wee Evie. Oh, I've booked a holiday for us on the 27th. Ranald's never seen the Northern Lights, and I found a wee cruise to Norway that guarantees you'll see them.

I patted her arm. "That sounds wonderful."

"Puts the kibosh on the wee Christmas celebration we were gonnae have after the Lochside Welcome guests leave," she added, "but all the other trips later in January and February are booked up and I dinnae know if…"

"Please don't worry about it, Caroline," I said. "I can

come round on Christmas morning with Evie, and Jack can bring the leftovers from the hotel when he finishes up at 4 o'clock. We'll have a lovely time."

Providing my husband and I was speaking to each other by then... well, even if we weren't, we would act our socks off in front of Ranald.

"Thanks, Gaby," Caroline said. "Ranald's got himself the Argos catalogue. Just say aye to whatever he offers tae buy Evie, will you?"

Given our lack of prep, I could hardly say no.

Ranald's appearance made me swallow hard, but his face brightened at the sight of Evie. He stretched out his arms, and she did the same. I settled her next to him, and he waved the catalogue at me.

"There's a playhouse in there I marked with the red pen," he said. "What do you think? We could put it in the garden here for Evie to play in whenever she comes round."

I flicked to the page—the playhouse an elaborate construction of swings, ladders, slides and monkey bars— almost £1,000 in price and only suitable for children over the age of four. Ranald was unlikely to ever see her in it.

"If you're sure," I said, congratulating myself when my voice didn't waver. "That would be lovely."

As we left the house, Evie pointed at the loch.

"Um, um!"

"Are you wanting a wander around there, Evie?"

The jiggling of her head I took for a 'yes' and we set off. The sky above us was icy blue, the same colour reflected on the water that rippled gently, the lack of wind a further sign snow was on its way.

In the distance, we spotted Stewart walking Scottie. Evie waved furiously, twisting to look up at me. "Ma-ma-ma!"

That was close enough to mummy to make me grin at

her. I was so busy dwelling on this child development triumph that I almost walked past him—Dexter huddled over and sitting on one of the large rock clusters close to the Royal George.

In his too-trendy outfits, Dexter always looked out of place here. The silver Puffa jacket made him stand out a mile and trainers that white wouldn't remain so for long on someone striding around the loch. He'd chosen low-cut socks too, bony ankles on show beneath cropped jeans. No-one ever did that in Lochalshie, knowing all too well that the wind whistled straight up your legs no matter how tight the jeans.

When I'd spoken to Katya the day before, she had said nothing about Dexter visiting. Was this anything to do with what I'd discussed with Caitlin? Or... oh-oh. Had he turned up to demand his share of the hotel back right now, even though he'd said he'd leave it until next year?

"Dexter. This is a surprise!"

His megawatt smile was much dialled down these days. Dexter attempted it anyway, straight white teeth flashing at me. "Hey," he said crouching down, so his face was level with Evie's. "She's changed so much, hasn't she? Still the spitting image of Jack, though."

I nodded, too mindful of whose spitting image Lucian was.

"Do you want to give her a cuddle? She's such a little flirt she loves it when men pick her up." Might as well remind him of the parenting stuff he was missing out on.

Dexter smiled and straightened up. "Go on then."

Evie, her little face the only thing visible in a padded all-in-one, woolly hat and mittens coo-ed obligingly once in his arms.

"How's work going? Will you be returning to the States?"

Thanks to the massive effort Blissful Beauty made every year to flog Halloween and Christmas make-up and skin-care, Dexter's marketing manager job kept him insanely busy May until November. The haggard look he wore would be attributable in part to that.

"I keep chopping and changing my mind. Do I return to the US for good or not? Hyun-Ki said I should go to South Korea—amazing opportunities there, according to him."

Hyun-Ki had been my boss when I first joined Blissful Beauty. He was now 24 and advancing through the ranks at a frighteningly fast rate. At some point, he'd look beyond Blissful Beauty and jump ship to whatever company offered him tonnes more responsibility and heaps more money.

"Are you going?" I asked.

"I thought I'd give it until the New Year. Then I'll decide for sure." He swung Evie up in the air, making her giggle. It was a mug's game—small children loved the move, and made it clear you must keep going. After a minute and your arms, shoulders and back shrieked at you to stop. Dexter, bless him, kept going, swinging her up and down. He must have tonnes of upper body strength.

"So… what are you doing here?" I asked.

He jiggled Evie up and down and making her giggle. "I'm flying out to LA tomorrow for Christmas, and I wanted to say goodbye to Lucian."

Oh dear. That did sound final. I'd need to pop in to see Katya later, who'd be devastated. Much as she pretended she was resigned to her fate, the reality of witnessing your boyfriend, the man who'd considered himself the father of your child, bid that child farewell forever would cut to the bone.

He hugged Evie to him. She leant her little head against his chest, his chin resting on top of her head, both solemn faced. Did babies gauge your mood—my wee tot working out that Dexter needed her peaceful and contemplative?

"Caitlin phoned me the other day. Delivered a super-long lecture about what fatherhood really means. That was nothing to do with you, was it?"

Oops. "No! Well, maybe a little bit. Sorry for interfering."

Scottie, who'd been let off his leash, joined us. He stopped in front of Dexter, sat back and barked.

Stewart hurried over. "Alright, Dexter. Havenae seen you for a while. You're right tae leave London. Filthy city, that. Shush, Scottie! Dinnae mind him. He probably thinks you're attackin' Evie."

I'd never realised Scottie felt so protective towards Evie. Most of the time, he ran a mile when he spotted her, terrified she was about to yank his tail—but when Dexter handed her back to me, he stopped barking immediately. Dexter ducked his head down and rummaged in the pocket of his silver coat. Tissues located, he blew his nose.

A brief lecture on cloud patterns and what they meant (imminent snow) delivered, Stewart squinted at Dexter. "Are you upset aboot something, Dexter?"

Ten out of ten, Stewart, for your superior observational skills! Dexter shook his head before nodding. "Yeah. I'm kinda upset, Stewart."

"What aboot?"

Again, wasn't it obvious? Katya had been here on her own for three weeks now, pushing around a baby that looked nothing like his alleged papa. Now, here was Dexter, whey-faced and casting the occasional glance at the Royal George as if he expected Zac to walk out any minute now, the two of them to fight it out. ('*I'm* the daddy!' 'No, *I'm* the daddy!')

"I've split with Katya," Dexter admitted, surprising me. Stewart wasn't a gossip, but he'd mention the news in passing to someone, and it would get back to Mhari who would bombard Katya with non-stop messages trying to weasel the truth she already suspected out of her.

"Have ye?"

"I don't... think... I'm Lucian's father."

Woo. Truth serum overdose.

Stewart crouched down and picked up a stick, flinging it in front of him. Scottie bolted after it, returning seconds later to dump it at his feet. Stewart nodded thoughtfully. "Aye. He looks awfy like that Zac yin, doesn't he?"

He had noticed, then. I glanced at Dexter, alarmed that people saying what everyone thought out loud might tip him over the edge. But he looked resigned, rather than suicidal.

"Mind," Stewart added, "Tamar's no' mine. Doesnae make any difference to me."

OOOOHHHHHH! How, how, how did I not know this and, more crucially, how had it escaped Mhari?

"He's not?" My pitch tipped over into squeaky. Tamar didn't look like Stewart as he'd inherited Jolene's dark hair and olive skin as per her Māori roots, but I'd always put Tamar's love of porridge and Scottie down to his father's genes.

Stewart threw the stick for Scottie, who bolted after it. "Jolene had a wee fling a few years ago when I was drinkin' a bit too much."

Everyone was on the truth serum today. Dexter elbowed me. I returned the gesture; he must be as flabbergasted as I was.

"We'd been checked oot at the hospital before that, where they telt me I had an awfy low sperm count. Jolene might no' have been able to get pregnant wi' me anyway, and she was desperate to have a bairn. The other fella doesnae ken she got pregnant and wee Tamar's fine wi' me being his daddy."

Good Lord.

Stewart whistled for Scottie, who joined us once more, tail waggling. Evie's little hands reached towards him. Protector, he might be, but he skittered away from the two of us. The distraction was just as well. I was lost for words.

"Thanks for telling us," Dexter said, gripping Stewart's arm. He looked down at Dexter's hand and back at the both of us once more.

"Aye, well. Youse willnae tell anyone, will ye? And dinnae say anything to ma Jolene."

Vow solemnly sworn (me deciding Jack didn't count as anyone), we watched him walk off.

"Oh. My. God," I said, mouth hanging open. "Mind officially blown. Um, does that mean you…"

Dexter shook his head. "Tamar's real father knows nothing about him. It's not the same, Gaby."

"But—"

I zipped my mouth shut. Not my business. When had my interference ever helped anyone?

"Well, um, I hope you have a lovely Christmas in LA," I said.

"Yeah, my sister's super excited about seeing me this year."

Too right she was. According to Katya, Dexter's older sister had received a lot of hand-outs from him over the years. She must be anticipating him bringing tonnes of presents for her and her kids.

"I wouldn't get my money back on that flight," he mused. "Super-expensive too because I booked it at the last minute."

O-ho! Was that an invitation for me to argue with him? I'd promised no interference, but why not?

"You can afford it."

"Do... do you think I can be like Stewart?"

"Absolutely. Caitlin's already lectured you about fatherhood. She and Jonno are dead close—much closer than she is to Adrienne."

He kicked the sand. "When I found out about Zac, I said super-vile things to Katya. She might not take me back. In all honesty, I don't know if I could do it. And it's unfair on Lucian for us to reunite and split all the time because I can't handle who his father is."

But you can! She will! Please get back together! I want you all to have a Merry Christmas! I kept my thoughts to myself.

"Well. I guess you have a few things to mull over."

Dexter leant over and kissed my cheek. "Y'know, if I didn't have such a weakness for complicated, flawed blondes who drive me crazy, you'd be right at the top of the women I should fall in love with list."

Katya had once told me that Dexter talking to her while they... ahem, was a come-on, the liquid chocolate of his vowels and consonants. Not 'alf.

I stepped back. "And if I didn't have such a thing for mean and moody red-heads..."

We smiled; neither of us meant what we said.

"Bye, Gaby." He headed off, and I turned away, making for the hotel. Time to concentrate on the one relationship it was within my power to fix. Apology to Jack coming up.

"Sound like a plan, Evie?"

She chirruped what I assumed was a 'yes'. As we

reached the hotel, Dylan emerged, mouth pinched, and brow furrowed.

"There you are! I've been phoning for ages."

Ah. I'd switched my phone to silent earlier when Evie was napping.

Dylan gestured behind him. "Guess who's here?" he said. "Mum and Dad. Desperate to play happy families with us."

I face-palmed myself. The corners of Dylan's mouth twitched upwards. "Nanna Cooper's come too. It's the Richardson full house for Christmas."

Chapter Thirty-Two

AN EXPLANATION FOR THE SNEEZES

I found myself oddly nervous, pushing open the door of the hotel. When was the last time I'd seen our father?

"How did they get here?" I asked Dylan.

"Private plane and a hire car. Tony still has friends in influential places apparently. Even so, how did he manage all that time with Nanna?"

A consideration indeed: Nanna would not have held back.

What did the hotel look like to a stranger? Tired, old and rubbish? And why did I care what Tony Richardson thought of it? This was my home. It helped, however, that when I followed Dylan into the public bar, it was packed with people. The fire radiated nuclear-like heat and chatter, and laughter almost drowned out Mariah Carey warbling about all she wanted for Christmas. Tired, old, rubbish— no, warm, welcoming and where I'd spent some of the happiest moments of my life.

He stood at the bar, hand wrapped around one of Colm's company's craft lagers and eyes flickering everywhere. "Have you told them about Colm?" I whispered to Dylan.

"No."

My mum nudged Tony's side, and his gaze met mine—a question and an apology in there.

He hadn't changed much. I'd finally worked out the last time I'd seen him. My 22nd birthday when he'd popped in to see me while I was still living with Ryan. Dressed in jeans and a thick jacket, he was the older version of Dylan. His hair had receded, and the lines around his eyes and mouth were more profound than I recalled.

Behind the bar, Jack watched me too. He might have pushed me into this reunion, but I knew he'd hover protectively all the while. He gave me a small smile and mouthed the word 'sorry'. I returned both. My mum's attention was on me too, her sucking on her bottom lip the way she did when she was anxious. Those people I knew had noticed also, and they stared.

Dylan slung an arm around my shoulders. As we were the siblings who didn't hug, the gesture bought the all-too-familiar itchiness to my eyes. "I'm not giving him an easy time," he said. "I haven't said much to him so far because I was waiting for you."

"I'm not ready."

"Me neither."

We walked forward, nevertheless. Stopped a metre in front of Tony. His eyes flitted from me to the buggy.

"The photos don't do her justice," he said. "She's gorgeous."

He looked up once more. "And she looks just like you."

No-one but no-one said that. Well, apart from Jack but then he would. I unstrapped Evie and handed her to my mum, who held her arms out willingly enough and showered the top of Evie's head in kisses, my daughter shifting her face upwards to beam at her.

"This was my idea," Tony said. "I'm sorry, but I was desperate to see you both and explain. And when you wouldn't speak to me on the phone or reply to my letter."

Dylan smiled sheepishly. "Evie threw it in a tub of tomato sauce, so we couldn't read it."

"Ah! Neither of you knows what happened in Spain, then?"

Dylan met my eyes. By the sounds of it, a Damascene conversion. Intriguing, but the Lochside Welcome, much as I loved it, was not the place for such a conversation.

"Come on then," I said. "We'll go back to mine."

Nanna Cooper, ensconced in the booth nearest to the fire and deep in conversation with Laney Haggerty about ponies, promised us she was fully recovered and putting on weight as per the doctor's orders. As the journey had taken just over three hours, it hadn't been uncomfortable either. She squeezed my fingers, leaning forward to whisper, "I might have got him a bit wrong, Gaby."

Next to her, the pile of suitcases and bags made me do a double-take. How long were they planning to stay?

Jamal was outside his shop as the five of us made our way back to the house. The Lochalshie WhatsApp group banging the jungle drums, no doubt, and Jamal as desperate as the rest of the village to nosey in on what was happening.

I unlocked the door. As Jack and I had been out most of the morning, the house was cold, my mum and Tony shivering as they stood in the living room as I bunged on the heating and Dylan boiled the kettle.

Tony admired the paintings on the wall—Jack's take on local scenery. He zoned in on our wedding photo, awarded pride of place on the mantlepiece above the fire. "You both look very happy," he said wistfully.

Dylan banged cupboard doors in the kitchen. He might have lived with us for three days, but in that time, he hadn't managed to memorise where we kept the cups, tea or coffee.

"I'll help him," Tony said. He walked into the kitchen, retreating immediately.

"Gaby, there's a cat in there and I—A-CHOO! 'Scuse me, oh, A-CHOO!"

His hands went to his nose too late to stop the spattering droplets, some of which landed on my face. My mum dug into her handbag and pulled out handfuls of tissues. Here was the explanation for something I'd always wondered about. When I first moved to Lochalshie as a cat sitter (no previous experience or indeed love of cats), I started my first day sneezing my head off. A few doses of super-strong anti-histamines later and once my immune system awakened, I didn't need them. My mum and Dylan were fine with Mildred and had been with her predecessor, Mena.

"Yes, Dad," I said, wiping my face. "I'll get you something."

In the kitchen, Dylan had sorted out the teas and coffees. He dug an elbow in my ribs, smirk firmly in place. I gave in and grinned back—the ridiculousness of it all irresistible.

I murmured apologies to Mildred, whose face expressed disconcertion. Why was her regular routine being disrupted by noisy cat haters? I tickled her under the chin and promised treats to come. Our first aid box—a shelf in one of the cupboards spilling over with plasters, TCP, headache and indigestion tablets—also contained an old packet of prescription-strength allergy tablets.

Reluctant to be splattered in snot a second time, I

handed them to my dad at arm's length. He was still sneezing like a plague victim, Evie watching him open-mouthed. The A-CHOOs eased off, and we sat down, Dylan and I on one side, our parents on the other, cups of tea in hand and a plate of shortbread on the coffee table.

Where to begin?

"I have not been a good father to you both," he said to us, voice dripping sincerity. Call it the mid-life crisis—optimistic of him to imagine he'd live to 104—he said, but he didn't want his children to despise him.

"Why now?" Dylan and I asked together. What made someone who'd managed to ignore so many critical events in his kids' lives experience a sudden epiphany?

"I met someone when I was in Spain. After Louisa and I split up." He turned his head to glance at my mum as he said it, her nodding slightly. While there had been rumours of various girlfriends over the years, Louisa was the one he'd eventually left my mother for.

Tony and Louisa moved to Spain after the global financial crash crippled the housing market. The property had been dead cheap, and they'd snapped up a bar, a restaurant and several cut-price apartments in a busy tourist town.

"A man called Robert. Local businessman. A bit older than me. He'd come out to Spain years earlier with his second wife, and he didn't see or get in contact with his children for years. His first wife finally tracked him down to tell him his oldest daughter had been killed in an accident and ask if he wanted to attend the funeral, which was due to take place two days later.

"He didn't go."

Whew. Cold.

Tony shook his head. "He wasn't brave enough—too scared of what his other kids would think of him for staying away all those years, and that it would upset them even more if he showed up at their sister's funeral. He figured it would be easier all round if he never saw any of them again."

Evie chose that moment to haul herself up using the side of the sofa and attempt to toddle her way towards me—the move earning her claps and praise all round.

"And I decided I didn't want to be that guy," Tony took up his tale once more. "Louise and I had already parted ways. But I didn't plan to get back with your mother. I thought she wasn't that much of a masochist."

He paused to look at her again. Revolting. Two overgrown teenagers, unable to stop the way their eyes met the whole time in the wonder of first love. Under his breath, Dylan muttered, "Yuck," making me smile again.

"We met up so she could tell me about you two and my little granddaughter, and the years fell away!"

"But he cheated on you all the time!" Dylan burst out, pointing at my mum.

Tony's explanation made sense, but I still didn't get why my mum would take back so easily after all those years she'd lived through infidelity. "Are you going to do something disgusting, like live in an open relationship or something?" I asked, appalled.

Dylan put his head in his hands. "Spare me!"

They shook their heads.

"He didn't cheat on me all the time, love," my mum said, turning to Dylan, "and he wasn't the only one."

If I looked at Dylan now, his expression would match mine—jaw dropped in disbelief.

"We got together when we were too young," she said, "a bit like you did with Ryan."

True. My last boyfriend and I started going out together

when we were both 15. Ten years later, I was thoroughly bored with him, and he was working his way through every temporary sales assistant who started at his family's business.

"Once you're older and wiser, it's often easier to work out what you really want."

The screaming and shouting years. The relief my mum had expressed when he finally walked out. An image, long forgotten, Tony's head on my mum's lap when they watched TV at night. The strict order to Dylan and me not to go into their bedroom on Sunday mornings because Mummy and Daddy were having 'special time'. (Urgh).

Other people's relationships… As Jack often said to me, no-one knows what goes on except the couple themselves.

Tony put his cup down. I snatched it out of the way.

"Sorry, love. I'd forgotten about households with young children. Never leave a coffee cup within grabbing distance, eh?"

My mum leant forward. "Dylan, Gaby—your father lost most of the money he invested in Spain. When he left, he was so desperate to return and make it up to you, he didn't quibble when Louisa asked him to make over the property deeds to her."

Tony looked sheepish. "I didn't want to tell you that. Not until I'd managed to make a bit more money. Bit embarrassing that your inheritance will be rubbish."

As Dylan and I hadn't expected to inherit anything from him in the first place, that hardly mattered, but my mother must have wanted to tell the tale to big him up. Kathleen Millar's daughter's work colleague's friend had got the story right, but only half of it. He was skint. But sniffing after money didn't seem to be the reason why he was here.

Dylan's phone buzzed at the same time as mine. Ten to one our partners had just sent us simultaneous messages asking us if we were alright or if they needed to burst in and throw my father out. Dylan checked his, glancing up to eye Tony defiantly.

"I've got something to tell you myself."

This would be a test. Years ago, I remembered Tony making bad taste remarks about a man at his work. Did Dylan recall that too?

"I'm gay. I'm in a relationship with a man called Colm, and I'm moving to Oban to live with him."

Mum stood up, eyes watering. She hurried over and flung her arms around him. "I'm so pleased for you! Though I'm gutted, both my children will be living so far away from me."

Tony wasn't yet at the hugs stage. But he nodded. "Whatever makes you happy, son. If you and Gaby decide to let me back into your lives, I'd like to meet the guy sometime soon."

There was our cue. I'd forgiven Tony for the moment, but another of Nanna Cooper's favourite sayings would apply here. I wasn't prepared to let go of the wariness around Tony yet.

"Actions speak louder than words," I said. "You'll need to take an interest in Evie, me and Dylan not just now but next year and the year after that, express admiration when I send pictures of Evie's first day at nursery, at primary school, high school, and show up at every major occasion."

I hoped my father knew that and regarded the opportunity with excitement.

He clasped his hands together. "Yes, love."

"The proof will be in the pudding!"

Oh heck. If I didn't stop the wise old lady sayings soon, I was going to change into Nanna Cooper.

Mum sat down once more. All of us were glassy-eyed,

Dylan, especially. Ever since I'd found out about Colm, Dylan had blossomed even more—his step lighter, the smile bigger and used more frequently and even the usual rudeness directed at me had been toned down. Of all the things that had happened in the last few weeks, the change in our relationship was the one that brought me the most pleasure.

(Though I kept my store of insults at the ready to be on the safe side…)

Evie crawled over to her grandfather, using his leg to haul herself up. "Hello, Evie!" he said, bending his head, so it was level with hers. "I'm your mummy's daddy."

Careful choice of words there. Family titles like granny and grandpa were reserved for those who did the job. Evie had two of them already, both devoted to her.

"Ranald is Grampy," I said, "and Jack is Papa Jack." Yes, we were aware of the pizza reference. "What do you want to be called?"

Tony blinked. It would take a while before I felt comfortable calling him 'Dad' again, but in the meantime, 'your mummy's daddy' was far too clunky.

"How about Grandpa then?" he asked. Mum hugged him and reached out for Evie, who chose that moment to thump down on the floor and turn red-faced. Next to me, Dylan sniggered, knowing what was to come. Grandfather duties were not limited to cuddling Evie and taking her for walks.

I got to my feet. "I'll fetch the changing mat."

When I returned, Dylan had backed out of the room, 'to be on the safe side'. He stood in the hallway checking his phone, a smile on his face as his thumbs typed out a message.

To be fair to Tony, he hadn't changed a nappy for years. Ever? And this was a humdinger of a stinky one. But he showed willing, getting down to the floor without hesitation as my mum instructed him. Tony took five times as long to change Evie as it would have taken me, but once she was clean and fragrant once more, he sat back on his heels, pleased with himself.

"We're booked in at the Lochside Welcome," my mum said. The mystery last-minute booking, then. "That way we won't get under your feet. I know you're going to be very busy over the next few days."

Crikey. Where were we going to hold the family Christmas celebration now? Jack and I were meant to be going to Caroline and Ranald's on Christmas Day once Jack finished work, and it wasn't fair of me to overwhelm them with all my family.

Dylan, back in the room now that there was no risk of being sprayed with poo, slapped his head. "I forgot to tell you, Gaby! Just before the Richardson happy family crew turned up, Jack got a phone call. The hotel's now fully booked for Christmas."

He was in the middle of explaining what had happened —Mum, Tony and I staring at him in disbelief—when Jack let himself in.

"Good grief," I said, revelling in the way that relief had unfurled Jack's brow and lit up his face once more. "Christmas is going to be very different this year, isn't it?"

Chapter Thirty-Three

BUCKS FIZZ AND UNEXPECTED GIFTS

"Wake up, Mrs McAllan. We've got a busy day coming up…"

I groaned and pulled the duvet up over my face. "I was in the middle of a seriously filthy dream where—"

"What?! Was I in it?"

Jack rolled on top of me, his face hovering above mine, sparkly smile in place. "I wouldnae like to think you cheat on me in your dreams. That would not be a good start to the day. Merry Christmas, by the way."

I reached up to kiss him. "Merry Christmas! Maybe you were in the dream, perhaps you weren't in the—no, don't, stop it, stop it!"

Jack's secret weapon was tickling me. I am, and always have been, ridiculously ticklish, from my stomach to under-arms, feet and even my blasted thighs. A determined tickler could torture me that way, and I'd agree to anything.

More so if the 'anything' was something I woke up in the mood for anyway…

When we eventually got up, it was still dark—the year's

shortest day only just past. Evie was fast asleep in her cot, furry coverlet kicked off. I pulled the blanket back over her, Jack patting the satisfyingly full felt stocking from Santa that hung off the end of the cot.

"Do we wake her up?" he asked, the question hopeful. This time last year she'd only been a few weeks old. Would she know what was going on—her eyes lighting up with excitement when she saw the stocking?

No. Parentally biased as we were, she wouldn't.

"Better let her sleep. It's going to be a long day."

In the kitchen, Mildred greeted us yowling. Like Evie, she had no knowledge or appreciation for Christmas either, especially if it meant the house filling up with unfamiliar people taking up space on all her favourite places to sit or sleep. Nevertheless, I dug out the gourmet turkey cat food I'd bought for her and filled her bowl. She rubbed around my legs, purring her head off.

"What do you want for breakfast?" Jack asked, "I'll make you whatever you like."

A generous offer, but I ought to save myself for lunch, which promised to be spectacular. Xavier had spent yesterday afternoon describing it to me in detail. After ten minutes I zoned out because food isn't that interesting even when you are as greedy as me. Still, our chef figured today would be the most significant opportunity of his cooking career so far, and he promised perfection.

Five courses. None of those poncy Royal George mini portions either.

"Toast will do," I said, "but put tonnes of butter on it. And peanut butter. And one slice with cheese on top. I'm starving."

Our tree in the living room, by now shedding pine needles crazily every day, had a satisfactory pile of gifts underneath. The bulk of them was for Evie—most of them bought after a frantic dash to Oban the day before.

"When will we open our presents?" I asked Jack as I polished off the last of the peanut butter on toast. Caroline had invited us to their house for coffee and cake so we could watch Evie rip into the gifts they'd bought her.

"Later? Um, you don't mind if mine is a bit rubbish, do you?"

"That's fine! I don't mind at all!"

Well, maybe a bit… Mine for him was epic. At least I hoped he'd see it that way.

Upstairs, we heard Evie crying. Both of us jumped up. She might be far too young to appreciate what day it was, but we both wanted to be there when she spotted the Santa sack. I loaded up.

Jack lowered the side of the cot and lifted her out, the cries turning to gurgles and smiles as she settled into her daddy's arms. "Merry Christmas, Evie," he said, kissing her cheek. I pecked her too, both of us laughing when she turned away, face screwed up—Daddy's girl through and through.

I unhooked the Santa sack from the cot. "Look, Evie! Father Christmas has visited you and left you all these presents. Do you want to open them?"

I swear she nodded. We set her on the floor, Jack and I down there too as I tipped out the presents. As Jack had predicted, the act of tearing off the shiny paper was Evie's chief preoccupation. Within minutes, a pile of purple, silver, red and green paper lay next to us, most of the toys ignored as she ripped up the sheets into tiny pieces. Hopefully, I'd be able to find all the stray bits later when I put them in the recycling bin.

"Do you want me to get her washed and changed?" Jack

asked, and I nodded, beaming at him. The pictures of Evie in the mini Santa suit would make her cringe in years to come. But Jack and I were delighted, both of us exclaiming about how cute she looked. I took a tonne of photos, firing them off to everyone I knew. Most of them would see her later anyway, but what was the harm?

MY LOVELY GRANDDAUGHTER IS THE MOST BEAUTIFUL GIRL IN THE WORLD! My mum replied. Still in need of lessons in the appropriate use of the caps lock key.

The WhatsApp notification on my phone bleeped. Katya. I showed the picture to Jack. Lucian wearing the same outfit and sat surrounded by a heap of ripped up wrapping paper. I'd popped round to the Airbnb the day before. Dexter opened the door, rolling his eyes when I threw my arms around him. "You lost all that money on your flight, then?"

"Yeah."

"We're taking it slowly," Katya told me sotto voce in the kitchen while Evie joined Dexter and Lucian in the living room. "But you should see him with Lucian, Gaby—the happiest man alive."

"Are they going to be at the Lochside Welcome?" Jack asked me now after remarking that Lucian didn't look half as cute in his Santa suit as Evie did.

"Yes. It'll be nice for Evie to have company her own age. And Tamar will be there too. Come on. We'd better head for the hotel and check Tony and Xavier are coping."

It had started to snow two days ago. Given that we were in the far north of Scotland, the weather was to be expected, but I'd never experienced a white Christmas. The picture-perfect scene as we left the house made me gasp. Maggie Broon's Boobs were coated in the stuff, white peaks against a sky that still had a slight pink tinge to the east, and the loch was glass smooth. The snow cocooned the entire village, muffling all sound. Our breath came out in puffs of smoke.

"Not sure what our guests will make of this," I said, "given the temperatures they're used to."

"All part of the experience. Mum wanted something different, didn't she?"

When Dylan had announced what would be happening on Christmas Day, Tony recovered first.

"Gaby, Jack, how about I take over the management of the hotel for the day, so you can spend the time with Ranald and Caroline, and your mum and your nanna?"

The bar in Benidorm had been much more extensive than we'd realised, and Tony was used to dealing with crowds of boozed-up Brits all year round. Christmas Day in the Lochside Welcome wouldn't involve that many people, but Tony had years of juggling multiple plates at once. When we asked Xavier if that would be okay, he nodded, happy to have Tony in charge if it meant he could spend all his time in the kitchen putting the finishing touches to the World's Best Christmas Dinner™.

Dylan and my mum volunteered to act as waiting/bar staff—the offer making me blub once more, Jack's eyes watering at the same time. Really, we might have solved all our money worries by buying shares in Kleenex, given the way we were currently getting through tissues. But the last-minute booking had cleared the immediate money worries, the party bunging us so much money we'd be able to pay off the tax bill.

Four gleaming Land Rovers with blacked-out windows were parked outside the Lochside Welcome now, having arrived in the village late last night. We'd spent the previous two days in frantic preparation, everyone drafted in as chambermaids, handymen and sous chefs, ensuring the hotel was as perfect as it could be. Jack and Lachlan wrapped up in multiple layers had even taken on the job of cleaning the outside, power-hosing the walls and repainting the sign so the black/gold letters of The Lochside Welcome —Fàilte stood out in stark relief.

"Look, Evie!" I pointed as Laney Haggerty's horse-drawn carriage pulled up outside the hotel. She'd kept on the décor elements from the Christmas fair, the carriage's sides adorned with tinsel and her ponies wearing the fake reindeer antlers.

She waved at us. "Merry Christmas, you two! Evie looks awfy bonny. D'ye want tae tell the first lot their taxi's here?"

Jack nodded. "I'll pop in and get them."

Mr and Mrs Simmons, a couple in their late 50s from Dorset, emerged staring in wonder at the scene. Jack piled their luggage into the back of the carriage.

"I've never been in one of these before!" Mrs Simmons said as Jack placed the small set of steps in front of the carriage door, and she clambered in.

"Can you take a photo of us?"

He obliged. Laney flicked the reins, and the carriage set off. As the Royal George was less than a five-minute walk from the Lochside Welcome, the mode of transport was well over the top, but when we'd phoned the Simmons two days ago to tell them about the chance of plans, they hadn't quibbled. To ensure their stay in the village was still outstanding, I'd come up with the alternative taxi idea.

The second couple disposed of in the same way, we peeked our head around the door. Tony, clipboard in hand, was deep in conversation with a man whose cap hid most of his face. Strangers milled about, me remarking once more that I had no idea it took so many people to make something like this work.

My mum appeared, throwing her arms around me. "Merry Christmas!"

I took Evie out of her buggy and handed her over.

"How are the VIP guests?" I asked, tipping my head up to the ceiling.

"Fine, fine. Lovely manners. They remembered me too!"

"Do you need us to do—"

"No! Tony, Xavier, Dylan and I have everything under control."

As if to prove the point, Dylan walked past a stack of chairs in his arms. He blew Evie a kiss.

"Goodness," my mum said once he was out of earshot. "Your brother's a different man. I wish he'd felt able to tell us earlier."

Me too, but Dylan's happiness now more than made up for everything. Yesterday, he'd sat down with Jack and repeated his offer to take on a share of the Lochside Welcome. Nae need, Jack said. We hadn't heard if Dexter still wanted his money back. Reunion with Katya or no, he still had to cough up for his niece's university fees, and they weren't cheap. But we were much better off than we had been a month earlier.

Dylan wanted to invest, no matter what. He outlined plans for the hotel. Years as a logistics manager had given him plenty of insight into business efficiency and the importance of diversifying your income. He'd be an excellent addition to the management team, easing the burden on Jack, so he didn't have to work nearly as many hours.

… which led Jack and me back to the argument we'd had the day after our anniversary. "I'm so sorry," I said, "I know how difficult it has been running the Lochside Welcome."

He shushed me. "But you're right. You do the bulk of the childcare and a part-time job, and you help in the hotel. Next year will be different. I promise."

It would need to be.

"Where's Nanna?" I asked now, and my mum rolled her eyes.

"Still in bed. Nanna insisted on room service. I had to take it up to her and then she phoned reception two minutes later to demand I return with brown sauce for her sausages!"

Tony, his chat with cap man finished, made his way towards us, taking Evie from my mum. "Everything's on schedule," he said. Enisa, huge carryall and massage table in hand, rushed past us and hurried up the stairs. Nice that other locals were benefitting from this gig too. Jamal didn't take Christmas off either, and I'd spotted some of the crew popping into the shop earlier.

"All you need to do is get here for 11 o'clock." Tony handed Evie back to me. "Okay? Off you go."

We took him at his word. Outside the snow had started again, that muffling quality it had intensified as the tiny flakes drifted around us. Ranald surprised us both by answering the door at their house—pleasure touching his features as he took in Evie in her Santa suit.

"Come in, come in! Caroline's made some Buck's Fizz."

And mince pies—the smell of fruit and baking drifting through from the kitchen. Their house offered the best views in Lochalshie. The French windows in the living room looked straight onto the loch and the hills behind it. All the seating in the living room was angled so that everyone faced the windows. The massive tree that took up the space to the right of the windows had presents piled up underneath it.

Ranald sat down, the whump as he landed too fast on the cushions giving away how much effort it had taken him to open the door. He flapped a hand as Jack noticed, his fingers curling into fists. "Not today, Jack. We're celebrating."

Caroline bustled in—the smile like the one Jack used when too many thoughts swirled around inside. But she dialled it up when she saw us, holding her arms out for Evie. Ranald plucked at the blanket on the chair next to him. Jack leapt up and draped it over his knees, tucking it around him. He dropped a light kiss on Ranald's head, one Caroline and I pretended not to notice.

"How's everything at the Lochside Welcome?" Caroline asked as she handed out glasses of Bucks Fizz.

"Fine, according to my mum and dad," I replied. "Laney's just dropped off the Simmons and the Murdochs at the George."

"Awfy good o' Zac to take them," she said, referring to the agreement that the guests we'd needed to turf out at the last minute could stay at the Royal George.

"He's being paid well for it," I said, though Jack raised an eyebrow. Zac had also stepped in to offer something for free. "Yes, well. Okay. Awfy good of him indeed."

A tray of warm mince pies appeared, making Evie haul herself up beside the coffee table. "You won't like them," I said, as she reached for one. Sure enough, she bit into it, screwed her face up and flung the pie across the room, making us all laugh.

"Shall we open the presents?" Ranald asked, pointing at the tree. A climbing frame wasn't possible to wrap up, but he'd outdone himself otherwise. Evie ripped into numerous shiny-wrapped gifts—clothes, toys, games, many of them intended for a much older child. He must have bought her Christmas presents for years to come.

As he'd ordered us to celebrate, I bit the inside of my lip determined not to cry.

"Here, Jack," Ranald said, shuffling in his chair and withdrawing an envelope from his back pocket.

Jack tore it open, gazing up and down at the piece of paper he held in front of him. "What's this?"

"You're a bright boy. You can see what it is."

I glanced over Jack's shoulder. Flippin' heck.

"I can't accept this."

"Yes, you can. Caroline will have enough to live on. You and Lachlan are my heirs, anyway. You're getting your inheritance early. The hotel expenses have been a terrible worry for you this year. Invest in upgrading the hotel, find some ways to diversify your income and put some money aside for the future."

"I ca-ca-can't…"

"Yes, you can. And no greeting either. That's an order."

He waggled a finger. "Caroline, can I get more of that Buck's Fizz!"

"Of course." She got up and turned away. The delivery of Buck's Fizzes round two might take a little longer, as I suspected Caroline would hide out for a few minutes to bawl, dry her eyes, re-powder her nose and return, wide smile in place.

Sure enough. Job's completed Caroline set the second tray down. Jack could drink mine.

Glasses in hand, we followed Ranald's lead. He raised his. "Merry Christmas! Here's to the best one ever, eh?"

"Merry Christmas! Best one ever!"

Do you know what? We all sounded as if we meant it.

Chapter Thirty-Four

LOVE AT FIRST SIGHT

"Is this going to be on the Netflix?" Nanna Cooper patted her hair. She had joined us at Caroline and Ranald's, happy to polish off the glass of Buck's Fizz I hadn't touched.

Last year, she'd missed out on an opportunity to appear in a Netflix documentary and never allowed me to forget it. Just in case she was about to find herself on the hallowed silver screen of Netflix, though, her hair had been styled by Enisa once she'd finished with her primary client earlier this morning and set rigid with an entire can of hairspray. Anyone lighting a cigarette within 10 metres of her was likely to set off a major incident.

"No, Nanna. It's going on social media, remember?"

Nanna tutted. "But lots of people will see it?"

"I expect so."

"Well, then, I hope you have a much smarter outfit planned, Gabrielle Amelia McAllan!" she said, taking in what I was wearing. I was in a woollen dress pulled over dark leggings. In the brighter light of Caroline's house, it did look scruffy, a thin coating of cat hair all over the front.

Her eyes swept over Jack, dressed in customary jeans and a Lochside Welcome fleece. "And you, young man, better put your kilt on!"

Chastised, Jack and I left Evie in their care and dashed home, Jack complaining that women never realised what a faff kilts were to put on. The formal outfit had so many components: the long socks; the sgian-dubh that was sheathed in one; the shoes and their complicated lacing; the plaid you wrapped around yourself; and the straps and the buckles that needed to be threaded through.

Jack had two kilts. One a casual version he occasionally wore behind the bar and this, the formal one, its material that much heavier and the colours—green, blue, red and yellow—more pronounced. Jack wore his with a dark blue ghillie shirt, black leather ties undone, and the apron of the kilt skimming his knees. I whistled, and he swept my hand up for a kiss. "You're not so bad yourself."

I was back in the turquoise dress—its second outing in less than a week. I mock curtseyed. "If you say so!"

"Much better," Nanna declared when we returned, breaking off from her conversation with Ranald, who looked perkier than he had done earlier. Caroline, with her access to the drugs off-limits to most, might have given him something to help make the day easier. Who cared if it kept him smiling?

The six of us set off for the hotel—a journey that took us all of 30 seconds. Jack Senior dressed in a kilt too was waiting at the entrance, arms out wide. "Jack, Gaby! So lovely to see you! Oh, hello wee Evie! Can I hae a wee cuddle wi' her?"

Jack Senior always asked. What had happened during my husband's childhood still made Jack shy away from ever leaving Evie on her own with Jack Senior, even though we were both 99 percent sure he wouldn't ever hurt her. But Evie's safety mattered to us more than anything else. Perhaps one day, Jack would ease off the wariness.

"Have you done this kind of ceremony before?" I asked as Evie's grandfather blew raspberries at her, triggering giggles. Last year, Jack Senior had qualified as a humanist celebrant. Another way, he told us, to atone for his past. In an older population-dense area like ours, funerals were far more common than anything else, though he had presided over a wedding and a naming ceremony in the summer.

"No," he said, "but it's easier in a lot o' ways because there's nae paperwork involved. I spoke tae them earlier, and we went through what they wanted. Nice lady. She asked after ye, Gaby. Wanted to know if you'd got the presents for Evie."

Yes. Designer clothing Evie would grow out of in weeks and a diamond necklace. Nothing remotely suitable for a one-year-old.

"Shall we go in?" Caroline asked, doubtless eager to get Ranald out of the cold and into a chair asap. Jack Senior handed back Evie, and we entered the hotel.

In the reception, two of the crew rushed past—one with a clipboard in hand and Bluetooth mike. What a life. Sacrificing Christmas day for filming, but they were all early 20-somethings. Maybe this represented the fastest way to get ahead in a fiercely competitive world.

I sniffed the air appreciatively—turkey roasting. No farty Brussel sprouts aroma, as I'd made Xavier swear on Lucas' life, he wouldn't put them on the menu.

Stewart appeared, Tamar pulling on a harness that looked like the one Scottie wore. He was on an extendable lead too, bolting over to see us and stopping when the lead ran out.

He let out a wail as his father hastened over to sweep him up. "Aye, you're alright, wee man."

He turned to me, thoughtful. "Jolene let him hae chocolate for his breakfast instead o' the usual porridge. I did tell her it was a mistake."

Jolene wandered past, lugging a gigantic bag of flour. She caught my eye and shook her head at Stewart's comment. I hoped my expression betrayed nothing. The Tamar paternity revelation still astonished me. When I'd discussed it with Jack, we'd both spent ages speculating on who might be Tamar's father. "Angus!" I said. "He gazes at Jolene with puppy dog eyes all the time." "No," Jack said, "Angus wouldn't do that to Stewart, but I remember there was this English fella who visited the area years ago who was awfy taken wi' her. If you're going to have a bairn wi' someone else, it's a lot handier if you never see him again, eh?"

In the public bar, presents had been piled up under the tree. I checked them. There was one for everyone. A long table had been set up in the conservatory to the right, portable heaters blasting out enough hot air to make the temperature bearable. Decorated with a tartan tablecloth, the spaces were all marked with handmade name cards cut from old Christmas cards. Mhari was busy swapping places around.

"What are you doing?" I asked. She turned, pointing her camera at me and snapping a pic.

"Makin' sure I'm no' sat next to anyone boring. Christmas dinner lasts for ages, doesn't it?"

"Who were you sat next to?"

"You. No! I'm joking. Dinnae greet. I've changed ma place, so I'm next to Lachlan."

"Oh-ho! Has he forgiven you? Nicola won't storm in

here later? Those blasted windows were expensive to fix. Are you and him back together then, finally and at last? The Mhari and Lachlan happily ever after I've been waiting for... Hey, why not ask Jack Senior if he could marry you today while he's here in a celebrant capacity? It wouldn't be official, but we could always have the proper wedding here in January once you've sorted out the paper-work. And seeing as Lachlan's a part-owner, you're entitled to mates' rates for the wedding package. I'd even design your invit—"

I stopped. Lachlan had slipped into the room, his expression as aghast as Mhari's.

"We're no' getting wed!" Lachlan, the fervent head shake mirrored by Mhari. "God, no! That's for mugs. Nae offence."

"None taken. But you wanted to sit beside him!"

"Aye, so he can diddle me under the table the minute the speeches start. Keep me awake and a' that."

"Or," Lachlan added, deadpan, "how about we try three-way phone sex with Hyun-Ki? That would while away an hour or so."

The twitch to his lips made me suspect the pair of them were winding me up. Or that it was an elaborate double bluff. Mhari's inherent nosiness made her the expert in covert tricks that hid your own doings from everyone else. Lachlan slung an arm around her. She shoved it off. "Save your strength. You'll need it for later."

About to walk out, I turned back. "You owe me 50 quid."

"What for?" she asked, screwing her nose up.

"That bet we had weeks ago. You said they'd split by Christmas Day."

"Too bad. We didnae shake on it!"

I should have known. But what did it matter? I didn't need the money.

Tony was behind the bar, laughing and joking with Dexter and the capped man I'd seen him with earlier. He was the director. Instagram live streams were most often amateur-looking, but this one would have that lick of celebrity polish and was expected to set the record for the most viewed live stream ever.

"Dexter's not involved in any of this, is he?"

Katya, Lucian in her arms, had joined me—shine back in her air and glow to her skin.

"Nope. But he knows Rudy," she nodded to the man in the cap. "How's Ranald this morning?"

About to answer her, I stopped as the door to the hotel opened, and Zac let himself in. Dear, oh dear, did this mean—

"Hey, man!" Dexter wandered over, expression relaxed. "Merry Christmas."

"Merry Christmas? D'you mind if I…?"

Katya and Dexter nodded, Katya passing Lucian over, and she and Dexter withdrew hand in hand.

I exhaled: No punch-up then. "There's no-one in the conservatory at the moment if you want to be alone with Lucian?" I said, taken aback by what flashed across Zac's face. Momentary elation disappearing under pain. He followed me through, ignoring the stares. Jack joined us, thanking Zac for putting our guests up when we'd needed to turf them out.

"No problem." He jiggled Lucian up and down, turning away.

Oh dear. Tears trickled down his face.

"Are you okay?" I asked as Jack mouthed the word 'argh!' behind him.

"Katya's the love of my life," Zac said. "When I first met her, I couldn't believe my luck. I was off to this village in the arse-end of nowhere—"

Jack cleared his throat.

"Sorry. Lovely little place, I meant. And there Katya was at the airport—a stunning angel in human form. With the most perfect peach of a bottom I've ever had the good fortune to see."

Jack caught my eye. Who knew that Zac had it in him to be so sappy?

"I flirted with her like mad."

Didn't I know it. Katya had made me laugh with some of the lines he came away with. He specialised in making the most innocuous inquiry sound filthy.

Zac turned to face me. "Do you believe in love at first sight?"

About to say no, I changed my mind. Jack nudged me. No. Yes, a bit? Jack and I clashed when we first met, but I reckon a lot of that was two people declaring vehemently they did not want to be in a relationship when fate said, 'Au contraire. Look who I've found for you!'.

Today, of all days, I wanted everyone to be happy. Zac wasn't about to get what he really wanted, but I might as well remind him of the plusses.

"Maybe that love at first sight thing will happen again," I said, "and it's great that you'll be able to see Lucian when you want."

He sighed. "Yes. Anyway, I'd better get back to the George. Five-course menus to finish and all that. And you've got your star guests to entertain. I left those amuse-bouches in the kitchen. Do you mind if I upload pics of them on Instagram once the video's live and say who made them and who they were for?"

"Not at all! The publicity will help us all," Jack said.

Zac kissed his son. "Give him back to Katya. I can't face her."

We watched him go, Lucian clinging to Jack. Evie glared at him. An interloper stealing her father's attention, tsk-tsk.

In the hallway, we heard Tony clap his hands. "If everyone could think about making their way to the staircase?"

Jack smiled at me. "This day reminds me of something. Can't think what."

"Oh, you! Two years ago. Almost to the day. A surprise visitor and a riotous party."

"That's it! We'd better get in place. Caitlin's due to appear any minute now."

Chapter Thirty-Five

THE VERY MERRY CHRISTMAS

For maximum dramatic effect, Rudy made us all gather in the hallway where we waited for Caitlin to descend the stairs, her arm threaded through her stepfather Jonno's. She'd dug out her original wedding dress—a short shift overlaid with broderie anglaise lace and a train at the back. Tiny in stature (never a more accurate sentence uttered than famous people are always much shorter and thinner in real life than they look on TV), she dominated the space, everyone's eyes on stalks.

"Hello, Lochalshie!" she beamed at everyone. "Merry Christmas to you!"

We'd all signed the NDA, promising not to tell anyone in advance, so her appearance wasn't a surprise. Still, it set off chatter anyway, everyone muttering about how wee/cute/glamorous Caitlin was and did she not feel she was missing out by not spending Christmas with her family?

The last, muttered by Nanna Cooper, Caitlin heard.

"Not at all, Mrs Cooper!"

That set off titters. The world's most famous family had

been filming their Christmases for years. The last one ended up with one person on a DUI charge, another vowing he'd never darken the family doorstep again, and a third confessing her cocaine habit was so out of control she was propping up the entire Columbian economy.

As a lab technician, Donal had always found Caitlin's life difficult to adjust to. The non-stop schedule, the screaming fans and the constant paparazzi made life as the husband to one of the world's most famous women a challenge. He acknowledged Brand Caitlin depended on keeping in the public eye but put his foot down from time to time.

This was one such occasion. The Cartier Christmas was something he would never do again, but what about something lower key... Why not recapture some of the magic of their earlier romance by returning to the place where they'd married, and renewing those vows? Film a small part of it for Instagram to satisfy the demands of Brand Caitlin. But once that was out of the way, the cameras would be turned off. Lochalshie had the added bonus of being miles from anywhere. Paparazzi photographers did not lurk nearby.

One phone call later and here we were. As the hotel's already booked guests were so few, Zac had agreed to take them, the pill sweetened when Caitlin offered to pay double for their stay. Those guests who were coming for lunch were all local, and they were here anyway, guests at a party they hadn't envisaged but were thrilled to attend.

In the function room, the chairs had been set up in rows with a red carpet through the middle. Tony and my mum, both dressed in the Lochside Welcome 'uniform' ushered us all in. Donal stood at the front, Jack Senior behind him, and he turned his head when Caitlin made her appearance, gliding up the aisle to stand beside him.

Tony shook a bell, and the chatter fizzled out. But small children find silence too tempting to maintain. The minute Jack Senior announced that we were gathered here today to celebrate with Caitlin and Donal, Evie started 'talking' the goos and gas that would form words in a year. That set off Tamar, telling everyone he wanted to play with his toys, which triggered Lucian, who began to cry.

"Sorry!" Katya and I got to our feet, but Caitlin waved a hand. "No, don't worry! It's all part of the fun!"

Rudy, the director, looked as if he wanted to disagree, far more used to scripted reality shows than filming when people were unfiltered. Still, the ceremony punctuated by cries and Tamar's chatter continued.

"I, Caitlin, renew my vow to have at least half a day a week where I don't look at my phone."

Mhari, busy staring at hers, glanced up. Lachlan snatched her phone away, making everyone laugh.

"I, Donal, renew my vow not to be rude to my in-laws."

More laughter. Jack leant into my Nanna, who was sat beside him. "No promises from me there, Lillian."

"I will be true to you in good times and in bad, in sickness and in health."

In the row in front of us, Caroline squeezed Ranald's hand. Jack spotted it too. We exchanged another one of those glassy-eyed smiles.

The ceremony concluded ten minutes later. Our waiting team stood in the public bar, their trays bearing glasses of champagne and Zac's amuse bouches. No one ever let me near plates and trays in the hotel as I always dropped stuff. The clumsiness didn't seem to be an inherited trait: Dylan and my mum and dad, aided by Tina and Russell, distributed glasses and the deep-fried langoustines without a single spill.

Caitlin wandered over. "Gaby!!!!! Thank you so much, you guys! This has been super-magical. Donal's, like, much happier than he's been in ages. We should come here every year."

You betcha! I'd just checked Instagram. Caitlin's film had indeed broken the previous record for the most-viewed Instagram live feed of all time. The Lochside Welcome's Instagram account had gained 13,000 new followers within half an hour of the film being uploaded.

Dylan, tray in hand, stepped forward. "Wo-would you like a glass of champagne?" When he'd told me about Caitlin's spur-of-the-moment plan to return to Lochalshie, he'd confessed she was one of his idols.

Caitlin put her hand on his arm. The slavish devotion in his eyes ramped up. "No, thanks. Please could you get me some mineral water?"

"Yes, yes!"

Once he'd sped off, she leant in. "Don't tell anyone, but I'm pregnant."

She winked. "If you wait until the new year, why not phone Pop Sugar and be one of those 'a close friend' says…? Might bring you in a bit of extra money."

She patted my hand and sauntered off, leaving me slack-jawed. We didn't need the money now, but perhaps someone else might appreciate an extra few thousand in their bank account. Mhari, say.

"Anything wrong?" inquired Jack.

"Other people's kindness," I replied, "bowling me over yet again."

"And turning you into an emotional wreck." He grabbed my hand. "They're about to serve dinner. Are you hungry?"

"Starving."

"Just as well I had a word with Xavier earlier then and told him to make sure you get Scooby Snack-size helpings. Come on, greedy guts. Let's eat."

"If I don't go to bed right this minute, I'm going to follow our daughter's example and scream the place down!"

At one o'clock in the morning, I prodded Jack. We were still at the vast central table, its surface piled high with discarded paper hats, pulled crackers, cheap plastic toys, dirty plates and empty glasses. Xavier's World's Best Christmas Dinner™ lived up to every one of his bold claims —smoked salmon, meltingly tender turkey and a brandy-laced chocolate torte I'd only managed a mouthful of.

Jack leapt up, mock alarmed. "Right you are, ma lady. Come on then."

Caroline had taken Evie at nine o'clock, by which time our daughter found herself unable to resist the lure of sleep, however much she tried.

"I'll tak her wi' us," she said, nodding towards Ranald. "He's awfy tired too." Her eyes glittered in the dimmed lighting, reflecting I guessed, on what next year might be like. She squared her shoulders. "Lovely Christmas, Gaby. I couldnae have wished for better."

And off she went, Ranald and Nanna Cooper in tow, the latter asking her advice on osteoporosis prevention techniques which would distract and delight her at the same time seeing as Caroline loved dishing out medical advice.

My mum at the far end of the table was deep in conversation with Donal, while Caitlin danced to the bar's jukebox hits. We'd never updated it, so Ashley's 90s favourites belted out. Caitlin bopped along to Whigfield's Saturday Night, aided and ably abetted by Jolene and Mhari. Oh yes, and there was my brother, arms resting on Colm as they swayed together, and he sang the words of the song to him. I hope it didn't put Colm off entirely; Dylan didn't so much sing as caterwaul.

My dad, making his way back from the Gents, stopped when he saw us. He grabbed me in for a clumsy whisky-scented hug, Lachlan having educated him on the finer aspects of single malt earlier in the evening. "I'm gonna be the best father and grandfather from now on, Gaby," he said, warm breath tickling my ear. "Promise!"

I shrugged him off. Dad must prove he was back for the long-haul, but he'd been super helpful the last few days, he adored Evie, and he and my mum floated in a love's young dream bubble.

Outside, the icy cold slammed against me. Thanks to all those bodies and an overload of food and drink, the Lochside Welcome had been roasting hot all night. Now, though the contrast between inside and outside turned me into a shivering wreck within seconds.

Jack stuck an arm around me. "Come here."

We inched our way home, the snow and ice making progress tricky especially as one of us didn't have their full staying upright capability thanks to too many of Colm's IPAs. The snow had lain, a pure white blanket on the edges of the pavements and paths and topping the hills. I'd taken pictures earlier—Jack and Evie, her in the Santa suit, him in a hat, both grinning at the camera as they stood outside, snow a bright and beautiful surrounding but not enough to detract from their central image.

My family.

"Just us and no Evie," Jack said as he dug in his pocket to retrieve the keys. ""Mildred will be awfy pleased."

Oh dear. I had terrible news for Mildred on the disruption front.

"I'm not taking my make-up off or my clothes," I said as he opened the door. "Too much effort. Straight to bed."

Mildred stood at the living room doorway and mewed for food, sniffing the air suspiciously—the wariness dying away when she worked out her owners were sans child.

Jack pecked my cheek. "I'll feed Mildred. Don't fall asleep, will you?"

Too much to ask, I told myself as I tramped the stairs. At the top, I found myself turning left instead of right—the instinct to check Evie first now automatic. In our room, I took my shoes off and fell back onto the bed, its soft, pillowy warmth so enveloping my eyes shut at once.

Jack rolled onto the bed next to me, also fully dressed.

"I didn't hear you come up!"

"I know. And you need to sleep. I won't keep you up long, I promise. But I wanted to talk about the Christmas presents."

I turned onto my side. We were nose-to-nose. The IPA fumes he breathed out didn't bother me this time. Interesting.

"You first," I said, reaching up to stroke his nose. He bit my finger gently.

"You are the world's trickiest person to buy for."

"Moi? Take that back, Jack McAllan. Easy pleased is my second name."

He tried to shake his head—a gesture not that doable when you're lying down on your side.

"No, you're not. I racked my brains. What do I get Gaby for Christmas? You only like cheap jewellery, and you buy hardly any clothes. The last time I bought you flowers, you forgot to top up the water. I got you a box of expensive chocolates once, and you threw them out when you thought I wasnae looking."

"Sorry about that."

He pressed his forefinger to my mouth. "It's no' a complaint."

Heartfelt. My predecessor, the dreaded Kirsty, was high maintenance. The sort of woman who only liked blingy gifts she could post on her Instagram account. BABES!!!! Look what the most fantastic, fabulous man in the whole entire world just bought me—like wow, thanks! #DiamondEarrings #Blessed!

"Then, I thought about what you've been up to for the past few weeks. Sneaky, like."

"What do you mean?"

He rubbed his nose with mine. "All that interfering in other people's lives. Trying to find them a happy ending."

Caught.

"I didn't succeed."

"Yes, you did…"

Debatable. Most people had come to their happy endings by themselves. And there was nothing within my power to do about Ranald and ultimately Caroline. Next year would bring serious challenges.

"My mum's offered your mum a job."

"What?" I sat up, sleep banished. How had I missed that?

Jack glanced up, face mischievous. "She's a receptionist for a GP in Great Yarmouth, isn't she? Mum's got a vacancy for the role. When she mentioned to me the other week that hers is leaving, I said what about Gaby's mum?"

All those accusations of interfering in other people's lives and here he was doing it himself.

"Seeing as my wife would love to have her mum close by."

"Did Mum say yes?" I asked, sure I would have heard about it if she had. My hand flew to my mouth. Did that mean she hadn't? Too cruel to raise that possibility and then snatch it away.

"Shush, shush," Jack grabbed my hand. "She did, but she wanted to talk to you first. Check you and Dylan were okay with it. Your grandmother's a bit unsure. Worried she'll miss her friends too much, but she's going to have a think about it too. Lochalshie might find itself with three new residents next year."

At that, his eyes slid away. "I say three…"

Back to mine. "It'll be beneficial for you if you've got plenty of family on hand to babysit next year, won't it?"

I snuggled back down to next to him so that we were nose to nose once more.

"When did you guess?"

"I've had my suspicions for a while," he ducked his eyes to my chest. "They kind of gave it away. But when you came into the hotel that day your family arrived, I spotted you cradling your stomach. The last time you did three tests before you told me so you could be 100 percent sure."

He reached behind him and opened the drawer next to his side of the bed and presented me with a cardboard box. "So, I bought test number three."

"I'm pretty sure I don't need it," I said. "If everything goes well. Evie's going to have a brother or sister in August."

I turned mock-serious. "But after that McAllan, we stop breeding, right? You take yourself to the hospital and have that thing cut off!"

To show him I didn't mean it, I gave 'that thing' a friendly squeeze. He responded with a kiss, his lips bumping against mine and the tip of his tongue exploring my mouth —beer and Christmas cake. Warmth and tingles, as the sleepy nerves in my body reawakened.

He broke off, propping himself up on his elbow and stroking the hair back from my face. "My shite Christmas present isn't any use then?"

"I s'pose I might do one more test to be on the safe side."

"There is one last thing."

"Yeah?"

"I don't think we need to stand in front of everyone and renew our wedding vows."

No. While Caitlin and Donal's exchange had made everyone exclaim at their cuteness, I bet if you calculated how many celebrities had renewed their vows over the years and split up shortly afterwards, you'd end up with a sizeable number.

"But it did get me thinking." He rolled off the bed and held out his hand for me, pulling me into his arms.

"I choose you," he said, making me start to cry yet again as he said the words he'd uttered to me two years ago in the registry office in Oban. The most prominent symptom of early pregnancy? The totes emosh thing.

"…to stand by your side and sleep in your arms. I'll laugh with you in the good times, and struggle alongside you in the bad, learn with you, grow with you even as time and life change us both."

Ditto.

The Grateful Thanks Bit

And I'm done! The book that was meant to be a one-off, then a trilogy and ended up five books long. Thanks to you for reading (and hopefully enjoying) the books. I have a lot of fun writing them, though this one proved trickier than every book before.

I have no further plans for additional books in the series —although as the saying goes, never say never—but I intend to put out a 'companion' book of short stories featuring some of the other characters next year.

Kristien Potgieter and Alison Jack provided expert critique services, for which I'm very grateful. Kristien has read and critiqued every one of the Highland books and her suggestions have vastly improved them. Sharon Bannister proofread the book for me and caught a couple of last-minute plot errors. All subsequent punctuation and grammar errors are my own and Enni Tuomisalo. I have a small but devoted following for these books on Wattpad, and they love Gaby and Jack. It fair boosts my ego when they read every chapter of the Highland series when I upload chapters on that platform. They are convinced that I won't be able to resist another book in the series…

Thanks as well to Diana Gabaldon, as I've continued to 'borrow' Jamie Fraser/Sam Heughan. The Outlander books are fabulous to read. If you haven't read or heard of them, you're in for such a treat.

Sandy continues to provide help in the way of patience

and understanding, and my mum's always been my cheerleader. I wish my late dad could have seen this.

Writing about a small, independently managed hotel in a rural part of Scotland now feels like a responsibility. Will places like the Lochside Welcome survive the pandemic? Fingers crossed they do, but if it is within your gift to give, please visit these beautiful spots and provide local businesses with your support.

About the Author

I'm in my 40s, married and 'mum' to a very spoiled cat. I live in Dumbarton near the bonny, bonny banks of Loch Lomond, and by day I'm a communications officer/freelance writer, by night an author. My biggest dream come true would be to be able to write full-time.

www.ingramcontent.com/pod-product-compliance
Lightning Source LLC
Chambersburg PA
CBHW011424010726
47494CB00011B/2485